WHAT HE BECAME

By
Eddie Generous

www.DarkInkBooks.com

First Published by *Dark Ink Books*, October 2024

www.AMInkPublishing.com

Dark Ink Books is a division of *AM Ink Publishing*. *Dark Ink* and *AM Ink* and its logos are trademarked by *AM Ink Publishing*.

*In memory of the Po-lins,
the best friend I've ever had.*

Chapter One

December 5, 1993 – Castoon, Maine, United States

Next to Troy Heen's half-finished breakfast was the Bangor Daily News, open to a page featuring the headline: **AIDS CASES, DEATHS INCREASE IN MAINE**. Beneath that, the subhead line read: **Total confirmed cases among Maine residents surpass 400. At the bottom of the column: Anonymous testing available to**... He sat at the counter at Cup of Love Diner and this paper was at least a month old and only appeared, open to that page, to that particular story, just a few seconds after Sheila placed his plate on the shining Formica counter. Cup of Love was not far from the home he should've left behind already, but he couldn't bring himself to go anywhere until he reconciled life after Alan.

He glanced at the paper for the twentieth time. Anonymity did not stretch very far in a small town, and he hadn't even gone to the hospital for the test he'd taken. Small as Castoon was, he didn't need to. Sticking around had become short term. Something had to give, and he needed an out.

Dead people on the news under sheets, and almost dead people with gaunt faces and too big gums and teeth, lesions like burn marks marring faces and arms, pleading to cameras. The plague was everywhere else, touching other people, in big cities. He'd ignored it the way people had always ignored that he never had girlfriends, never posted up in bars trolling for skirts. AIDS was scary in the way things were scary for strangers, but couldn't hurt you, yourself. Not until the plague showed up in Castoon.

A deep voice hummed words like daggers into the back of Troy Heen's head. He winced. It had begun to sound like radio static turned up high. Those around him had changed so drastically since the news broke, that the slurs seemed to mix, swirling together piercing darts of noise. He didn't always hear the words but never misunderstood the meaning.

"Hear me?" said that same deep voice wading through the static.

Troy had and he hadn't. He'd eaten most of the huge breakfast, pretending not to notice the strategically placed newspaper, and awaited the bill from Sheila, the manager. He licked the fuzzy coffee sensation from his teeth and reached for his wallet from the front right pocket of his Levi's.

"Don't need no AIDS in here, why don't you just git?" This voice came from a smaller frame. A little buddy voice. The kind of voice that only rose above polite indoor volume when there was a big boomer voice nearby, calling for the same action.

Troy was lucky despite this recent torment. He'd sidestepped the virus, physically, and it came so close, but here, in places like this diner, the plague still touched his life. Rocked it. Ruined it.

"You better hear me."

Troy had eaten meals and drank coffee at Cup of Love a few times a week since he was twenty, when he moved to town with three buddies. They'd rented a house and had all worked at the turkey plant. Troy outstayed them and had a pretty steady stream of roommates over the years until one came to live with him for a little longer.

He withdrew a five from his wallet and set it under the napkin dispenser next to his dirty plate. He hopped off the padded blue leather stool and turned to face the men. There were four of them, all guys he knew. Three of them worked at the plant. One had even lived in Troy's home for a few months when his girlfriend called the cops on him over a black eye and a cracked rib.

Troy looked at the door and marched. He stiffened as he passed the foursome but tried not to show it. He put his hand out to push open the steel handle and a boot connected with his ass, sending him sprawling through the door. Gravel dug into his palms and knees, the door swung back and bounced off his shoulder. He didn't turn for another look. Instead, stood up and let the door close behind him, sealing off the vicious sniggers.

***

Troy lingered between asleep and awake, wanting to die and wanting to kill. From far down the hall came a single clang, followed by the whoosh of a door opening and closing. He blinked his eyes wide. Mostly dark around him, he ran his fingers along the heavy seam of the mattress' edge as he looked at the empty closet across the room from where he lay. Moonshine cast a faint blue line against the tops of three left behind wire hangers on the rod.

Footfalls squeaked gently over linoleum in the kitchen; from the total sum of about thirty paces away. Silently, Troy kicked his feet out from beneath the bedsheet—pulled from a box and placed over the naked mattress—and stood barefoot in plaid boxer shorts and a white t-shirt. He turned his head in partial-circles, surveying options.

A flashlight played yellow on the brown carpet of the hallway. Troy watched it growing larger until it was too close, and he took three long strides to stand behind the open door. He bumped a box along the way, but it did not move. The footfalls turned from carpet and resumed motion over more linoleum. The sound of piss hitting toilet water explained the change and Troy took the moment he had with the intruder's noise to tear a strip of brown packing tape from a heavy box stacked by the door. The stream ceased mid-piss, but resumed a few seconds later, as if no other sound had polluted the otherwise silent home, and that the man in the can had nothing to worry about.

Troy reached into the box for something heavy and found the Junior Division Cumberland Country Roping and Riding Championship trophy he'd won in 1976. He held it by the tall, steel cowboy, and waited.

The toilet flushed and the man stepped out of the washroom and into the hallway. The flashlight beam shined enough to illuminate through the door crack to where Troy stood. The man drew closer and closer, but turned right instead of left, into the master bedroom, rather than the spare room where Troy had been sleeping on a flopped down mattress. The light went on and the door closed. Tape sounds growled.

Sweat began to trickle into Troy's armpit from holding the heavy trophy over his shoulder. He lowered his arm to soak up the sweat with the cotton of his t-shirt. The man in the bedroom began tossing boxes and grunting. Objects tumbled, something glass hit against something steel.

"Shit sakes," the man said and kicked the master bedroom door back open.

He stomped across the hall. Troy lifted the trophy high again and waited. The man stopped on the far side of the door and flicked the light switch.

"Dammit," he said and hurried past the mattress to close the blinds.

Troy started after the man, moving quickly, running on terror. The man turned and waved; he got out, "No. No," doing jazz hands as he pleaded. Troy brought the trophy down in less time than it took to exhale and smashed the intruder's forehead. He dropped. Troy stood over him blinking while the man rolled drunkenly on the carpet next to the mattress.

"Nobody wasn't 'sposed to be here," the man said, groaning.

Troy had his eyes hard on the bloody face. The man had a stubble beard and thin eyebrows, and a terrible gash that ran about three inches in length—about half the length of the marble slab on the bottom of the trophy. Aside from that, he was near enough to identical to Troy that only close family would know the difference, and as of that week, Troy Heen no longer had anyone he considered close family.

"Don't hit me no more," the man said, obviously not

seeing what Troy saw. Too preoccupied with pain. "Nobody was 'sposed to be here…just wanted cash, I didn—"

Troy stopped the man's words with a fresh swing. The man kept rolling despite the quietness of his mouth and Troy swung again. The man stopped. Troy swung and swung and swung until there was a hole in the man's skull just above the stretched orbital opening of his left eye. Blood had spurted all over the wallpaper.

Troy dropped the trophy and fell onto the mattress. He lay back and looked at the gentle cobwebs that had come to exist amidst the spackle texture of the ceiling. He remained stretched out until his heart slowed and he got to thinking clearly.

Up and pawing at the dead man's pants, Troy found a wallet. Simple black leather, worn, but not overly. In the wallet, he found three cards and nine bucks in cash. The license belonged to Ben Wesley Lynch, address being in a small town in New Hampshire.

"You didn't come all the way from New Hampshire to rob this house, did you, Ben Lynch?" Troy rolled the name around his mouth. "Ben Lynch. Ben Lynch."

The next card was a hunting license. The last was an NRA card. Troy ran his index finger over the slightly raised letters while again gazing at the ceiling. He then put the cards and cash back into the wallet and searched the dead man's other pockets. His coat had a tissue and a pair of sunglasses. His pants had a set of keys, including one to a Ford. Troy sat back once more and began tapping his lip with his index and middle fingers. He dropped the keys onto the mattress next to him and got busy fixing up the mess, in a manner.

December 6, 1993 – Castoon, Maine, United States

"You want this emptied?" The woman on the other side of the till partition was named Marge Plimpton. She'd always been sweet and cordial. Wasn't anymore. The smaller the town, the bigger the gossip.

"Yeah. Every penny." Troy tapped the counter.

"You leaving town? Heard your house is for sale."

Troy nodded. "Isn't mine. I only rented it."

"Probably for the best."

Troy closed his eyes and exhaled. "How come you say that?"

"Just, you know." Marge began counting out twenties.

"No. I don't know. Why don't you fill me in?"

"Look, I don't want no trouble. I just meant this is a family community. A moral place." Marge then counted out three tens, then a five, and pulled change from the tray beyond sight.

"And I'm immoral? You didn't think that after the tree lighting a few years ago. You said something about mistletoe being everywhere on special winter nights like that. Remember how you said that to me and then put your hand in the pocket of my jeans?"

Marge pushed the money over. "That never happened," she said and kept her eyes down. "Sign this slip and get out of here, okay?"

Troy signed his name. He took his stack of cash and the twelve cents in change and turned. Everyone looked at him. A woman with a stroller wore a ghoulish terror mask and screamed a wordless cry when Troy fake coughed over the baby.

"Just get out of here," Bob King said from his desk. He wrote mortgages and business loans. He once loaned Troy three hundred dollars in the ninth grade so he could buy two heifers for his father's bull. That was before the bank foreclosed on the farm and before his daddy shot himself and his mama took off to Florida like an especially stinking fart in a windstorm. "I mean it. I won't have you in here bringing that filth with you." Bob King then nodded to the old man who worked as security.

The old man stood on shaky legs. He put a gnarled hand on a holstered beltline pistol.

***

The snow was thin and sloppy on the roads, but Ben Lynch's Ford Econoline van had little trouble. Troy had two more stops to make before heading home, neither happened in Castoon.

In the rearview mirror, he watched his town shrink. He'd spent his childhood and youth in the country, spent the last eight years in town. But that was over. They didn't want him, and he couldn't stay if he wanted to.

His foot eased into the gas pedal and the town became a speck and then a nothing. He settled his eyes on the back of a rust bucket Chevy going the same way and rolled just under the limit until he got into Portland.

Different worlds. Castoon had two stoplights, a credit union, a public skating rink at the only park, and a single school that ran from kindergarten through high school. Portland had everything. The lampposts featured festive wreaths and storefronts had fake frost sprayed to the edges, leaving only ovular views through the middles. The sidewalks were on both sides of the street and people were busy getting on with whatever their lives meant. Anonymity. Troy could be anyone if he so chose.

Troy could be Ben Lynch.

Ben Lynch.

The bell on the door jingled and Troy stepped up to the first glass counter and looked in on a world that had always been aside from his own. For the most part. On the farm, he'd used a .22 to shoot groundhogs, skunks, and raccoons, but never got into guns the way so many others did.

"You're nuts." The man talking to the employee behind the counter was red-faced and clenching fists.

"I'm sorry, but the right to bear arms has nothing to do with you wanting army guns. If you can't hit a target with a regular rifle, you need practice, not a damned Kalashnikov."

"So, you won't order one? You know I can go across

town—"

The man behind the counter interrupted the red-faced customer. "I didn't say I couldn't or wouldn't, I'm only saying it's unnecessary and silly. The Civil War ended one hundred twenty-eight years ago, my friend. America has a proper army, the slaves are free, you don't need to defend against an uprising."

The man sneered harder before softening. "Be in by next Tuesday, if I order it today?"

The man behind the counter sighed. "Sure thing. You put two hundred down and I'll get it for you."

"You're damned right, this is America." The red-faced man dug out his checkbook and leaned over the counter.

It was another three or so minutes before the employee—likely the owner given that he offered his opinions so freely—asked Troy if he could help him.

"Yeah, umm, I guess I need a three-fifty-seven Magnum." Troy pointed at the big revolver behind the glass.

The employee grinned. "To what end do you need such a heavy gun? Don't get me wrong, but you don't seem the type."

Troy lifted his gaze. "What type is that?"

"The gun nut." The man pointed toward the door.

"Ah. No. I'm not. I'm going fishing with my mother's second husband. In Florida…well not fishing. I don't know what you call it."

The man nodded after a second and let his grin stretch. "Gator baiting?"

"That's it, exactly. I was told I need to be able to blow a hole in a dinosaur, but I need to do it with a handgun."

"Sounds like your mother's husband is a bit of a showboat. Lots of people use rifles, but enough use high caliber handguns, too. So, I hear. You have the right excuse, so I won't try to sell you something else."

Troy said, "Yeah, okay. So how much?"

The man bounced his head on his shoulders, thinking.

"Holiday spirit and all. Three hundred even, and you can have five boxes of rounds, on the house."

***

The snow was heavy and falling fast by the time Troy rolled up to Lover's Lane. The houses were sparse, and at the dead end of the road was a place to park and watch over the river and the farmlands further on below. Troy passed the bungalow he'd had his sights on moving into only three weeks earlier and kept going until pulling up to the dead end. He turned without even a glance at the mostly darkness where the river flowed through the scenery below and headed on back toward the bungalow.

As he suspected, two cars sat in the stubby driveway. Troy kept on going and parked about a quarter mile up the road, not far from another bungalow, this one rundown and lifeless. No vehicles were parked in its driveway.

It took some pawing, but he found the switch for the ceiling's dome light. The Magnum was heavy, and the cartridges were heavy. He opened the spinning cylinder and began popping the rounds in. He closed the cylinder and then reopened it. Trying it like TV cops, he flipped his wrist twice to get the thing to close.

The falling snow made the cold bite less than it had when he first set out on the journey. A flake landed on his eyelash, and he blinked it away once it became a drop of water. Quick steps, he had the weapon inside his jacket, the material of the jacket drooping like it suffered the effects of Bell's palsy. He was suddenly at the side door of the bungalow. Knocking.

The door swung open, and an unfamiliar face answered. "Yes?" she said, looking past Troy, probably for his vehicle.

"I need to talk to Alan." Troy sniffed. He knew of this woman, but they'd never met.

"Are you Troy?" She folded her arms, but not confrontationally, more like as if to avoid the cold forcing her nipples to stand at attention. "You're Troy, right?"

Troy did not answer, simply took a breath, and exhaled loudly through his nose.

"He's in his room. Has to work the early run from Portland to Bangor and then..." she trailed and then said, "but he just went to bed. Probably it's okay." She stepped sideways.

Troy entered, ran the sleeve of his coat under his nose.

"You know he's been beating himself up like crazy. And I know it's not fair, but he needs support. He needs..." the woman trailed again.

Troy stomped snow off his boots and continued up the short flight of steps. He knew the way. He'd helped pick out the place. Planned on using all the lawn at the back for a deck and a hot tub.

The door closed behind him. He kept right on going. At the space between the living room and kitchen, he hooked a left and made for the master bedroom at the end of the hall. The door opened with a click and closed with a click.

"Sharice, what's up?" Alan said. His words wet and slow.

"Not Sharice," Troy said.

"Troy."

"Maybe. Or maybe it's one of the boys from the bus lots." Troy had his hand on the Magnum.

"Troy."

"Maybe." Troy withdrew the weapon and stepped closer.

A bedside lamp flicked on, and Alan gasped. "Troy." Alan sat up and lifted the duvet to his chin in the way a child might on a stormy night. "You don't have to do this."

"What's it matter? You're already dead." Troy raised the Magnum. It was now pointed at Alan's chest.

"There's medicine...it was a mistake...I'm paying for it every way already...please."

Troy pressed the muzzle to Alan's soft chest. He said nothing else. Alan wrapped his hand around the barrel, trying to shove it away a half-second before Troy squeezed. The report banked off everything in the smallish room and Troy's arm reared back from the recoil.

Troy had blood all over him. The heat from the shot let loose tendrils of gentle grey smoke. The door opened behind him, and he turned. Sharice made a face but didn't move otherwise.

"Come in here." Troy pointed the Magnum at her. "Move it," he added when she wasn't moving, only staring, wearing her shock like a Halloween mask. "Now."

She got going then and once in the door, pressed herself against the paneling on the far side of the room. Her eyes fell onto the body and the smoking hole in his chest. Big enough to sink a fist.

"On the bed."

"You killed him," Sharice whispered.

"On the bed."

Sharice remained pressed against the wall.

"On the bed, you goddamned fag hag cunt!"

She moved then and sat gently enough that she did not disturb the corpse.

"I'm going to go out to the living room for an hour or so to think about what to do with you. If I hear you moving, at all, I'm coming back and blowing your head off. Got it?" Troy was calm in saying this.

Sharice only nodded.

"Tell me you understand."

"I understand," she whispered.

Troy closed the door behind him as he left and moved with tender, quiet steps. Once outside, he ran. At the van, he leaned and tried to catch his breath while he worked the door handle. The overhead light came on and he climbed in.

The drive home was about thirty minutes and passed in a flash. Troy parked the van across the street from his place.

"Dammit," he said.

Everything had to fit neatly, or questions might occur. His

car wore a stovepipe hat of snow. He found his keys and unlocked the door. Cold powder whoomphed down over him as he leaned in for the snowbrush. He closed the door and got to work.

Sweat ran down his face as he stripped off the bloody and snow-damp clothes he wore. Ben Lynch's clothes—jacket, pants, and sweater—had soaked in the tub and then went into the dryer before Troy set out. In only his underwear, Troy dressed Ben Lynch in the bloody pants and jacket. That dangerous blood. The effort was difficult and took almost nine minutes.

From a box sat atop the fridge, Troy grabbed a bottle of absinthe he'd purchased years earlier as a party gag. He took it to the bedroom and poured it all over the corpse and the sheet still half on the mattress. He put the bottle on the floor and returned to the kitchen for a lighter and a candle, forgetting that he'd only unpacked the essentials. He hurried around, looking for the box where he'd dumped the everything drawer.

In the bedroom, lighter in the pocket of Ben Lynch's jeans, he took the Magnum he'd sat on the bare mattress and put it against the corpse's mouth. He angled it up and blew a hole through the dead face. The previous damage was minor by comparison and the head blew out like a smashed pumpkin.

The Magnum fell onto Ben Lynch's thighs. Troy nodded while inhaling through his nose and then took a box flap and held the lighter beneath. Once going, he set the candle down sideways, as if it had fallen.

***

The trip to the address on Ben Lynch's license took nearly four hours. It was a slumlord's apartment building. By the door, eight names filled the slots next to the buzzer options. He tried two keys from the chain before finding the right one. On the second floor, next to the stairs was apartment E. An eviction notice dated six days prior was taped to the door.

Troy got the lock right with the first key he'd tried.

Inside was a shithole. Bare pipes and a dated Maytag refrigerator. A hot plate on the counter and an empty slot where a stove should've been. Dead roaches were all over the floor. The sofa had no legs, and its seat sat about a foot off the threadbare rug.

Troy began hitting light switches and looking through cupboards and closets. He found an ancient rifle, cruddy with rust, and threw it on the couch. He found clothes. He found mismatched dishes. He found nothing of value.

He didn't bother locking up before he left, didn't even close the door all the way.

Chapter Two

December 17, 1993 – Copper Falls, Ontario, Canada

The cattle in the basement of the barn were bawling as Jake Gerber clomped down the stairs, knocking free the snow that had clung from as high up as his thighs. He was late to feeding the twenty-nine head, thanks to a sheared pin in the blower mounted behind the tractor. He had to get the lane blown first thing because the trailer was coming for nine young heifers he had going to market the following Tuesday. The truck and trailer weren't as bad as the phone company—be home between eight in the morning and nine at night, please and thank you—but the guy wasn't exact; if anybody ran a schedule pretty similar to the do-it-all-yourself farmer, it was a day-trip trucker.

"All right, all right," he said, then tipped the five-gallon pail like a scoop into the mixed chop—grain, oats, and corn ground into a lumpy powder and milled together—bin at the front of the barn. He did the right side first, where he'd sequestered the cows, the steers, and the bull. The heifers on the other side had their heads through the rusty and shit-spackled bars, trying to get their overlong tongues into the powder across the aisle.

"Just hold it, okay?"

He returned to the bin for another scoop and ran it along the feeding aisle for the eleven heifers. They butted and snorted, interrupting each other in case one of the sisters had a tastier serving of chop.

Once the nine went on the trailer, he'd open up the middle and give the whole head free range, which would put the bull in with the three remaining heifers. Hopefully that would get them pregnant sooner than later, the cows too. Maybe give him all girls and he'd have some luck turn for the better.

He tossed the pail back into the feeder bin and before he closed the lid, he looked up the auger chute to see how far from the top he'd gotten. Too damned far.

Losing nine might make it last. He took off a rough leather glove and wiped at his nose and mouth, gave his head a scratch beneath the black and orange Ski-Doo toque. He'd been wearing that same toque every winter since he was seventeen. He'd purchased a Ski-Doo Safari 377 with the sum of his teenaged life savings from a Ford tractor dealership just north of Copper Falls—about twenty minutes east of the Gerber farm. Back in 1988, he was the envy of his entire shop class, but since then, he'd sold the sled for fifty bucks to a man with eyes on restoring the cracked hood, yellowed windshield, torn seat, and finicky carburetor.

He straightened the hat, put his glove back on, and climbed the stairs to the main floor of the barn. In the daylight, even on grey mornings, the light poured in thickly through the cracks between the century-old boards that made up the walls. All winter, snow drifted onto the bales, making them look like jumbo Frosted Wheat cereal. Along the beams in the rafters, pigeons hunkered down against the cold. The dozen or so barn cats had kept to tunnels between the bales that morning. They'd come out once Kit showed up to feed them after the bus let her out at the end of the school day.

Jake pulled the three-inch jackknife he kept in his pocket 365 days a year and cut the strings from two bales already piled near the feeder hole, which was directly above where he'd just laid the chop. He looked down the hole before he pocketed the knife and took up the pitchfork that leaned against the granary wall—the granary was a relic leftover from the days prior to when the steel silo went in, which happened long before Jake's parents bought the farm, back when he was still just a hope in his mother's head. His parents died in February—found themselves in a short game of chicken with a drunk snowplow driver—and left behind enough life insurance to cover dual burials and then an additional twenty-grand in cash. The twenty-grand went to the bank. The mortgage writer wouldn't rewrite the farm with only twelve-percent equity unless that money went into a payment account specifically setup for the monthly dues. That man in the suit told Jake he was doing him a big favor, most banks, he'd said, would make Jake sell the farm and pay off the mortgage.

The cattle were looking up at him hungrily, through with their milled chop. He kicked down one square bale and then the other, he then moved some loose, snow-covered hay to the hole. Back downstairs, he spread out the sum and checked the water troughs.

"Goddammit," he said and slipped off his glove to rub his face and then beneath his toque.

Something must've shifted in the winter earlier because the underground water line had been frozen since mid-November and nothing ran from the barn tap. He and Kit had to lug buckets of water down to the troughs nearly every day.

He looked across the pen to the door leading outside. A creek ran behind the barn and the cattle drank from it the rest of the year, but come winter, if he didn't keep the door closed, he'd probably come out one morning to see the whole head frozen in a huddle.

"Need a spring," he said to nobody. "Like a screen door."

The sound of a heavy engine outside changed the subject. Jake redonned his glove and climbed into the pen with the heifers. Shit had frozen around the bottom of the ramp door and Jake started running. Those truck drivers did not like their time wasted.

He grabbed a spade from next to the feeder bin and returned to the door. There, he got busy at breaking up the rock-hard shit.

"Jake, you down here?" a voice called from the head of the steps.

"Yep. Just give me a minute," he said, slamming the spade home.

Footfalls trailed closer. The trucker said, "Howdy. She

frozen?"

Jake looked over his shoulder, past the heifers monitoring his work, and recognized the man leaning on the pen bars from times his father had sent cattle to the same market. "Yeah, be just a minute."

"Uh-huh." The trucker remained where he was, watching. "Your daddy always did that the night before and had it ready by the time I got here."

Jake kept his head down as he worked at the holy irritation.

***

Kraft Dinner macaroni and cheese with Highliner fish sticks—Heinz ketchup to dip for Jake, Heinz ketchup all over the plate for Kit. She was twelve and her brother could only cook hot dogs, brown beans, and freezer pizzas, so she fixed Kraft Dinner and fish sticks often.

"There's a trip to Toronto. To see art and then go to the science center," Kit said through a mouthful of bright orange mush. "It's in March."

"How much?" Jake kept his eyes on the plate. When he was twelve, he went to the Ontario Science Centre for a class trip. His parents gave him a check to cover it.

"Thirty, plus whatever I eat. They have restaurants and stuff."

"Yeah, okay, but first kind of warm weekend you got to help me pull old cedar posts. We'll split those fifty-fifty."

Kit swallowed. "Like for fences?"

"Yeah, old fences from before people were using electric. The heavy posts are worth a buck. The other ones we pull out hopefully we can get fifty cents for."

Kit frowned at her plate. "Nobody else has to pull old fence posts to go to Toronto."

Jake looked at the part in her dirty blonde hair. It needed a cut. "You don't know that. But also, what am I supposed to do?

Not like Mom and Dad left us anything worth anything."

"We could move into town."

Jake blew a heavy breath. "And what, live in an apartment and I get a job at the veneer plant or the goddamned furniture factory. Come on, we'll get this going. It's just tough for the first bit."

Kit pushed back from the table, the feet of her chair screeching on the linoleum. "How long? Been almost a year! How long? Everybody else gets new clothes and a purse, and a Timex with a Velcro band! Nobody else has to pull fence posts!" Kit didn't stick around for the fallout and stormed away right after she'd finished.

Not that any fallout was bound to come. Instead, Jake got up and plucked a pen from the cup by the phone and took his mother's address book and started writing a list of what Kit needed. He'd managed to get her a new coat and boots for Christmas with money he made helping one of his father's friends put in a new furnace and oil tank. They sat beneath the fake tree, wrapped in blue paper leftover from the year before.

KIT
-clothes ?
-purse ?
-trip $30
-haircut $10
-better food? (cookbooks?)

He started a second list then, things he might be able to get out of the farm, sideways.

-fence posts $1/each
-do chickens?
-clean shed for storage rental?
-clean out old stuff for yard sale?

"Kit?" Jake picked up a cool fish stick and bit the end off after dipping it in warm ketchup. "Come out here, please."

Kit stomped to the kitchen. She'd been crying, had track marks running down to her chin. "What?" she said and wiped at her face.

"How much clothes do you need? Do you know how much clothes cost?"

The question caused a visible shift in her emotion. "Umm, I don't know."

"Okay, but let's say like fifty to one hundred. If it's more, I think we're screwed. I guess you don't know how much a purse costs either?"

Kit shook her head.

"Okay, well, we'll see about that one anyway. How much is a Timex?"

Kit shifted her mouth to the left and then said, "Maybe I don't need a Timex."

"Yeah, probably not. Clocks are everywhere anyway. Now, how do you feel about taking care of some chickens?" Jake had the pen tip pressed next to the word *chickens* on the list. He then tapped the pen five times, waiting for Kit's answer.

"And I get money?"

"Yeah, but chickens cost, so you got to earn them."

"How?"

"You can work around here for the Christmas break, but it's gonna be worth it."

Kit frowned again.

"Don't give me that," Jake said. "First, we clean everything out of that little shed. Whoever had the farm before Mom and Dad did chickens. That little shed was a chicken coop. So, we're gonna clean it all the way out and get it ready. Then we're gonna clean out the big shed and go through everything that might be worth something and put it in a pile and then we put the rest into a junk pile. Maybe there's some scrap metal worth something in there." Jake added *scrap run* to the list of potential money makers.

"But when do I get money?"

"You don't get money until the chickens start laying, but I wasn't done. We're also gonna get some cookbooks so—"

"We got cookbooks."

Jake looked at his plate. "Then how come it's always this?"

Kit shrugged.

"Okay, so you get out the cookbooks and then look in the garage deep freeze and figure out how to cook some of that meat. Half a damned cow in there."

"Am I going to have new clothes before school starts?"

"We can go Wednesday. Those nine heifers go up for auction on Tuesday, so I'll have some money Tuesday night. We can go shopping on Wednesday, but you got to trust me."

Kit's expression soured again. "We can't go shopping at the Salvation Army. We can't. That's where the welfare kids go, and Sandy Lawrence saw one kid wearing her old sweater and they made fun of that kid all week!"

Jake tapped his temple. "What, you don't think I know? We ain't going to the store in Copper Falls, we're going to Andover. We'll stop in at the Salvation Army, see what's what, but if there's nothing good, we'll go to Zellers and get you a haircut in there too."

"Can I get it dyed?" Kit's eyes were full moons.

"What? No, we're scrimping like hell, you nut."

"But we're going to Zellers for sure?"

Jake started a slow nod and spoke through it, "Uh, yeah, but we are gonna work 'til Christmas. Now, get your boots on. We got to take water to the barn."

"Okay…but, really. I get new clothes?"

Jake shoved the last bit of cold fish stick into his mouth. "Yes. Get your boots and coat on."

Kit did.

Chapter Three

November 29, 1993 – Winnipeg, Manitoba, Canada

On the eastern outskirts of the city of Winnipeg, Darren Mullin pulled his mother's Chevette into the rear parking lot of the McDonald's where he worked the two PM to close shift. He got out, shivered as he sucked hard on the last cigarette he'd get to smoke for three hours, and hurried across the icy asphalt. Before he reached the door, he happened to glance in the side window of a huge Winnebago parked in the lot. What he saw stopped him dead for a total of eleven seconds, right until the bare breasted woman riding atop a mostly unseen man looked at him and grinned. It wasn't a nice grin.

Darren tossed the cigarette and rushed inside.

"Out in that big old camper? It's been here since before I came in at ten," Scott Waylon said, smiling wide, revealing the silver shine of his braces. "Were they nice tits?"

Darren put his hand to his chest, covering the McDonald's logo on his uniform. "I swear, by God, they were the greatest tits I'll ever see until I see your sister's tits."

"You fuck." Scott was still smiling. "My sister's in the sixth grade."

Darren then laughed. "And I'm taking her ass to prom."

Scott made a gagging sound and put his hands to his throat, sending a carton of fry sleeves sideways, which then knocked the manager's tin ashtray to the floor. The door opened.

"What are you doing?" the manager, Gerry Robinson, asked. He had a cigarette, unlit, between his lips. There was a green Cricket lighter clenched in his right hand.

"Darren said there's a primo mama in the camper with huge tits. Says she was riding cowgirl in front of a window," Scott said.

Gerry looked at Darren with his eyebrows raised. "Is that right?" He lit the cigarette.

Darren nodded, put his hands out to measure in the range of double Ds. "Beauty nips, too. Pink and small. Not like the wagon wheels Scott's mom's got."

"You never saw my mom's tits, you fuck head."

Gerry exhaled, spoke with smoky words. "You watch your mouth, customers might hear. And who did this?" He pointed to the ashes and butts on the ground.

"He did. I just told the story—" Darren started but was cut off.

"Yeah, well, you're not even supposed to be on break for another hour and a half."

"Dead out there," Darren said.

"Get out, clean something maybe, unless you have more to tell about the tits." Gerry waggled his eyebrows.

Darren tilted his head, pouted his bottom lip, then said, "Nah. They were primo though."

"Then get outta here and let me enjoy my dart in peace." Darren slipped by, opened, and closed the door behind him. "Better clean that up," Gerry said to Scott, kicking near the ashes, but not into them.

Scott took a fry sleeve and a scrap of cardboard and bent down to clean.

***

"Welcome to McDonald's, what can I get you?" Rachael Dawson said from the till.

Two women and two men, all in loose fitting green coveralls and bare feet stood before her. In the back by the burger trays, Darren took his right hand from the mop he held to elbow Scott.

"That's her. The blonde," Darren said.

Scott looked. From their vantage, it was much easier to see out to the front than to see into the back, and yet, the woman waved with just her fingers at the pair of them. She appeared to be the youngest of the foursome. She looked to be in her twenties. One of the men looked a little older, while the other two were older yet. In their forties or fifties according to the light wrinkling on their faces. They were all trim and practically swam in the coveralls.

The younger man said, "Cheeseburgers. Forty cheeseburgers." He then inhaled through his nose. "Working here would drive me crazy; that smell's like heaven."

Rachael said, "You serious?"

"About the smell or the cheeseburgers?" the man said.

"The cheeseburgers." Rachael wore bug eyes that darted between the bare feet sticking out at the bottoms of the overalls and the faces. Grey puddles of snowmelt had formed around them.

"Oh, hun, Ryder here never jokes about food. Not ever," the younger woman said.

"Okay. Drinks?"

"Four waters," the man said.

"To eat in or take out?" Rachael said.

"Eat in," the man said.

"Okay, that'll be forty-four, ninety-nine. It'll be a little while to get them all ready."

The man put three green twenties on the counter. "Keep the change," he said.

Rachael said, "Thank you, but it's against policy." She made change from the register and the man pointed to the donation bin for Ronald McDonald House Charity. She dropped the change in and turned to get four cups of water.

"Am I reading that right?" Gerry stepped from the fryers.

Rachael put the drinks on the tray, pulled four straws from beneath the counter, and turned her back to the customers. "Yes. Forty cheeseburgers." Rachael made the face she made when customers were freaks. She then all the available cheeseburgers—six of them—and put them on the tray. She turned to face the man called Ryder. "We'll bring you the rest as they come."

The young man nodded, almost curtsied, and took the tray.

The weather outside had begun whipping up snow over the last hour and only two patrons remained at other seats. Both were truck drivers who visited that particular McDonald's about twice a week. One got up to leave, tray in hand, as the foursome plunked down near the ball pit near where he'd been sitting. He waved to the employees after dumping his trash.

"All right, I'm done," Scott said, taking off his apron. It was four o'clock.

"See ya!" Rachael shouted from the burger line.

Scott shouted back and went into the manager's office to punch the clock. He stepped out, nodded to Darren who was mopping half-assedly, and called to Gerry who had just returned from delivering twelve more cheeseburgers: "Bye!"

Gerry gave him a salute.

Scott held the door for the second truck driver—he hadn't bussed his tray, never did—and moved out into the cold, near dark night. Scott was the last human being to do so from that particular McDonald's location until the police arrived the following morning.

Chapter Four

December 24, 1993 – Copper Falls, Ontario, Canada

Jake left Kit in the kitchen. She was covered in flour, and he'd had an epiphany. It was to be their first Christmas with only the two of them—grandparents long gone and the invitation from the aunt in Montreal got a sincere thank you, but no can do. Change was proving to be difficult, more so now during the holiday season.

Three o'clock had come and Jake called over to Copper Rentals to see about hours. Duke who owned the place—kept the rental store in the basement of his house—was downright rude until Jake said his full name. "I'll open for you, since it's Christmas," Duke said. "But you got to be quick in picking."

He was quick. Most of the new releases were already rented, but after about three minutes of standing and looking, he had a stack of three-day rentals. Duke told Jake that he was real sorry about Jake's folks and that he could have the movies for a week.

Jake tapped the steering wheel of the pickup in tune with something new by Reba as he pulled in the laneway at home. The fields wore snowy blankets that rose up higher than the ditches and drifted in the way, making the lane blowing business a near daily chore. The house was three quarters of a kilometer away from the road, making regular driving in take a solid minute. He was most of the way back when he saw the little red Pontiac parked by the main door to the house.

"Who in the hell would be here on Christmas Eve?" he asked nobody.

Jake shifted out of gear and pulled the hand brake. He took up the white plastic bag of eight rental movies and hurried inside.

"Kit?" he said once through the door. "Kit?"

He set the bag on the wash machine to his left and bent to untie his boots.

"Sherry Robison's here. She brought us cookies!" Kit shouted from somewhere beyond a wall, probably the living room. The fireplace aided the furnace and kept the living room the warmest spot in the house, when there was wood burning.

"Oh. Okay." Jake walked in socked feet—the toes drooping like hound dog tongues—through the kitchen and hooked a left into the living room. "Hey there, Sherry," he said and slipped out of his coat.

Sherry had a younger sister Jake's age and they'd gone all through school together. Sherry was thirteen years older and divorced.

"Mr. Jake Gerber," Sherry said, rising from the couch. She wore a long red sweater with a white snowman knitted into the front. It dragged midway down her thighs. Beneath that she had on tight white jeans and fuzzy red socks that came above the pants' ankle cuffs. "Long time no see."

"Sure is. What brings you around here on Christmas Eve?" Jake said this with his back turned as he hung his coat in the closet by the front door, the one only Jehovah's Witnesses and insurance people ever knocked at.

"Just bringing by some holiday cheer, but I see little miss Cathy here has already been baking up a storm."

"Kit," Kit said.

Sherry clicked her tongue, didn't so much as look at the girl.

"I brought you some cookies to go with the ones little miss has been baking."

Jake still had his toque on, partway crooked, which was his normal. He rubbed his chin and then continued up to his head, beneath the hat. "That's awfully nice of you."

Sherry looked at Kit, and then stood from the couch. She walked over, got close to Jake, and said, "I know how lonely this time of year can be. You just call me if you need me to come by and playhouse with you for a couple days."

Jake inhaled her scent through his nose. Something flowery, but not cheap. "Oh, I think we'll be all right. Won't we, Kit?"

"What?" Kit said, looking at the powered down floor model TV set next to the chintzy Christmas tree.

"Nothing," Sherry said over her shoulder. She put a piece of paper into Jake's hand and then kissed him on the cheek. "Call me and I'll come."

"Yeah, sure."

Jake rubbed his face, smearing the pink residue from Sherry's kiss. He watched her leave. He and Kit both remained silent until the door closed and the starting of the engine could be heard through the walls of the home.

"Jesus, where'd that come from?"

Kit rolled her eyes. "I think she wants you to be her next husband."

Jake shivered. "She's nothing like Mom, that's for sure."

"I think she's a B-I-T-C-H."

"She's something." Jake rubbed his hand under the toque, noticed it was still on his head indoors, and tossed it onto the seat next to the telephone. "What do you want to watch first?"

"What'd you get?" Kit was up and crossing the room. "You have lipstick on you."

Jake rubbed some more.

***

Kit was all cuddled up. She cried at the end of *Hook*. Not a sad ending unless you didn't also get to reunite with your own family.

Jake tried to soften the mood. "Sherry's cookies are terrible."

Kit wiped her face on Jake's arm. "Promise me you'll never let her move in here."

"Oh, hell, never. That woman is all kinds of wrong." Jake patted Kit's free shoulder.

"Good. Are you ever going to have girls over?"

"Sure, but I haven't been thinking much about it this year. Mostly been thinking about how I can make the farm work."

"Yeah."

"Yeah. Bedtime?"

Kit nodded and let Jake stand her up. Together, they climbed into their parents' bed.

***

"Jake?"

"Yeah?"

"How come you're not asleep?" Kit asked. The moon hid behind clouds, and the bedroom was full dark aside from the red numbers on the front of the clock radio.

"Guess I'm just thinking."

"About Mom and Dad?"

"Yeah, and the farm."

"I didn't have any money to get you something for Christmas, but I was looking at how to make a roast in the Betty Crocker book. Okay?"

Jake whistled. "I haven't had a roast since…been a good while anyway. You think you'll get it right?" He gave her side a tickle poke.

She jerked away, smile in her voice, and said, "Yeah. Better than kissy-kissy Sherry's cookies."

"Pfft. I've eaten motor oil better than Sherry's cookies."

"Jake, promise me again you won't let her move in here. I know that's what she wants."

Jake exhaled. "Never in a million years. She's not the first lady to wag her butt at your big brother and won't be the last."

"Gross."

"Mostly. Go to sleep."

"Goodnight."

"Goodnight," Jake said and flipped over.

December 30, 31, and January 1, 1993/94 – Copper Falls, Ontario, Canada

The Knechtel was the only grocery in Copper Falls. Through the entry to the right were four cashier tills with conveyor belt counters, behind them were the manager's office and the wall of cigarette cartons. To the left was the produce section, further up being the meat department, but not the deli department—that was at the other end of the store, in with the bakery and hot food take-away counter. The meat department smelled like cold blood and made all the produce smell like cold blood too. A fat man with a moustache worked the meat counter where patrons bought fish, whole chickens and turkeys, and then carved livestock by the portion—half of lamb, quarter cow, whole pig, and so on.

Jake had the cart waiting. He was hefting ten pounds of potatoes from the display—Kit found a book on cheap potato recipes in the cupboard above the stove—when Lee Anderson came over and clapped him on the shoulder.

"How's it hangin'?"

Jake dropped the potatoes into the cart. "Hey, Lee, pretty good, and you?"

"Long, loose, and full of juice."

Kit looked up at the man.

He blushed behind his fiery orange beard. "You got plans for New Years'?"

The money from the sale of the cattle went into thirds. The second of those thirds was about to be gone with the shopping trip.

"Going to take it easy at home. Me and Kit," Jake said.

"Ah, right. Rad. If you get bored and Kit falls asleep or something, Jane Patterson's breaking in her new place. She

31

bought that house up the hill, on Douglas. That white one?"

Jake nodded.

"She's single. Going to be plenty of single chicks. There's four nineteen-year-olds, all just started at Rayfield's, like nurses or whatever, they're from Walker's Forest. Prime chicks."

Jake offered a grin and said, "Sounds like fun, but me and Kit are gonna hang out, and watch the countdown on Global."

Lee Anderson shrugged. "You're only young once. Soon all these chicks'll be old."

Jake looked at the cart with the potatoes and jar of Jiffy peanut butter. He upturned his head with a sudden jerk. "How about you bring some of those girls out on New Years' Day and we go skating. I'll get a patch of ice out there and we'll get some coffee—"

"Irish coffee...ooh, Bailey's too. Kahlua, that shit's good in coffee. Or hot chocolate." Lee Anderson's smile began widening.

"Whatever, you bring some people and I'll get the rink ready. Sound good? Like, come after lunch."

"All right, man. All right. See you then." Lee Anderson gave a wave and headed up toward the frozen dinner cooler.

Kit said, "Can I invite some people, too?"

"Hell yeah," Jake said, nodding and smiling.

***

Jake had to replace another sheared pin in the snow blower. An instantly chilled sweat trickled down his neck by the time he got the tractor out. A good rink usually took a few weeks to set, but a few days was doable. The temperature was fourteen below zero, so he had that on his side. The hayfield next to the drive-in shed was flat and it took three passes: one pass to cut down every foot of snow, to clear it right down to the grass.

Kit was in her old snow pants and puffy new coat and boots. She'd been at the side lawn where the well tap rose from the ground about thirty inches. It had a lever function rather than a twist nozzle, which kept it useful once winter set in. This was the same tap they used to take the water to the cattle in the barn, some hundred feet and a set of stairs away. Kit had shoveled a path straight out to the designated rink space so their mother's garden hoses would reach without trouble.

"Do we put water on it now?" Kit asked.

The hoses hung on spikes driven into the framework of the sheet metal walls of the drive-in shed. They'd been in the old chicken coop before the great three-day cleanup occurred.

"Yeah, the earth's frozen hard. Thought we might have to wait because the snow came so fast, but nah, it's frozen hard." Jake climbed down off the tractor. Snow sparkled from his head to his boots, even on his eyebrows. "I can do that if you go start on supper and feed the cats."

"Okay. Lisa and her big sister are coming. Same with Chrissy and her mom. But Donna and the Susans can't come. Nobody answered at Jesse's house."

"That's pretty good then, huh?"

"Yes."

"Better get it pretty thick then, huh?"

"Yes."

"Gonna make supper for us then?"

"Yes." Kit turned and started for the house.

Jake pulled all four lengths of hose off the wall and headed out through the big sliding door of the shed.

***

"Supper's ready," Kit said, startling Jake.

He had ice all over his boots and pants, an icy sheen on his jacket front. His leather gloves were solid.

"Geez, you must be freezing."

Jake blinked at her. "Takes a lot of water. Go kill the tap. I've got to bring the hoses in, or they'll freeze."

***

Ninety minutes after going inside, Jake was in a change of clothes—his father's heavy canvas barn grubbers he'd worn in wintertime—with fresh gloves and the wet hoses looped over his shoulder.

The sun was down, so he moved the truck to shine on the thin sheet of ice. He rolled down the window of the truck and turned up the radio. Billy Ray came on just after the DJ said there'd been a snowmobile accident down near Burlington, three dead, a fire at a hall in Andover, and that the weather in Saugeen County was minus-nineteen with a wind chill of minus-thirty and a two-percent chance of flurries.

Jake unspooled the hoses and hooked them to the tap. He took the open end and began walking. He'd already crossed the driveway by the time the water started flowing. He watered the hard packed snow leading up to the rink. The wind had his cheeks red. He went on spraying the rest of the ice for about half an hour until Kit came out in her mother's grubbers.

"I can do it some," she said.

Jake said nothing, just dropped the hose and ran to the garage. He stripped down to his underwear and hurried inside. He stood in front of the fireplace, wiggling his toes and fingers. Ten minutes later, he was in dry clothes and back outside, turning off the tap. Kit's teeth chattered and she sprinted inside ahead of him. He boiled water and they had Carnation hot chocolate.

He set the alarm for five in the morning to get a fresh helping of water on the rink before the sun came up.

***

All day he and Kit took turns watering the rink. Jake moved six square bales of straw over to the side of the ice so people would have somewhere to sit and put their skates on.

The dryer in the house ran most of the day, though the outer layers never went in—they'd take days to dry anyway. At nine that night, Jake called it and sat on the couch with Kit after she did the barn chores for him. They each had two beers while watching the musicians and pre-coverage before the New Year hit but were both long asleep by the stroke of midnight.

***

Out at five, and then seven, and then nine, and finally at noon, the last time with a five-gallon bucket of recently boiled water. Kit had the big shop broom, flipped over. Jake had affixed a piece of weather stripping to the back of the head.

Quick as they could, they poured the water and dragged it along, smoothing out the worst of the pebbles and bumps. Once finished, they stood back and looked at the sum of their efforts.

"Kind of nice to see it done, huh?"

"Yes," Kit said. "It sure was a lot of work."

"Yeah, but people will love it."

***

By two o'clock, the girl named Lisa had gone home because her sister was bored. Chrissy had skates on while her mother sat on the straw bales, bundled up, drinking the coffee Jake offered. He had his skates out but sat in his boots and offered polite chatter to the woman.

If Lee Anderson had told anyone, they didn't show.

***

At four-thirty, just as the sun was setting, Kit watched out the living room bay window as her brother skated alone, a shadow beneath a pale blue sky.

Chapter Five

Troy Heen hadn't been Troy Heen since the night he staged his suicide and murdered his ex. He'd become Ben Lynch. Ben Lynch purchased another Magnum—this time without rounds—from a pawnshop in Littleton, New Hampshire. He then filled the tank of the van and drove through the night, taking the I-93 to the I-89 before getting on the I-81 and riding it out all the way to Rochester, New York. He parked in a Dunkin' Donuts lot and napped for four hours.

By two in the afternoon, he figured out the next step. That night, he put the Magnum in the face of a young woman working the till at a Mobil gas station. He ordered her to cut the telephone cord from the wall and empty the cash register. He wore a paper plate with two eyeholes cut out, tied to his face like an old goalie mask with a shoelace he'd found in the back of the van. The plate had a triangular grease stain from a piece of pizza. The woman emptied the till: only ninety-five bucks.

Ben Lynch then said, "Open the safe or I'll blow your head off."

The woman said she couldn't and then said she'd get fired if she did.

"Now I know you can open it. Be fired or be dead. Up to you."

That got her moving and Ben Lynch ran down the road to where he'd parked the van with close to five hundred dollars in his pocket, which would sit with the one-eighty he had remaining after buying the gun.

He let the paper plate mask get sucked out the window as he drove.

January 25, 1994 – American Interstates and Queen's Highways

Ben Lynch sat up on the Motel 6 bed and swiped at the bug beneath him. He'd been dreaming about police and about prison. The clock told 5:23. That was AM. He hit the lamp's switch and hurried to the shower. He'd taken a long soak in the tiny tub the night before. An additional shower was necessary.

Dressed, he surveyed the room, though he hadn't brought more than a grocery bag of clothes in with him, and then left. The key went into the return slot, and he got behind the wheel of the van. His last stop before the border was at Dunkin' Donuts for a coffee and a pair of chocolate glazed donuts.

A pile-up had traffic moving about a foot an hour. The wipers swished and squeaked at the steady snowfall just southwest of Rochester. The voices on the radio suggested he'd been on the highway already three hours, and he took the next exit. Through Oakfield and then onto the 77, not slowing a tick to peek for animals as he burned through the Iroquois Nature Reserve. He rode the 31 all the way to the I90 where he hit traffic again. Now he could see the Rainbow Bridge in the distance.

***

He told the Canadian border guard one truth: he was not bringing any fruit or vegetables into the country.

***

The border behind him, he kept to the highway past the exits for Niagara Falls and then Welland. Ontario was barren, maple trees and snow, same as New York State. The traffic moved a bit quicker, probably because there was less of it. After passing a sign that read St. Catharines 6KM, he had to slide into the left lane to go by a tow truck pulling a Toyota from a snowbank.

The woman standing next to the tow truck held a baby to her chest, bouncing it. Her hair stuck up in irregular intervals.

"Don't envy you," Ben said. "Don't want to end up you either."

He took the first exit into St. Catharines and rolled by several signs for Brock University. No interest there. The students milled about the sidewalks and crossed the streets without consideration, forcing drivers to stop and wait.

Away, though not far, he found signage for a mall and followed it. He needed Canadian cash. He needed more clothes. He needed a thermal sleeping bag. Motels and hotels were too damned expensive.

A lady in a box built into a wall took his American cash and swapped it for a little more than seven hundred Canadian dollars, mostly in brown and red bills. He found a Zellers department store and mingled with the elderly people and the obvious mothers of young children until he found everything he needed.

Shopping, being around people, trying on clothes, these were normal things. Shooting people and jacking gas stations were not. In a hurry, he paid and got back out to the van. He drove side streets until he found country. There were flat white fields and farmhouses. Every barn was red. He found a river, swollen with winter. He looked around and dug the Magnum out from the springs beneath the passenger seat. He unloaded it and dropped it from the cement bridge where he stood. The water moved so quickly there wasn't a glub or a splash. The cartridges went in next.

January 26, 1994 – Grimsby, Ontario, Canada

Ben slept in his van and woke up cold. The cities followed one after the first, second, third. He got back on the highway once fueled up and took the Skyway over Lake Ontario. Exit signs for Toronto started to draw shorter numbers. That was more city.

Everybody knew Toronto, so at the next exit that had nothing to do with Toronto, he took it.

More city, but not big city. Guelph was slow going, and he stopped for coffee at a Tim Hortons and got Chinese in the same plaza. Aimlessly, he bummed around, even bought a pack of cigarettes for something to do—he'd quit smoking in January of 1989, a New Year's resolution.

Before sundown, he found another mall and department store. He purchased a second sleeping bag and a little kerosene heater.

January 27, 1994 – Queen's Highway 6, Ontario, Canada

The cities were all behind him and the highway was down to a couple lanes. The houses were moderate, and the vehicles were getting on in years. Ben Lynch lit a cigarette. He pulled into a town called Arthur and parked. He walked one end of the main street to the other, looked in every window, and only burned a couple hours.

Back in the van, he got another coffee from a drive-thru window and then pulled in to park. He went inside and sat on the can for twenty-one minutes.

***

Circling like soap in a sink drain, he stalled and clung, never really getting anywhere. He stayed close to Highway 6, veering off to see towns or farms, but trailing back when he'd gone a few miles.

Winter had the run of the place and nothing was happening.

At a quarter after five, he pulled into an A&W in a town called Sprucemont and parked a few spots down from a Cadillac convertible that had no business being out in the winter, and an enormous Winnebago.

The girl at the till wore thick glasses and grew pimples in lively pink clusters, whiteheads sprouting like snowy mountain caps. She said nothing and the closer Ben came, the more her eyes crossed. Her apron had been pulled sideways and the left seam was stuck around one of her big breasts. As if she was about to breast feed through her orange and brown employee sweater.

"Can I get a Papa meal?"

The girl looked down and began punching fingers into the register. "Root beer?"

Ben scrunched his mouth a second and then said, "Sure, why not?"

"In a frosted stein or to-go cup?" Her voice was nasally.

"What?"

"A stein?" She turned and pointed at a picture but kept her eyes on Ben.

The picture was of the goofy bear mascot holding a big glass beer stein.

"Yeah, sure."

"Did you want to purchase the stein to take home, only...?"

"No."

"Four-forty-nine."

Ben pushed across a red fifty and the girl sighed, side-eyed him, and then began making change. He pocketed the change. It took several minutes for his food to come up and he stared at the minefield of pimples on the girl's face. It was tough to look away. Once the food was finally ready, he took his tray and paused to get a look at the shoeless foursome in green coveralls as they entered the restaurant.

***

A kid buzzed circles near where Ben sat and eventually collided with his elbow, sending the heavy stein to the floor. He caught the handle just as the cup shattered. The bottom remained intact, same with the handle and one side, but half the mug had broken away in three long slivers. It gave the stein a set of teeth.

"Oh my gosh. I'm so sorry. Billy!" the kid's mother shouted across the restaurant. She was short and thin. The kid was short and fat.

Ben sat three tables from the exit. The glass on the floor was in a small puddle of slivers and a few small hunks. He was nearly done with the drink when the kid bumped him.

"Let me buy you another," the woman said.

"No worries. Just foam left, pretty much."

The woman was shaking her head, standing behind Ben. She leaned in close then and said, "You see those freaks? They ordered forty little cheeseburgers and aren't wearing shoes."

"Really?" Ben turned to look around. It was obvious which freaks she meant, but their table was vacant.

The kid had a car in his hand and was flying it, making airplane noises. He stopped suddenly and let his arm drop to his side. The woman shouted, "Billy, will you come eat your supper?"

Billy spun on his heels and took one step. A loud snapping turned him back around. Ben rose from his seat but couldn't see past a set of booths. He could only see the kid.

The mother started over. Her meal and the kid's meal were on a tray at a table just behind Ben's seat. More strange, wet sounds came from the blind spot. Then moaning. Then groaning. Then growling.

The woman was a few feet from her kid when a furry claw shot up and slashed at her flesh, letting out a fantastic red backwash. In a flash, two huge, furry creatures in green coveralls broke for the counter and leapt over. The pimply girl screamed for three seconds before the only sound she made was gargling. A manager rushed forward and one of the beasts was on its hind legs with its jaw wrapped around the man's throat. A pair of boys with knives tried to side-walk out from the employee door when a third beast cornered them and began slashing. The claws carved deep gullies, bone white reflecting under the fluorescents, red pumping and spilling, body parts thrashing.

Ben turned slowly, like a drunk about to put his car into a tree. A blood-smeared beast leapt from a tabletop onto his, sending his mostly empty tray to the floor. Claws sank into his stomach and teeth punctured the back of his neck. Automatically his arm jerked around and planted the A&W stein into the beast's cheek. It howled and rolled off him.

Ben staggered backward to the exit, made brief eye contact with the beast devouring the cooks by the employee door, and then pushed out of the restaurant. He planted hands on his wounds until he reached the van. He lit the engine and yanked the shifter, getting on the road as quickly as possible.

From behind, lights came on him quickly. The vehicle was huge. He couldn't drive faster. The injuries were bad enough that he should've been looking for a hospital.

He winced as the big vehicle pulled up next to him.

There were now canine beasts at the wheel and—he exhaled although the dairy tanker sent the van into shakes with the drag. Seeing things.

He took a left and drove ten miles from the highway. Took another left and drove sixteen miles. Took a right that meandered around a river for nine miles. He took another right for two miles. Then a left for five. A right for two. He then pulled over on what seemed an utterly dead stretch of county road. He spilled into his sleeping bags and turned on the kerosene heater.

Outside, the moon was high and full.

Chapter Six

Outside it was so brisk, Kit's nose hairs clung together as she hurried out to the chicken coop in her pajamas, rubber boots, and old coat. They'd purchased five laying hens and Jake cornered the man who put them up for auction to ask about tending to them. Jake relayed what the man told him to Kit, and it was all pretty simple. Chickens, especially in the winter, kept to themselves.

The glowing red heater was an expense that Jake hadn't considered, but he'd found a used one at the same auction house—though on the market side of the building—for twenty-nine bucks.

Kit stood in front of the heater, soaking in rays while she dumped water into the bucket on the floor. The chickens were all up on a shelf, sitting on straw beds, watching her with beady eyes, their wrinkles and neck skin rippling with the constant twitchiness that was their nature.

"What're you looking at?" she said to them once the bucket was empty.

In the house, Kit washed up and dressed and ate a bowl of cereal, packed the sandwich, cookies, and the apple she'd put in the fridge the night before, and climbed into her new coat, boots, and hat. The clothes she wore were only new to her. They'd gone to the Salvation Army first, and she was in a grouch over it but saw mostly the same clothes at Zellers and then stuff not nearly as nice, so they went back to get the items second hand. Jake's relief was all over his face and Kit had never worn Nike anything before finding it used—many of the cool kids had Nike. Most in fact.

The walk down the lane took seven minutes on cold days. She huddled into herself beneath the pale purple sky and watched every breath plume from her mouth like cap gun smoke. She got to the end and to her right, the bus's lights were just tipping over a gentle hill three-quarters of a mile away. She shivered and pinched her hands in her armpits, pivoted her hips, rocking back and forth trying to get warm. The bus engine roared, closer, and she kept rocking.

She stopped moving mid-rock. Down the road to her left, about a quarter-mile, was a big blue van. There were no houses back that way, not unless you drove for about ten minutes, and nobody really had a reason for coming up that direction to make for the highway, unless they got lost on the winding backroads.

The bus door opened and Kit crossed the slim road to climb aboard. She got to her seat, one spot before the middle on the driver's side, and the bus started moving again, pulling into her lane to turn around. One other kid lived on her road, but right on the highway corner. He was in the second grade and the bus picked him up on the way out, which gave him about ten minutes of extra sleeping time.

On Highway 6, the bus headed north to the next concession and turned onto a highly populated side road. The bus filled steadily until there were thirty-six butts in seats before they headed back south to Copper Falls Public.

***

Kit was in art class when the PA system declared there was to be a class assembly first thing, and all the kids from grades one to four had to go to the gymnasium to talk about being nice. Bully was a term that came up sometimes in class, but not so much at recess. Kids could be mean. The word bully still didn't seem right, was too harmless sounding.

The vice principal, Mrs. Coke, stood on the lip of the stage and spoke at the hundred or so students gathered into the space. Rhonda Bernhard had been a short, fat eighth grader whose parents made her wear long denim dresses and bonnets. There were nine Bernhard kids, but Rhonda was by far the youngest—the others were all out of school, staying to the provincial minimum of sixteen before dropping out to focus on servitude to their god. Everybody knew they were freaks. Some girls picked on Rhonda. Homemade underwear marred by a period stain was stolen from the change room the Friday preceding and wrapped around a big red dodge ball. Other eighth graders kicked the ball at kids. It had gone on all lunch recess.

Kit was in the hall. She'd been asked by her teacher to run down to the janitor's closet for a fresh pack of brown paper towels. She paused by the gymnasium doors to listen.

"On Saturday night, Rhonda Bernhard left a note stating she was never coming back to school because of how horrible we all were," Mrs. Coke said, her eyes down.

"No more Fat Rhonda!" a boy shouted, a fourth grader named Ronnie who had two brothers, one in the sixth grade and the other in the eighth grade.

Kit pivoted, leaning her head on the doors so that she could peek through the crack.

On stage, Mrs. Coke sighed. A heavy sound into the microphone that quieted the errant laughter. "Rhonda left her home in the middle of the night and began walking. About a mile down the road, she slipped on ice and according to the doctor, broke her leg. She froze to death."

Kit gasped. The gymnasium was silent. The air was poison, and nobody breathed until they had to. Then, as if unable to exist otherwise, that same boy, the one with the big brothers just like him, just like their mother and father, said, "Stupid Fat Rhonda."

Mrs. Coke lifted her face and looked at the boy. She pointed a bony finger with an inch-long press-on nail painted maroon. She said, "You did this. You killed her. And you and you and you." The finger pointed in a wave. "And me and all the teachers. Bullying cannot be tolerated."

Mrs. Coke continued, explaining how important it was to

tell someone if another kid bullied them. In all, the assembly took half an hour. Once the younger kids started toward the doors, Kit ran back to the art classroom. The PA system sounded and called to the gymnasium the rest of the classes. Kit didn't tell anybody what she knew; it was too horribly fantastical to be true, she had to have misheard or imagined it.

On the stage, Mrs. Coke wiped the slate and started from the beginning. Kit sat near the front and gasped when Mrs. Coke said Rhonda Bernhard had frozen to death. A couple girls began crying. Ronnie's eldest brother shouted out, "What's that got to do with us?"

Mrs. Coke pointed her finger and said, "You. You killed her." This time the finger stayed put. "You and your brothers." It held steady for a ten-count and then got into the rest of the blame game.

***

The bus let Kit out at the end of the lane, and she stood aside as it turned around. The sun was only an idea on the western horizon. It had gotten much colder as the day progressed. Cold enough to make her lungs ache.

Still, Kit paused a few extra seconds to look at the van. The windows were white, though it hadn't snowed enough to stick around against the wind. She dipped her chin and pulled at the drawstrings of her hood. Head down, she charged in the long, straight laneway.

Jake was on the ice rink, stickhandling a puck. The big shed blocked the wind chill.

"You know the Bernhards?" Kit asked

"The Mormons?" Jake said.

"Maybe. They all wear dresses and bonnets."

"Yeah. I think they're Mormons."

"Rhonda Bernhard snuck out of the house to run away and broke her leg. She died of cold."

"Holy crow." Jake stopped playing with the puck.

"We had an assembly and Mrs. Coke said it was everybody's fault because we let people be mean to each other."

"Yeah?"

"Then everybody told on everybody else for being mean and Mrs. Gardner told us that we didn't need to tell everything, only when someone really hurt our feelings."

"Yeah."

"It was a bad day."

"I bet. Did they like your new clothes?"

"Nobody noticed." Kit turned toward the house then but turned back. "There's a blue van out on the road. It was there this morning, too."

"Hmm. I wonder who owns it." Jake pushed the puck over to the single straw bale he'd left out by the rink.

Kit had the fridge open and pulled out a pot of leftover Kraft Dinner. She took a fork from the drawer and began plucking noodles by the twos to nibble at. Though she'd been using the cookbooks—even Jake had tried to fix a couple recipes—the mainstays remained.

The door opened, and Jake stepped in. He had his skates in his hands. He set them on the plastic drainer mat and kicked off his boots. "You want to take water out to the cats when you do chores? I don't think they eat snow how dogs do and getting to the creek is pretty tough going."

"Okay." Kit put the pot back into the fridge. "Are you going to see about that van?"

"Guess I'd better."

"Can I come?"

"Yeah, guess you better. You might need to drive the truck back. Who knows, maybe the van's full of money."

"Maybe it's full of cow poop."

Jake made a face. "Hope not."

"Are you going now?"

"Yeah." He opened the closet, pulled out his heavy barn

overalls. He took out his jacket after he'd stepped into the shit-stained coveralls and set it on the washer, then bent to put his boots back on.

Kit took a big Coleman water jug with a spout on it out from a low cupboard—they hadn't used it since the summer, during haying. "This is enough water for the cats, right?"

Jake leaned in around the half-wall to look. "Yeah."

"Hot water will last longer."

"Smart."

Kit filled the jug from the tap and joined her brother at the door. He was ready to go and said he'd go feed the cattle while she did the cats and checked the chickens and then they'd go out to see about the van.

***

The sun was almost all the way down by the time Jake pointed the truck's headlights on the van. "Ready?" Jake asked and Kit said, "Yes." They got out and Jake went to the driver's door. It was frozen but opened with a jiggle of the handle. Kit stood behind him, shivering. Jake tried the key and the battery click-click-clicked.

In the temperatures they'd been getting, the truck's block heater needed plugged in just about every night. So, no wonder.

"Christ almighty," Jake said. "Let's put the chain on and pull it into the shed. Plug it in then. I guess call someone about it, or something. If the plow comes tonight, it won't be able to get past."

"Okay."

Jake ran over to the truck bed and pulled out a chain. He slipped onto his belly, sliding on the snowy road, to get a look under the van's bumper. Fat rivets held the bumper to posts. Jake wound the chain around the posts and hooked the claw.

Kit was popping up and down and swaying her upper half, pivoting on her hip, hands in her armpits.

"I'll back up. You put the loop over the hitch ball and then get in the van, put it in neutral and steer how I steer the truck."

"What?" Kit shouted.

"Just steer how I steer. Like pulling a wagon, okay? I'll go real' slow."

Jake ran to the truck. The steamy, smoky exhaust cloud engulfed him momentarily. He shot forward and spun into a sliding skid behind the van like a stunt driver. Then came back around. Jake overshot, backed up, and Kit popped the chain over the ball.

The van went into neutral, and she kept her eyes pinned on the rear end of the truck through the icy windshield. Jake was going about three miles an hour and took the turn at half that. Once on the laneway, Kit relaxed some, but was still tense and sitting up tight against the steering wheel.

"Ummm."

Kit stiffened and turned to look for the noise.

"Ummm."

Her teeth chattered from cold and terror. She looked at the bundled body in the back, the top of a head poking above the covers.

"Errr."

Kit's breaths came fast. Puffing before her.

"Errr."

The bundle was marred by dark red and black stains.

"Uh."

Jake honked and Kit faced front. She turned the wheel to match the truck.

"Ummm."

Jake pulled up by the barn and faced the nose of the truck down. He parked but left the truck running and hopped out. Kit swung open the van's door and the impact between the bumper and trailer hitch was a dull, but heavy thump.

"Whoa, you got—"

"There's someone in the back!"

Jake's eyes stretched enough that the cold brought tears forth almost instantly and his jaw hung slack, mouth steaming.

***

"We'll let him get warm before we worry about the wounds," Jake said.

The man couldn't hold a conversation and only moaned when Jake pulled him out by the armpits and Kit took his feet. They carted him in and stoked and fueled the fireplace until it blazed. They then made a pile of bedsheets and an old quilt and lifted him off the cool floor. He was about a foot from the flames.

"Any more blankets?"

"Only on the beds," Kit said. "I can get Mom and Dad's?"

"Yeah, okay."

Kit broke away and returned with the queen-size duvet and bedsheet. She draped them over the man. He'd begun shivering.

"Should we call the ambulance?"

Jake picked the man's wallet up from the floor. "Yeah. Yeah." Jake turned from the man and made for the telephone bench. "Hello. I need an ambulance."

"Emergency?" The voice was tinny and high.

"I think so."

"There's been a party go through the lake at Hotchkiss Corner. The teams are all over. Going to Sprucemont and Owen Sound. How serious?"

"I don't know. There's a man. He was in a van. Could be he was out all night and day. He's got blood on him, too."

"Any broken bones?"

"I don't know... He's chattering a bit now. Wasn't awake before. Cold as ice, but we got him in front of the fire."

After a pause, the switchboard operator said, "Nothing we can do for the next hour and a half, at least. Young men at a fishing hole. They lit the cabin on fire, drunk, and went through.

Nine of them, the youngest was only sixteen."

Jake whistled and rubbed his face, looking at Kit.

"So wait it out. Hold on. Get the man warm and call back if anything turns for the worse."

"Oh. Okay."

"Sorry."

The disconnect was loud. The electronic pulse was louder. He hung up. "Guess there's been a bunch of people go into some lake and all the ambulances are busy going out of town."

"What does that mean?" Kit leaned in to look at the man's face. He'd begun shaking like a hockey card between bicycle spokes.

"We watch him awhile. I guess."

"Should I get Mom's kit for in case he wakes up and needs bandaged?"

"Yeah. Guess so."

Chapter Seven

The papers on Detective Marc Foster's desk were organized chaos. The little red light on his telephone blinked steadily because the last three times he'd checked his messages, they were all from the school, calling about his son. He'd then called his wife, but she did not want to talk about the kid or about coming home. Instead she yelled like he'd told their son to act up, like he'd uprooted the boy and took him to his grandmother's place.

At least she spoke to him, albeit briefly and angrily.

He'd told her he couldn't think about Freddy skipping, smoking pot, or threatening to run away with the girl he'd been dating. The thing with the bodies and the camper was all he could think about, at least until a lead stumbled into the office or the situation blew into a new jurisdiction. Marc leaned in to read the chicken scratch of the officer who'd taken the tip. Somebody saw that Winnebago come into town, saw it leave heading south. Another saw it leave heading west. Another north. Another said it was hidden in plain sight at a scrap yard down in Conn.

"Foster, come with me. Bring your jacket, grab yourself a coffee." Charles McCarthy waved with a DuMaurier pack and a white Bic brand lighter in his right hand.

"Sure thing, Chief," Marc said after nailing down where the voice was coming from. Since the blood and the absence of bodies, the station was the goddamned Metro Toronto Zoo. "Give me a sec."

"You know where I'll be."

Marc slipped his cigarettes and lighter into the pocket of his jacket after he plucked the jacket from the chair back. He put it on as he made his way to the lunchroom. An empty Tim

Hortons' donut box sat in the middle of a Formica-topped dining table. He gave a look inside to be sure he hadn't missed anything.

The coffee maker on the counter had dual pots, and one pot was empty while the other was down to a quarter. He dumped the coffee—grind laden as it was—into a plain white mug grabbed from the top row of the dishwasher. The mug cupboard was usually empty.

He lifted the cup to a few inches from his mouth and noticed the lipstick smear. His eyes fell back onto the cracked door of the dishwasher. It was nearly full up top, someone needed to turn it on.

He wiped the lipstick into a dull smudge as he headed for the side door and the picnic tables next to the parking lot. They were isolated. A fence cordoned the lot. They had privacy.

The chief had a folder with him and a stainless-steel travel mug full of tea—coffee attributed to his ulcer, so said a doctor, and he'd told the world he was trying to cut back. He had a cigarette between the index and middle fingers of his right hand—he'd confessed that the same doctor told him cigarettes were likely the root cause of his ulcer.

"You called the other employees?"

Marc slipped onto the seat of the picnic table's open side, straddling. His coffee cup sloshed, and black liquid tipped over the edge in a wave. "Sure," he said and then fished a cigarette from his pack.

"Anything special about the people working?"

"Nah. One kid had a three-day suspension last October for showing up to class stoned, but nothing from the others. Nothing from the missing woman and her kid either."

The chief inhaled and spoke through an exhale. "Any chance of a drug angle?"

"Nah."

They sat in silence for close to a minute, sipping and puffing. Then the chief said, "Anything concrete on this

Winnebago?"

"Can't even place the age. It was dirty. Nobody saw the driver. Don't even know if it's really got anything to do with anything. Hell, it was there half the afternoon, could be the driver went in, got his burger and rings and root beer, ate, washed up, took a dump with a flush toilet, and then went out to sleep. Left after he woke up, totally unaware that people had died just inside the building."

The chief tilted his head. "You believe that?"

"No. I believe it's connected. I also believe this isn't just, you know, like, a one off."

"Oh?"

The chief looked out to the traffic beyond the fence. People took Highway 6 all day and all night. Thousands of people passed through town every week. Come summertime, multiply that number by a hundred.

"It's too clean."

The chief turned around and looked at Marc for this one. "Clean? You call that mess clean?"

"Not clean how you want to eat off the floor, but clean as if someone, or more likely a few people, went in killed and disposed of the bodies before anybody had a chance to place a call or notice. Old what's his name said he was at the door at nine after eight and they were locked and the lights were off, and he hung around the parking lot for an hour waiting for the date that was supposed to meet him."

The chief stabbed out his butt into the ceramic ashtray. Water had mixed with the leftover ashes and had turned the white grey, permanently. A color close to that of the weathered picnic table.

"Now, there's another mystery. How did Adam Petes get someone to agree to go out with him?"

"Want ads in the paper, or lonely hearts. Whatever it's called."

"Was the Winnebago there while he was there?"

Marc shook his head and finished his cup.

"Any of the calls amount to something?"

Marc laughed humorlessly at this—a quick double burst. "Nothing at all. Glad we didn't put the thing about the huge paw prints. Every dog in the county bigger than a Chihuahua would be on the chopping block."

"What do you think of that? The paw prints."

"No shoe prints in the blood. I think they're wearing shoes with dog prints on the bottoms. I saw a bigfoot documentary where this guy in Colorado was wearing plaster molds of their feet and selling prints and stuff to tourists."

"Did they find any sasquatches? Wait, is it sasquatches or sasquatch, like deer?" The chief withdrew another cigarette and lit it. "No, sasquatches is right."

"I don't know, but no. The show was more on the people obsessed with bigfoot."

"Okay. I can get behind that, otherwise we're looking for dogs bigger than I ever saw. Bigger than wolves."

Marc squinted. "What about werewolf imitation. A few freaks go into A&W, maybe they praise Satan or the moon, then slip on the crazy shoes and get busy killing folks. They steal the bodies to make it seem like a werewolf feeding frenzy."

"Dogs always eat the bones and all," the chief said.

"Yeah, sure, they eat them and choke, but nobody choked here."

February 3, 1994 – MacGregor Point Provincial Park, Ontario, Canada

Raymond Jackson had on a tan hat with matching waterproof tan slacks, a brown and orange, down-filled vest, and Merrell hiking boots. Shirley Carver wore an almost identical outfit, though her vest was grey and pink. They'd left the trail and moved through the stiff snow beneath the canopied ceiling, toward Lake Huron.

A twitcher caught sight of a northern goshawk a few days earlier and sent a blurry shot into the paper. Raymond showed his girlfriend Shirley the picture. They were at the community care facility for an old age day program. Most times folks just talked about Elvis or Christmas or grandkids or how the world was going to shit or how there were so many Chinese and Blacks around these days. Raymond and Shirley talked birds and sometimes snuck away to fool around under a staircase like a couple of teens. Mostly kissing, but Raymond promised if they went for it, he'd get enough blood to the right spot. Some mornings he even woke up with a hard-on, so it still worked.

Sticks snapped in a semi-constant rhythm underfoot. The few birds that stuck around for the winter were quiet and the wind played a low tune through the trees.

"Damn," Raymond said.

The lake was suddenly right there, and they'd gone further than they wanted to.

"Oh, dear. We've gone too far." Shirley leaned against a tree. Spry for sixty-six, but visibly tired from the thirty-minute hike. "Perhaps we ought to sit still and watch the—"

"Holy God up in Heaven." Raymond lifted his binoculars and panned over the half-frozen water. "That can't be, can it?"

Thick ice filled from about thirty feet out to beyond their sightline. The Saugeen River flowed into the lake, the natural motion of the water below and a couple days above freezing created breaks in the coverage. Partway frozen into the ice were at least two human corpses.

"Looks like A&W," Shirley said, she had her binoculars up as well. "See the shirt? Very nearly the same colors of your vest, and the uniforms at A&W."

Raymond looked down at his vest. "Huh. Hadn't thought of that when I bought it... We better go tell somebody, right?"

February 4, 1994 – Sprucemont, Ontario, Canada

"Could be we have some people you're looking for," the RCMP officer said to Marc Foster.

"Oh yeah? Who's that?"

"We've got bodies. One's in her A&W uniform. The others are naked."

"Others?"

The RCMP officer said, "Sure, others."

"How many?"

"Total: two female and two male."

"A baby?"

"No baby."

"How do they look?"

The RCMP officer exhaled. "Pale and chewed."

"Fish?"

"No. I'd say mammals, like dogs or a cougar. Probably more like a cougar. Got a couple up here."

Marc rubbed his face. Dogs. The prints. "Fuck. Okay. Fax me some shots. That shirt have a nametag?"

"No, but the pants were partially intact. Legs below the thighs were mostly gone, but the wallet was loaded with coupons and cards. Had a library card, a student ID card, a beginner's license, a health card, a SIN card, all matching the name. Laurence Andersson. Two *esses*. Nine-one-nine Cotton Way, Sprucemont, Ontario. Born April eighteen, seventy-nine."

"No need for shots. We'll need transport. There's a baby missing too."

The RCMP officer exhaled into the phone's receiver. "These are big teeth marks. Not saying we won't look, just saying we won't find. Probably a baby is like fine veal to whatever eats people."

"Jesus Christ, man."

"Hey, don't shoot the messenger. They died long before they ever went into the river."

"The Saugeen?"

"Sure. Shoots out into Huron right near where they were

found."

"Well now, that's something to grow on," Marc said.

The Saugeen River wound hard west just south of Copper Falls, twenty-five kilometers north of Sprucemont.

"You'll look for the baby? Maybe put out a call to look for something suspicious?"

The RCMP officer huffed. "Not my first day."

Chapter Eight

September 19, 1899 – Dawson City, Yukon, Canada

The legs weren't under Leslie Autry as he shambled along. He hadn't eaten in days. The gold rush boomed, but only when it struck. Otherwise, Dawson City was an immoral hole where a man might find Hell on Earth and emptied pockets.

Leslie was a man gone over the ledge. He'd sold his life and left his family, made big promises and burned nearly every bridge he crossed on his way to fortune. Dawson City sucked him dry and put him out of everything he owned, right down to his panning gear and a second set of clothes.

He stumbled sideways on a muddy road and dunked his face into a murky horse trough. He swished water and lifted his head to spit. A quarter to take a bite of horse shit. Another quarter to sit beneath the horse until it pissed on him. Ten dollars to wrap his mouth around a horse's cock and do a whore's work.

The men who hit it big in Dawson City were not the type of men who were used to having money. The men who hit had more money than entertainment.

Leslie Autry was desperate and horse cum was a steeper price than he originally thought. He'd drank about a buck of that money, only to wake up outside, naked and penniless.

"Look at you," a voice said.

Leslie didn't turn, didn't need to face the shame any longer. He dunked his head and exhaled his breath. He held under there as long as he could, but fingernails dug into his shoulders and reefed him backward.

"I saw what they did to you. It was not very nice."

Leslie squinted up. A woman. She had long black hair and pale cheeks, high cheekbones.

"I need a drink," he said.

The woman leaned over the naked man. "No, you don't. What you need is revenge. Most times I stay out of things, but some folks deserve to die and others deserve to see some retribution. Would you like to see those men die?"

Leslie Autry licked his dry and cracked lips. "I need money. I'm thirsty. I can work."

The woman bent back at the waist and laughed. After a few hearty seconds, she bent forward again. "Sir, you can't even stand. Hell, you can't even suck a cock worth a damn. Mind, it was a rather large cock."

"Please."

"How about this. I'll free you from every endless need and every sordid memory?"

"I need a drink."

"No, you don't. You need to crawl into Lucy's and sit in the corner, in a shadow. Try to find a blanket or something to cover yourself."

"Drink."

The woman rummaged into the folds of her dress and produced a dime and a nickel. "Lucy's or you will be very sorry."

Leslie Autry nodded, his slug-like tongue playing back and forth over his lips.

***

The population was down significantly thanks to the fires back in May. But where there was gold, there were men looking to do whatever it took to get it. Many men.

Lucy's was a scandalized place. During the daylight hours, the pastor visited on the regular to offer words of damnation and hellfire. The locals scowled and scorned. When the sun went down and the streets of Dawson City bathed in shadows, those same scowling faces showed up for the burlesque dances, the half-hours stay in the rooms upstairs, and for the kind of music that would move Satan himself to dance.

Leslie Autry had a hunk of filthy poncho draped over himself where he lay in the corner. He'd long finished his first drink. A young man in skins bought him a beer, told him it would help get that taste out of his mouth, then laughed and kicked Leslie in the side. Leslie cradled the mug and spilled not a drop.

The sun was gone, and the gas lamps shone a gentle golden glow over the various shades of wooden interior. The piano player earned the latest nickel in his cup. The door swung open while *Breaktime* was winding down.

"The cocksucker's back!" a voice shouted, and a chorus of men laughed.

"Hey, boys," a syrupy voice called out from upstairs. The whores leaned over the railing in their underwear, breasts just about spilling.

Leslie Autry sat up and said, "I need a drink."

The men laughed.

A man big and rough as a lumberjack spoke from beneath a wiry black beard. "We find a second drunk, think what they'd do for money."

The men laughed some more and then made gagging moans.

"Your father should've shot you into your mother's ass, instead of—"

The door burst open. The piano ceased playing. Like a whipped wind, the thing flashed inside. The big man screamed, holding his throat. Another man said, "What in the Lord?" as blood streamed from between the big man's fingers.

"Did you see? Was it a bear?" this came from another of the party.

The whores slammed doors. The piano player and the bartender hid in the office, behind a quickly barricaded door. The sound of dragged furniture swirled in next to the heavy breathing of men, poisoning the still quiet…and something else. Another sound. Something large.

One of the panhandlers standing next to the big man had a revolver out. A second did likewise. A great, furry shadow broke from beneath a table, sending it flipping. One man took aim and put a shot into the airborne furniture. The second man fired into the floor as claws peeled the skin from his face, fish-hooking his mouth and reeling it back to his ear. He fell sideways and lay stunned and seeping. The flap of loose skin ran almost to his shoulder.

Glasses on the bar top shattered and claws scrambled beyond the sight of the three men who remained standing in the group and the patrons who'd had the ill luck of being in attendance.

The young man who'd kicked Leslie Autry after providing him with a beer broke for the door. The furry shadow leapt from behind the counter and cut him off. Slashing and biting. He wailed and the man who'd fired into the table rang off a shot in the direction of the wolf—it was out in the open, no doubts, a wolf.

It bounced from a pivot and took a shot as it leapt across the room. It growled and sank teeth into the man, severing his shooting arm from his body with a jerky tug. People gasped and screamed.

"A wolf!"

"A devil dog!"

"My eyes! I can't see, it got my eyes!"

"Where is it?"

"I don't know."

"Look o—!"

The lamplights fluttered with the chaos of the barroom. Tables flipped and chairs screeched. Men wept and wailed. Blood pooled.

The big man held his neck. He came to lean against the bar. He had his knife out. Men were dead all over the room. Only men. Only panhandlers. "You," he said. Across the room was the drunk, unharmed in a filthy poncho.

Leslie Autry's eyes darted around the slaughter. The giant wolf stepped with a slight limp. Blood dripped from its jaws and paw prints littered the once dry flooring. Blood trickled from the beast's right fore-shoulder. Its eyes were cold brown, almost gold. It snarled as it crossed the cleared barroom.

The big man waved the knife. "Git! Git!" he hissed. The blood continued pouring from around his hand.

Upstairs, a door opened briefly. The wolf turned and the man looked up. The door had already slammed closed.

"Fuck away," the man said.

The wolf stopped moving, bending almost imperceptibly at the knees, before launching onto the man's throat. The knife clattered as it fell.

The young man who had kicked Leslie Autry was crawling. The wolf quit lapping at the big man to prattle across the room and take off the man's right calf with a single bite. The man rolled and screamed. The wolf was on him. It ate and drank.

Only the wet lapping sound and pained moans remained. Not another noise. Methodically, the beast went from man to man and made meals. It ate until it had its fill—eating faces and fingers and throats mostly.

Leslie Autry began crying. He didn't move more than his hands and shoulders, wiping tears and bobbing for breath. The feast took many minutes. Now and then, a door would open and close quickly. Eventually, the sopping beast ventured close to where Leslie sat.

"Please." The only word left to him. "Please."

The beast stopped and turned its snout to the ceiling. Its fur ran in courses, as if the rivulets of blood followed destined paths after release. It then began to shake. Blood splattered everywhere. Leslie wiped his face, licked his no longer dry lips.

The forelegs widened and the hair sank back into flesh. Elbows bent and breasts ballooned, also reeling hair into pores. The rear legs grew in drastic proportion, stretching to five, maybe six times the width. And pale. Pale everywhere that the fur was no longer. The stretched neck came next, and bones snapped and crackled. Skin sagged and reeled in. A low howling became a feminine moaning. Like sexual release impending.

Hair fell in great wavy brown layers over…the woman's shoulders. She lowered her head and played her brown eyes on Leslie Autry. Her mouth was full of huge teeth and then they began receding. Her toenails played a tink-tink-tinking on the floor as she crawled. New, human teeth filled the gaps.

"Please."

"I gave as I promised," the woman said. "Or most of it." She wrapped her long, slender hands around his throat and squeezed.

The man turned red beneath the dirt crust and water grime. His arms danced and pawed. He tried to gasp, tried to say please.

The woman gripped him for seven minutes. She then made quick work of every pocket. Dead men could not spend money and dead men could not unlock doors to cabins. There was gold in some of those cabins, and gold was worth stealing, sure as her name was Polly Harp.

Chapter Nine

January 30, 1994 – Copper Falls, Ontario, Canada

Overnight, Jake and Kit had taken turns checking in on the man in their parents' bed. The contents of his wallet told them his name and that he was an American. It also told them he had cash, but not likely anything beyond the billfold section. No credit cards or bank cards.

Kit had the blanket peeled back to look at the gash on the man's side—four deep gullies with red and yellow weeping scabs. His musk emanated heavier while uncovered. It reeked of mannish sweat and sour sickness.

"Where is this?" he said, his voice like a pebble rubbed against cement.

"Jake!" Kit backed away from the man and his open eyes.

Jake had been in the kitchen and came running in socked feet. He stopped by the door. The pale, gaunt face and the scruffy beginnings of a beard fit with the bloodshot eyes.

"Hello," Jake said.

The man smacked dry lips. "Where is this?"

"Kit, go fetch a water glass and a straw." Kit hurried away and Jake continued, "This is our home. You parked on the road, and we were bringing the van in, so the snowplow didn't smack it. You were inside. We tried to get you an ambulance, but there was a bad accident, so they couldn't come."

Kit returned and handed the water to Jake. The red and white straw stood comically several inches above the lip of the cup. Ben Lynch leaned forward to take the straw into his mouth. He swallowed and then pushed the straw away with his tongue.

"I can't go to the hospital," he said, slowly.

"Why?" Jake let his hand drop a few inches before setting the cup on the nightstand next to the clock. It was six-fifty-two in the morning.

"I can pay you, but I can't...I...don't have health insurance." It took a while to pass this statement.

The eggs had not sold—there had been an underestimation as to how many chickens were necessary, and then the packaging, and then that nearly every one of the farmers Jake saw at the diner on the highway or at the coffee shop in town or at Ruby's had chickens—the rental space in the shed hadn't met the needs of two separate men demanding a climate controlled environment after they'd pulled a tab from the flyer pinned up at the grocery store, and there had been too much snow and too much cold weather to pull cedar rails from the bush.

"This is a farm, right?" the man asked, and before Jake decided on an answer added, "I used to live on a farm. I can help, once I'm a bit better." His voice had sped to a typical, conversational pace.

Jake looked at Kit and said, "I don't think that can work. Look, I'll call the ambulance, and we can hold your van in the shed, for now—"

"Let me stay in my van then."

Jake shook his head. "Too cold."

"In the shed. I have a heater...I need to rest. Please?" Ben Lynch was helpless as a flu-addled boy.

Kit elbowed Jake and he closed his eyes. "How about you stay a few days and then just ship off."

"Okay."

***

Kit fed Ben soup while Jake went through the mail. The heating bill came, and he'd never seen anything like it. Triple what it had been for October-November. He exhaled a heavy breath. That third chunk of the heifer proceeds would only just cover it, but what of life beyond that?

Kit came back with a mostly empty bowl and dumped the soup dregs into the sink. The feet of the chair squeaked as she pulled it out and sat down. The fridge kicked on, and Jake winced.

"What's wrong?" Kit asked.

"Everything," Jake said and turned in his seat, pulled open the fridge door, and reached in. Beer bottles clanged and he withdrew a Labatt's Blue. The cap hissed and he dropped it on the table next to the electric bill. He took a mouthful and said, "Ahh. Money."

"He doesn't seem bad, you know," Kit said, fingering a flyer from Canadian Tire.

"No, but he's laid up." Jake took a mouthful and swallowed. He didn't drink very often. "He might be different later."

"You're bigger than him. You could kick him out later if he's different."

"Maybe. Who knows?"

"We need money. If you want to keep on being a farmer."

Jake sighed. "Yeah, and what, you wanna move into town?"

Kit shrugged.

"Then I, what? Like I get a job at the plant or be a janitor or garbage man or something?" He slugged the beer. "I just wanna be a farmer like Dad."

Kit popped up, sending the chair screeching backward behind her. "Dad's dead and maybe you can't just be Dad!" She began stomping.

Jake said nothing, only finished his beer, then opened the flyers to look at all the stuff he couldn't afford.

January 31, 1994 – Copper Falls, Ontario, Canada

"Did you hear about the bodies?" Francesca vibrated with the news. She leaned over the brown, vinyl bench seat of the bus to talk at Kit. "Bodies washed up. Half-eaten, or like, made to look that way. A killer staging things for a *tableau*."

Kit blinked. "What?"

Francesca divulged the information as her father had spilled it to her, complete with unsubstantiated theories and her learning of the word tableau.

"Wow," Kit said. She'd never been to the Sprucemont A&W—or any other A&W—but she'd seen it, plenty of times.

At school, everybody talked about the bodies. At recess, some kids pretended to be bodies, using a squeeze bottle of ketchup for blood. The stories grew nastier and more vivid as the day progressed. One boy in the ninth grade told his friend— Kit was within earshot—that the police knew who did it, but were covering it up because it was a cop. "Cops are almost always the killers," the boy had said to the nodding friend.

By the end of the day, Kit stood in the cool, early afternoon air, waiting for her bus to pull up. Her teeth chattered; hands stuffed under her arms. On the street, teachers scooted, and parents scooted and kids on bikes meandered, which kept the routine evacuation of the school by way of buses, slow.

In seats, the children were instantly mollified by the soft confines and some tipped heads against windowpanes. Kit had a seat to herself, and it was rare that anyone popped up to chat on dreary winter days, on the ride home anyhow. The rumble of the engine overpowered the general hum of the discussions between seatmates. Kit let her forehead press against the frosty glass.

Copper Falls hardly ever changed, but folks had recently been talking about how the Tim Hortons that was coming in was going to bring jobs, but also kill businesses. Kids at school regurgitated parental opinions on the subject as if they'd cared one way or the other, as they had with the killers and the dead A&W employees.

Teenagers. Teenagers did not die often and if more than one died, it was almost always in a drunk driving incident.

Kit pulled her hood down to keep her forehead pressed against a window, but also warm, as the bus pulled up behind two other buses at the only stoplight in Copper Falls. Ahead of the buses, two transport trucks had left their blinkers on to follow Highway #4. Southbound traffic was heavy from the fourth part of the veneer plant's shift change. The light turned green, but the buses didn't move.

The first truck forced a Hyundai to stop and honk. The second passed through the amber light. The buses pulled forward about thirty feet. The front bus took a right turn onto Highway #4, and the remaining buses pulled up again.

Kit watched this without seeing much until they stopped in front of Benny's Pizza and kids she knew exited with fat slices on greasy white plates. Her guts grumbled. A police car pulled in to block her view. A fat cop got out, and she whispered, "Mink, Mink, the barnyard stink," just like her mother had said it, before.

Robert Mink was the chief of the laughable Copper Falls police department. His fatness had been his identifier for his entire life. Jake liked to point out he looked like Gailard Sartain, the robust, angry, straight man from the Ernest P. Worrell movies who always held up one-sided conversations with his pal Bobby. Gailard was also in *Fried Green Tomatoes*. They had that one on VHS because her mother…

Kit snuffed back hard and looked around. Nobody was looking. Nobody would see if a tear spilled. She snuffed back again and pressed her right cheek to the glass. The light changed, and the two remaining buses pulled through.

Once beyond the light, there were no more town kids walking home, but there were some mothers with strollers and men with briefcases. One man stepped into the Olympic Diner, and Kit watched him intently, but scrunched her face once she thought she knew who he was—a man from the grocery store who hated his job and took it out on customers.

Next to the Olympic was the wooden walking bridge, and several people walking. A boy and a girl had stopped and threw bits from the cedar boughs wrapped around the bridge's framework over the edge to watch them fall to the frozen,

Saugeen River below. The bus was past them, and Kit's head pushed back and the engine chugged as they rolled up the steep hill out of town.

The one benefit to her bus ride was that she was second off since the driver kept the order instead of reversing it and letting the last off first—which was what Rachael Plummer told Kit happened on her bus route to the southwest of town.

***

"Hey, I think we gotta let him stay," Jake said. He had strands of straw stuck to his heavy coat and frozen shit clung to his boots.

"For money?" Kit said.

She hadn't made it inside. Jake stopped her in the garage. Cigarette smoke lingered. Like with beer, he was irregular, but did partake.

"Yeah. Sure. But here's what I'm thinking. Once he's better, he can sleep in his van in the shed, with a space heater. He can use the old outhouse—"

"Are you going to let him pee through the cracks?"

"Yeah, why not?" Jake said.

The walls of the shed were ridged sheet metal. It was possible to piss down a crack and straight outside.

"Or maybe not. What do you think?"

"I don't know. Might be lots of pee."

Jake began nodding, eyes squinted. "Hmm. Okay. He can also pee in a bucket if he wants. Then, in the mornings, he can come in and eat breakfast. Once you're gone, or later, when you're not home, then he can use the shower."

Kit blushed.

"Trust me on that. Sometimes, guys get weird and show girls, even middle school girls, their dicks. I'll kick his ass if he does, but, you know, better if it doesn't happen."

"Yes, it is."

"Does this sound okay?"

"Yes."

"Of course, if it turns out he's weird or looks at you funny or anything, I'll give him the boot. We'll have to start locking doors at night, but it will be good. He can give me help. I was talking to him more today. I think he said he was a rodeo champion as a kid. He was kind of out of it. I gave him some of the pills from when Dad got his wisdom teeth pulled."

"Wow. Think he'd want to ride Jacques?"

Jacques was the bull, a comparatively docile beast when measured against to those on TV rodeo programs.

"Nah, what's the point? Don't matter. I just wanted to make sure you were okay with it...and, maybe you had other ideas?"

Kit shrugged.

"Okay. I'll go tell him."

"How much are you going to charge him? Kit leaned her head against the wall.

Jake scratched beneath his toque. "Umm, thinking seventy-five a week until he can help, then like forty a week, or fifty. I doubt he'll stick around long. I'll get him to help us get posts and everything."

"Same deal though? I get fifty-fifty for my trip? Especially since the eggs aren't selling...and there's not enough."

Jake grinned. "The chickens are okay though, right?"

"Sure."

"Good."

"Good."

"All right. I'll go tell Ben."

"Good."

***

"Could you help me to the bathroom?" Ben asked.

Jake nodded, eyes downcast. It was the only way. He stood by the side of the bed and leaned his shoulder for Ben to latch onto. The man was light but had big hands and long fingers that dug gently into Jake's neck. Once upright, Jake buried his shoulder in Ben's armpit and together they hobbled to the washroom.

"Could I take a bath, too?" Ben said this through a wince. "I smell terrible."

"You're getting better. Quick, given how we found you." Jake leaned again and helped Ben down onto the toilet.

"Could you maybe wash these…no sense putting them back on dirty."

Jake straightened. "Oh, umm, been thinking. I'm going to need some money."

"You mean for how long I've been here or for my staying longer?" Ben was on the toilet, underwear still on, cotton bandage drooping at his side. It had run pink and yellow, and bits of scab clung to the material.

"Both."

"Money's in my wallet…take what you think's fair. I'd like to stay until I'm all better…stay until I figure out what I want to do next. It's too damned cold to be sleeping in a van."

Jake coughed, fingered at the pink rose wallpaper his mother put up about a decade prior—it had bubbled in spots. "Well, actually, I was thinking you could stay in your van, with a space heater. You could use the old outhouse by the shed and come inside to shower and use the toilet when Kit's at school. Got an old black and white TV you could set up, and a radio, they're just sitting in the garage. Probably you can get CBC and TVO and maybe Global. Once you're feeling better, I mean. You're not much danger to Kit like you are now."

"Or you." Ben had begun leaning to get a grip on his underwear so he could pull them down. The washroom was a place of business.

"You like a serial killer or a Kung-Fu guy or something?"

Ben looked up. Squinted. Shook his head gently.

"Then I never really need to worry about you, not with me

anyway...you an escaped mental patient?"

"No. Can I shit?"

"Just a minute. You said you got those cuts from a dog or a bear, but you were delirious. Where they really from?"

Ben swallowed and his chin quivered. "I can't remember. I was driving, coming up, across the border...even that's fuzzy. Then I'm hurting in the van. I hardly feel like myself at all."

"Really?"

A tear fell down Ben's cheek. "It's the damndest thing I ever felt. I know my name, but it feels funny too, but I was looking in my wallet and at my license and dammit all, I can't remember why I came to Canada or where I got that cash. Hell, I don't remember owning a van, not until I was driving." He began sniffling, more tears fell. "I must've sold my car. I rented a house, but the owner put it up for sale..."

"Okay, shout if you need anything." Jake backed out and closed the door behind him. He popped his head in quickly. "Towels in—"

Ben stopped. He was halfway back down to sitting, underwear coiled around his feet, off-white and overwrought.

"Sorry." Jake pulled the door closed. "Towels in the closet."

Chapter Ten

September 9, 1973 – Redwood Valley, California, United States

There was a bag hidden beneath the fold-out bed with almost $20,000 in it. The Winnebago bounced, and stones pinged off the undercarriage. One more night in the wild, come morning, they'd be at the gates of their destiny. The death of Martin Luther King Jr. had been the first brick to crumble in their suburban wall. The world seemed louder, the crimes of its people more obvious, more blatant, more horrendous.

Turning right at a stop sign, the Winnebago pulled into a dusty campground that worked on the honor system. Three bucks got a night, a recharge, the evacuation of a camper's tanks, and use of the showers and toilets.

The second brick came in the form of Maya Angelou and a conversation she had in a St. Louis bookstore that made it into the local paper. The reporter who'd penned the feature suggested something along the lines that the anti-establishment, anti-white, perhaps anti-Christian writings of Maya Angelou should be ignored. At the office of Johnson & Briggs, where Cynthia Slater worked as an assistant to a junior attorney, the place was abuzz more than normal, concerning where the Blacks might stick their books.

Gary Slater pulled the parking brake and looked at his wife. "We're close," he said.

They'd been married twenty years. It was on their third anniversary, only one month prior, that the final brick smashed and their will to contribute to such a horrid society crumbled. The story of rapist and murderer Dean Corll was all over the news. He was dead—so where at least twenty-eight boys and young men—but the world was no less sick.

"Tomorrow," Cynthia said and then screamed, gleeful.

They'd sold their home. They'd sold their cars. They'd

called upset children. They'd purchased the used Winnebago at a steal. The journey began in Kansas City, Missouri, and they took it slow. It was a huge leap, giving up everything in exchange for utopia.

"Are you ready?" Gary asked, adopting a playful gameshow host tone.

"Am I ever!"

***

The small fire burned at the center of a rusted truck tire rim halfway buried in sand. On lawn chairs, the Slaters held straightened coat hangers dangling hot dogs. Each had a beer next to their feet.

"Howdy."

The couple turned their eyes on an older woman in blue jeans, a western shirt, silver belt buckle, cowboy boots, and a well-worn Stetson hat. Her eyes were brown with shimmery flecks of gold.

"Hey, hi," Cynthia said, not getting up.

"That's quite a rig," the woman said, and nodded. In the shadows of twilight, it looked bigger than ever.

"You like it?" Gary said and turned over his wiener.

"She's a beaut'."

Cynthia made to get up then. "I'm sorry. Where are my manners? Would you like a beer?"

The woman waved this off. "I've been thinking about getting one of these. I just have my bed camper on the truck, you see."

Gary nodded, head tilted, eyebrows up. "Now, now, now. This here is destiny, because that there camper is up for sale and it's cheap."

Cynthia looked at him and then got it, nodded with her whole body. "It is, isn't it?"

"How much?" The woman took a step closer, her eyes

darting from the sky to the Slaters.

"You can have it for two grand, but it has to be cash and it has to be no later than six in the morning." Gary reeled in his wiener and slipped it into the bun that had been on his lap.

"Why so little?"

Cynthia followed Gary's lead and brought in her dog, pulled a bun from the bag on the ground. "Tomorrow, we'll be members of the Peoples Temple. Giving Mr. Jones every cent we have, and another two-thousand will look good in the pot."

"Damn. It sure will. I'm going to make some calls. I have a couple cousins out here, might be able to loan me for a few weeks. Holy that's a steal. Now, don't you go selling it to someone else." The woman turned to hurry off.

"Wait." The woman stopped and looked at Cynthia. "What's your name? I'm Cynthia and he's Gary. Slater."

The woman was all smiles. "Polly Harp. Don't you go nowhere!" She hurried off, eyes on the sky.

***

Micky Orsot fiddled with the radio, trying to get the Dodgers game. It wasn't going well and Linda Orsot sat next to him, adding commentary to the failure. "Will you shut the hell up, woman?" he said and then tossed the little radio across the small space to the messy bed they'd share just as soon as they'd done enough arguing.

"I don't know why the hell you expect so much from that damned thing. It's from Japan for cripes' sake."

"I don't know why the hell you don't shu—"

The camper rocked, cutting off the rebuttal. It was nearly ten and the park was mostly quiet. A ways away, someone listened to rock music on a tinny radio, but they only heard it when they held their breath.

The camper rocked again.

"Go check it out," Linda said.

"Who's there?" Micky said. He got to his knees and looked out the tiny window.

"See anybody?" Linda asked.

"No."

The camper rocked again.

"Go see," Linda whispered. She pushed at Micky's arm.

"Fine," he said and pulled a knife from the sheath he'd taken off and set on the small, foldaway kitchen table that remained down much of the day and all night. "If someone's screwing around out there, you better move it, 'cause I'm coming!" He swung open the door and hopped down into the grass.

Linda got to her knees and tried to look out the window. A loud snap echoed inside the small camper, coming from the doorway. Wet smacks followed.

"Micky?" Linda said and then sat down. She looked to the door. Saw nothing. "Micky?"

She got up and walked the short distance, taking all the time she could. She stood at the top of the two stairs and tried to make sense of what she saw. A huge, furry beast was eating something in the camper's doorway.

"Micky?" she whispered.

The beast looked up, snarled, and then leapt. Linda fell back into the steering wheel, hitting the horn for two seconds before claws dragged her to the floor and teeth tore out her throat.

September 10, 1973 – Mendocino County, California, United States

Polly Harp sang along with the tunes coming from the stereo dash of the Winnebago. The machine bounced and shook, rode almost like it was floating. In the passenger's seat, pale and holding her arm, was Cynthia Slater.

"Where are we going?" she said, dreamy. A glaze filmed

her eyes.

Polly grinned, facing the blacktop. "I saved you from joining a wack job cult. Now, where's the money?"

"The money?"

Polly side-eyed the woman. In the back, Gary was retching into the toilet, taking great whoops of air before expelling nothing much. Not anymore, at first there'd been many splashes.

"The money. You said something about a pot."

"Pot?" Cynthia said.

Polly tapped the steering wheel of the Winnebago to the tune of the song coming through the speakers. "You know, I've never bit someone without eating them, not on purpose. Maybe you'll become like me. I've only ever met one like me before and I didn't know it at the time because they weren't human; a gold miner shot him dead. Hear stories though. You'll never believe them until you're furry as a gorilla yourself."

"Gorilla?"

"No, money. Where's the money?"

"Money? The bank?"

Polly huffed. "It'll come back. I think. It did for me anyway. I was a plum idiot for a while…if you're changing and not dying on me… I guess I'll have to rip this place apart if you die." Polly peered into the rearview. Gary was outside the bathroom, sitting on the floor. "Hey, Gary! Where's the money?"

"Money?"

"Yeah."

Gary's stomach clenched and he jerked forward but was able to control himself. Blood stained his right pant leg purple. "Wallet."

"Yeah, I have your wallet. Where's the pot of money?"

"Leprechauns have pots of money?" Gary said this with teary, smeary-faced sincerity.

"Yeah, they sure do. I guess I'll wait and maybe you'll

become like me. Could be an interesting change. I bit off a lady's hand once and she locked herself in her bedroom and I ran off. I got sick after that, and something compelled me to go check on the lady, by the time I got back to the estate—some la-di-da plantation place—the husband had killed her. I felt fine after that and I always wondered if it was a piece of the same thing, ya know?"

Cynthia put her hands to her head. "We were supposed to meet Mr. Jones." Her words treaded syrup before coming out.

"Jim." Gary mumbled this into the linoleum.

"That guy's a fruitcake. I did you a favor. Two, if you count me eating the old couple instead of you. I guess you could say I saved your lives."

Cynthia looked at Polly and reached across the aisle and touched her knee. "Thank you."

Chapter Eleven

February 7, 1994 – Copper Falls, Ontario, Canada

Jake and Ben stood by the fence line that ran alongside the path to the back forty. Holding steady by the culvert and creek, two oversized posts rose about ten feet apart. The other posts and rails were slim, though sturdy enough to stand, even against the bull's minor, exploratory pushes.

"See, you can use this pair and build out." Ben slapped one of the oversized posts. The top was a couple inches higher than the top of his head. He'd moved out to the shed five days earlier, started slowly with the work, but had come to follow Jake the total of the last two days, forcing him to find things needing done.

Jake looked at the posts and then up to the fat flakes drifting overhead. He slipped off his right glove and rubbed his chin, and then up his cheek, then beneath his toque. "Huh, think it matters if the other posts are just in the shit? On the shit even?"

"Sure, but you can make do. Not good to leave the cows pent up, plus we won't have to lug water."

"That's what I was thinking. I guess we could put it up and I take it down in the spring, then get some proper posts in. Better dig some of this ice with the loader or bale spear, and then shovel it out. Gonna be a pain."

Ben's eyes bounced around the frozen and snow-covered shit in the barnyard. "No cement under here, is there?"

"Not there, no. Stops a few feet past where the feeder is."

A round feeder made of tubular steel sat empty.

"You have round bales?" Ben asked.

"Not many. Swapped them for squares."

"That's probably okay. We'll want to stick a feeder carriage on the front of the lean-to, make sure they come out. They won't come out unless there's food, even if they're thirsty."

Jake slipped his glove back on. "We can make the feeder bit in the shed and cart it out, zip-zip a couple screws in once the lean-to's up. That way we don't freeze to death."

"Not so bad today. The other night I was sitting out of the van and fell asleep on that old car seat that's out there, was having a few smokes and trying to get a clearer picture for the Browns and Steelers by putting the TV up on top of the van. I woke up so cold my feet ached, and the little bit left in my beer was ice."

Jake laughed and then stopped abruptly, his eyes widening. "There's an antenna post at the back of the shed. We could probably go to the dump and rescue an antenna and some wire."

"Well, damn, that would be handy and—"

"And we can get some sheet metal for the lean-to. My old buddy is the manager. Meet me by the truck in five." Jake had on snow pants that had double as much caked and crusted shit as it had clean spots. Couldn't dress like that, not going to town.

"Mind if I come in and do some business?" Ben said.

"Oh yeah, sure thing." They started up the slope next to the barn toward the yard. "Hey, you know how to skate?"

"I don't think so."

Jake was halfway over the fence, resting his crotch and ass on the top rail. "That's really something. But you remembered about how to build a lean-to..." He kicked his other leg down.

"I guess I do, we had cows when I was a kid, and horses, and a mule called Pete. But I don't even remember what my parents look like or their names or if I have brothers and sisters. It's the most fucked up thing I ever... At least I think it is. Shit, maybe I am some kind of mental patient."

"Seem all right to me," Jake said.

***

Yellow vinyl siding and a chimney the size of a car exhaust, the little shack at the dump had a single man, a cash box, a woodstove, a table, a chair, and a radio inside. The attendant, John Oates, leaned by the door, smoking a cigarette with the lid of a stainless-steel thermos in hand. Coffee steamed. He'd told Jake *sure thing* about grabbing some sheet metal and *take your pick* to the antenna. For metals, there was usually a moderate fee.

"Who's that guy?" John said.

Ben was over by the aluminum pile, pulling at antennas. A couple bent or broken units would come together as one without much effort at all.

"He's helping me at the farm. For board." Jake eyed a stuffed Care Bear. It was pink with one ear and many brown stains. It sat in the void of an ATV tire.

"Where'd he come from?"

Jake scratched beneath his toque. "He's American and hit his head or something. Kit and me found him on the road the night those snowmobilers went through, so there was no ambulance coming. He doesn't have anywhere else to go and knows about farming, so…why not, eh?"

"That's awfully white of ya."

Jake exhaled a slow huff. They probably had the right man for the job when it came to minding the county's trash. A bit backward, no aspirations, no social sense. Which was odd since the Oates were upstanding. All of John's siblings worked in offices or were in college—his parents were senior members at an insurance firm down in Sprucemont.

"Anyway. Alley was asking about you at New Year's."

Jake straightened and cocked his head a touch. "Is that right?"

Alley was John's older sister. She was about seven months graduated university and had a job for the county as some kind of administrator. Former homecoming queen. Former prom queen. Former fuel to a good many wet dreams of the boys on either side of her grade at school.

"Yeah. She likes sad saps. Was dating this guy with a big

burn scar on his face for a while. His whole family died in a house fire, but he lived."

Jake squinted. "So, what, she asked about me because my parents died?"

John snorted and then horked up a greenish gob onto a bent piece of tin. "Probably, and that you're looking after your sister. Alley's way too hot for you, so it's got to be something. If she weren't my sister, I'd have already fucked her."

Jake laughed, disbelieving, but believing.

"You want her number? I could call my mom tonight and call you."

"Absolutely," Jake said.

Ben came up to the shack with two antennas, same model, both slightly busted. "Cool if I take them both and put them together?"

"So, you're like one of them TV memory loss people. Can you do *Dead Zone* or anything, like if you touch someone?" John asked, searching his pocket for his cigarette pack.

"What?" Ben said.

Jake rolled his eyes and waved to John, then started toward the truck. His footfalls crunched over the compacted garbage mysteries beneath the soil and snow.

***

"The man's a goddamned idiot and total fucking asshole. When I said buddy, I used it pretty loosely. Buddy how you're a buddy because if you put up with a guy you get to go scavenge at the dump sometimes."

Ben nodded. "So, what? You told him about me?"

Jake turned into the parking lot of Ruby's, a family restaurant on the steady verge of closure. "Sure. Some of it. That a problem?"

"Guess not. No, guess not. Think I'm maybe a secretive person, but it could be I'm defensive because this thing scares me like you wouldn't believe."

"I suppose it would. Come on, my treat." Jake pushed open the door, and the grease scent from the deep fryer invaded the truck's cab. "Food's better than the building suggests."

They stood in the doorway and kicked the winter from their boots. A man approached them with a brown paper bag in hand. He nodded to Jake and Ben. They hadn't reached the second door when they had to stop again. Jake stepped sideways, and Ben leaned to a wood-paneled wall as one of the owner's sons came rushing out with two small polystyrene containers.

"Troy! Troy!" He wore a damp white apron. "Your 'slaw!"

Ben spun, and his breaths fell short.

The man who'd only just left jogged back and saluted with the hand holding the bag after he collected his coleslaw. The man in the kitchen whites turned on a pivot and held open the door.

"Going in?" he asked.

Ben stared after the man, stiff as a maple, and Jake said, "What is it?"

Ben scrunched his face up and shook his head. "Don't know that I can say exactly."

Jake led the way through the second door past the take-out counter and bakery display. The display had a couple signs and two bundles of paper napkins inside. To the right were the His and Hers toilets. The employee crossed behind the counter and through a swinging door, into the kitchen.

To the left of the entrance was the worn smooth carpet that led into the dining room. Ruby's had the home cooking vibe down to the mismatched wooden chairs you might see at a relative's on Christmas when the whole family came and one dining set wasn't nearly enough. At capacity, Ruby's sat up to seventy-two patrons. Now, in total were six old farmers having lunch.

As it had been with his father, Jake took a seat at the long communal table. He didn't introduce Ben, not right away, and no one asked.

"How's Mr. Gerber?" Rory Donaldson asked. He had hair white as paper and had only ever hobby farmed. He'd made enough back in the 'sixties to never hold a proper job: fixed the ponies—as the old timers called it—and leant money to folks who couldn't manage a traditional mortgage.

"Fine. Looks like I'll have to blow out the lane again tonight."

"You see that Bret Easton idiot? He's driving around with six feet of snow on the roof of his van. Goes everywhere at about ten clicks an hour," Adam Hillier said. He was the youngest at the table until Jake had shown up. He had a pig operation south of town that his father sold him when he moved to Florida.

Larry and Mark McMurphy sat across from each other and began talking snowfall with Dan McKenzie and Phil Herman.

"Oh Bret's all right," Rory said.

Dana Petrovich was a chunky woman with breasts big enough that even the men empathized with the back pain she must've felt. She wore a white sweater, blue jeans, and a black apron. She pulled a notepad from the apron. "What can I get ya?"

Jake plucked the stubby menu from in between the napkin dispenser and the condiment caddy. He handed it to Ben. "I'll take a coffee and cheeseburger, only onions and lettuce, no mayo or tomato or pickles," he said.

"Uhh, coffee," Ben said and then paused. "I guess the same as Jake, but with tomato."

Dana hurried off with the slip of paper. She stopped at the little window to the right of the dining room. Nash Mohamed took the note. He owned the place and had for more than a decade. Karaoke night, wing night, ladies' night, and tequila Tuesday had all proved a bust.

"See that?" Rory pointed to the furthest end of the room.

There was a shape beneath a big blanket and several large foam blocks piled up against a wall.

"Yeah, what is it?"

Rory laughed. "Nash is turning this place into a country bar next. That's one of them mechanical bulls."

"No shit. Ben used to ride bulls." Jake pointed to Ben. "Rory, this is Ben, he's helping me out at the farm."

Dana came by with the coffee pot and filled two off-white porcelain mugs.

"Getting things under control then?" Phil Herman asked, his German accent tinged his words like an afterthought. He'd been in Canada close to thirty years but still spoke like an outsider. "Must be doing okay to have help." He began nodding.

"More like can't afford not to get some help, for a little while anyway."

"So you rode bulls professionally?" Rory asked.

Ben said, "No. I was only amateur. But I won a contest when I was a kid."

"When was that?" Rory wore a grin, showing off two gold teeth.

"Uhh, don't remember, to be frank." Ben shrugged.

Rory frowned. "Oh. I see."

Nash hurried out of the kitchen with two plates of food. "Jake, my friend. You have cedar rails for sale? Little skinny ones?" He set the plates down but got them backward. "I need some to go around Maurice."

"Yeah, I can get some. How many?" Jake looked at the tomato poking out and switched his plate for Ben's.

"Who's Maurice?" Rory asked.

"Enough to make a little fence, but pretty, you know?" Nash pointed to the mechanical bull beneath the blanket and then looked at Rory. "Maurice, that's him."

"Need me to make the fence?" Jake asked as he shot ketchup onto his burger and then onto his fries.

Nash squinted. "How much?"

Jake squirted mustard onto his burger. "Five meals. These two and then three more."

"Done. But not beer or liquor." Nash held out his hand, skinny and wrinkled with long yellow fingernails.

Jake shook.

At the far end of the table, the McMurphys prodded at Jake that he'd low-balled himself since Nash agreed so quickly. Nash only grinned and said, "I'm a businessman," and then, "Can you have the fence in for next Friday night? Not this Friday, but next Friday?"

Jake nodded, chewing.

Rory pointed at Ben. "You should get this boy to ride your Maurice before the big night, make sure it's sound. He was a champion bull rider."

"It works!" Nash said. "It damn well works. The company's out of Guelph, they gave me a guarantee. They'll come fix it as soon as it breaks, for one year. I made them agree to that when I bought it. Got it on a steal already but made them do some insurance for me. I'm a businessman."

"I haven't ridden anything in a while," Ben said.

Dana came up with the coffee pot in hand. "That's a real shame for you," she said and then cackled, high and heavy. The rest of the table laughed along.

February 12, 1994 – Copper Falls, Ontario, Canada

"Where's Ben?" Kit asked as she pulled on her boots, beneath her snow pants.

"He's helping at a pig farm for the day. Don't worry, this'll be easy. Plus, you get a free meal at Ruby's, and we'll pull out some extras to sell."

It was a warm day by February standards. The snow was crunchy, and the icicles wept steady trickles. The rails in the bush would be soaked, but not snow-covered. Not all the way.

The tractor with the loader bucket bounced along the trail

over the slick-packed snow. The rails were collected, but scattered in a few spots, only feet from the fields. Whoever took the old rails down, tossed them into piles. They'd been out for decades, thinning and rotting. The ones buried in dirt would be useless, soft as soggy matchsticks, the ones with any separation at all from the soil would be good. The in between ones could go to Nash.

"Are we going out for Ruby's tonight?"

"Gotta do tomorrow. I'm going out with Alley Oates tonight."

"You." Kit was off the tractor and her eyebrows had climbed up under her toque. "You have a date?"

Jake climbed down after tilting the bucket so the maximum number of cedar rails would fit above. "Yeah. I have a date."

"Thank god it's not Sherry Robison."

"You don't have to worry about me, okay?"

"Okay."

"You worry about not letting any dick weeds trick you into screwing around. I don't need to be an uncle anytime soon."

"Ugh, gross. I'm not stupid you know. Also, the guys only try to fool around with Pam, Stacy, and Jen C."

Jake led the way into the bush, ducking beneath sopping pine branches. "Why's that?"

"They all have big boobs."

Jake sighed and offered a half-hearted grin. "Some things never change. Don't worry, one day you'll wish the guys would leave you alone." Jake cleared his throat as he bent to lift the end of a fat rail partway raised on an ancient tree stump. "Ben hasn't tried anything with you, has he?"

"No."

"He talk to you when I'm not around?"

Kit got on the smaller, but dirtier end of the rail and lifted it to about mid-thigh. "He doesn't. I hardly see him. Lisa tried to tell me he'd climb in my window and rape me."

Jake shivered and started walking backward out of the

bush. "Lisa Granger?"

"Yes. She's crazy though. Her summer boyfriend took her virginity at Load Park, in the sand under one of the tractor tires."

Jake laughed. "And she's what? A year older than you?"

"Same age, just in the other class. I don't know if I believe her. She's sex crazy. It's all talk. She has more freckles than not freckles and her boobs are smaller than mine."

Jake dropped his end of the post into the gap between the bucket and loader arms. "That means so much less than you think. Some guys'll screw anybody."

Kit made eye-contact with Jake. "Not you."

"No, not me."

"You're not a virgin, are you?"

Jake rubbed his gloved hand over his toque. "No. Plus that's none of your damned business."

"Who'd you do it with?"

"Get out of town."

"Tell me."

"No."

Chapter Twelve

October 5, 1990 – Moreland, British Columbia, Canada

Jody Penrose opened the door leading to the unfinished basement. Her footfalls thumped, the nails moving audibly despite her slight stature. She'd used the excuse of her size and weight to explain how she came to get so far only to fall apart in the final stages of agent examination. Likely on some official forms somewhere it suggested stress or a breakdown. Maybe those forms would have an official seal, emphasizing the failure.

The basement floor was smooth grey cement. Cobwebs filled the corners and between the beams and framework on the underside of the main floor. There were two windows, small but busy with light. The grass growing against the glass tinged the space in green. There was a washroom the size of a closet and nothing else. Four cinderblock walls.

Jody looked at the space. A consolation prize for moving back to Canada, unfit, mentally, to deal with the weight and expectations of agents of the Federal Bureau of Investigation. The participation ribbon of a life's goal failed.

She stepped into the washroom, flicked the light switch off and on three times, flushed the toilet once, and made her way back upstairs to where the realtor awaited her.

"I'd like to make an offer."

The realtor smiled. "Is there a Mr. Penrose?" He was a chubby man, head of hair in the shape of a horseshoe. He had both hands in the pockets of his loose slacks.

"No, I killed him," Jody said, her eyes dulled by boredom and disinterest.

October 26, 1992 – Moreland, British Columbia, Canada

8x10 photographs cluttered the walls. The first was a bird's eye shot she got from a cop in Alaska. The body had chilled quickly making the decay slow. The image was of a jaw, bone white, spine scrubbed clean, pink and blue tendrils hanging limply between the gap where the throat should've been. Blood analysis on top of the last known whereabouts put this discovered body in league with a string of missing bodies. This shot wasn't where the pattern initially clicked, but it was the oldest incident that she knew of. September 23, 1991. Nine missing persons. Nine big, nasty bloodstains. There were six photos of the scene and reports from two witnesses. Both saw a camper in the area, but both also said they saw campers all the time. They couldn't believe such a grisly murder could happen so close and they not hear it. The next set of photos was a twosome. Also, in Alaska. Missing, bodies never recovered, home ransacked for anything valuable or easily sold. The missing couple were both in their seventies.

The third set was where Malcolm Harris sent out feelers and found Jody Penrose's private investigation business. He had a missing daughter who'd been involved in something bloody while camping in Mehatl Creek Provincial Park. The incident occurred on September 11 of that year, but she didn't get involved until the first week of October.

Malcolm Harris was a wealthy man and gave Jody everything she asked for, and quickly. The cops decided it was grizzly bears who'd taken off with the four missing individuals, leaving behind blood and folding chairs and two canvas tents. Jody sent out preliminary feelers of her own and learned that an elderly couple were found to be missing just days later outside the town of Merritt. Strange for a quiet county.

She had eleven pictures of the campsite and two of Olivia Harris. She had one picture of the farmhouse from where the elderly couple had gone missing, but little to go on, until October 11.

Five McDonald's employees went missing sometime after the closing hour. Five bloodstains and a dozen photographs.

Three people witnessed a camper parked across the road much of the day. The cops laughed Jody off when she said to mind the local old folks in isolated homes. They laughed until the Minskes went missing and their home had been looted.

Jody took this information to Malcolm Harris, and he'd told her, "Whatever it takes, but you come to me with names, not the police." It was another week before she got lucky when an Alaskan fisherman happened to be passing through while she was asking around a diner in Cherryville. The locals had nothing to say, but this fisherman remembered the date and the number. "Full moon that night, that's how come I remember the day."

Ping-ping-ping: she was onto something. Each of the dates she had coincided with a full moon. It gave her something to go on, a reminder of when to watch newspapers.

February 8, 1994 – Moreland, British Columbia, Canada

Her ear burned. She'd been on the line all morning, making the rounds. The black receiver of the telephone created an especially irritating suction after a while. But it had to happen. Malcolm paid her thirty-five thousand plus expenses not to take any other cases. Maybe she could've cleared more, but the man paid for her vehicle—a 1993 Jeep Cherokee—her fuel, her phone bill, and subscriptions to seven newspapers from across Canada and another twenty from across the border.

She kept track in blips. Got lucky, really. In 1993, she spotted four cases with identical outcomes—though not the same number of missing persons. The routes were irregular and strange. Houston, Texas. Pine Bluff, Arkansas. Fort Scott, Kansas. Dickinson, North Dakota. Most times the cops weren't willing to share photographs unless she paid a visit, levelled with the men, showed them she wasn't any kind of threat to their authority or manhood. Malcolm covered plane tickets as well.

"Winnipeg Free Press, Janice speaking. How can I direct your call?"

"Hello, Janice. Maybe you can help me. Any strange disappearances lately with lots of blood?" Jody was bored, but diligent, because diligence bred success. Her voice revealed as much. She'd started playing guessing games with major cities, trying to anticipate based on last known whereabouts.

"Ooh, you're gonna want to talk to Buddy Maroon. I'll put you through to his line," Janice said and then clicked.

Jody sat up and fumbled for a pen and paper. She reeled her calendar up close and got ready. Buddy Maroon answered on the ninth ring. He exhaled audibly and then said, "Buddy here."

"Buddy, my name is Jody Penrose." She got into a brief outline of the situation. Buddy offered what he knew, and Jody's heart pattered. There'd been disappearances and blood, and a poor old couple halfway between Winnipeg and Steinbach were gone as well. The cops had kept everything tight for a month. Panic avoidance. "You have anything else? Anything from the inside?"

"Notta. This a thing? I'm doing all the talking. This a thing?"

"Get yourself a pen and paper and I'll give you some dates and locations. I don't have time to get to everything. I need to book a flight."

"All right. You coming here? To Winnipeg?"

Jody was on her feet, almost bouncing. "You can bet your ass."

"Wear something warm."

February 10, 1994 – Winnipeg, Manitoba, Canada

The room was in the main building of a Howard Johnson with bright green carpet. Outside was a row of fifty-five single, motel-style units. Construction trucks lined the front like pigs at a trough. Inside, Jody took her two suitcases—one full of clothes, the other contained her research and copies of her photographs—up the stairs to the second floor. Room 216 was at the end of the hall. The room smelled like muted Old Spice from the carpet cleaning powder. The atmosphere was dry and close to freezing.

Jody dropped her bags inside the door and hurried over to the heater. The setting on the dial was nineteen centigrade. She turned it higher. The heater remained lifeless. The heavy plug dangled. She plugged it in, and a puff of dust billowed. She sneezed.

Scotch tape in hand, Jody looked around the room, and then back to the open suitcase on her bed. She tossed the tape into the case and began gathering the pertinent photographs and notes. If the cops were ever going to play nice, she had to play nice.

***

The station was like any police station in a small town, but Winnipeg was a city. The women sat at desks and cops in uniforms mulled around, a few more sat at desks. She asked the pretty, young woman on reception for Detective Todd—Buddy Maroon gave her the name.

"Are you the lady who called earlier?"

"Maybe. I called yesterday."

"The lady with the theory?"

"Probably. I called and spoke to Detective Todd, and he said he'd be here to meet me."

The young woman pursed her lips and began looking at the long purple nails she wore. "He's gone on vacation. Left this morning."

"What?"

"On the moon, said he'd catch you there."

Jody closed her eyes and breathed through her nose. "My guess, he'll be back from his trip real fast."

***

"Ms. Penrose?"

Jody looked up. The man saying her name was short and chubby. He had a full head of brown hair and strong looking arms. He wore a striped button up with the sleeves rolled to his elbows. She stood then and said, "Buddy?"

As if she was performing, Jody brought out the photographs and explained the intricacies. She explained the similarities. She explained what was missing and let it hang and stick. It wasn't a contest; fresh eyes were welcome eyes.

"That's incredible," Buddy said, tapping the tip of his cigarette against a steel ashtray mounted atop a plaid beanbag. "I need to wrap my head around this. I wrote a piece, but it's small. Can I use these photographs?"

Jody nodded.

"We missed tomorrow's edition, but Saturday's our biggest. Front page. Serial killers in Canada, bodies never recovered." He gazed vacantly at a far wall.

They were in his office with the door closed, but it was loud enough that the newsroom rumbled like a backhoe engine outside a window.

"Also, I tried to play nice and fair, but I need access, so you'll have to write me in and explain my visit to the police station."

Buddy's eyes fell on Jody and his head tilted sideways ever so slightly. "I've been in town a long time. If that works, it'll be a first."

"What do you think I should do? I have to see the notes if I'm ever going to connect things. Forever I've looked at the missing people and the elderly people always seemed secondary—no signs of violence, no great outcry for the loss of youth, just plain looking robberies with a side of missing persons—but I think they're the key. I can't wrap my head around how they're chosen. I think the killers don't just pop in and out. I think they hang around after they kill the people."

"I know it's work, by why are you on this one so hard?"

Jody sucked at the inside of her cheek. "You nailed it, nothing more: work. This is my job."

Buddy pointed and squinted. "No, there's something more and I'll figure it out."

"You do that."

Buddy leaned back in his chair, grinning, and then bolted upright. "How about this?" He stared hard at Jody then, all humor gone. "We get supper and spend all night together seeing where the facts take us? We get some beer...or gin. You like gin?"

"Or you could keep your head on the facts and your pecker in your pants. We work to the same goal, parallel, but in different spaces."

Buddy lifted his hands as if shoving an invisible wall. "Whoa, who said...? Yeah, fine." He picked up a pen and grabbed a sheet of lined paper from a tray on the corner of a huge, messy desk. "No room for error. Word for word. Now, what did the detective say?"

***

Jody got back to the Howard Johnson. She lay down and got up six times before tossing her jacket back over her shoulders and heading out of the room. A young man worked the front desk. He'd had a cleft lip surgery that had healed into a V. It muffled his S sounds.

"What's there to do around here that isn't just eating and drinking?" Jody said.

The man tapped a white Howard Johnson pen against a white Howard Johnson stationery pad. "There's that movie *The Getaway*. It's playing. I'm taking my girlfriend tomorrow. I guess lots of movies playing, but that looks real' good to me."

"I need something more engaging."

"I don't know. The Jets are out of town. It's not like New York City. I don't... Did you try the paper?"

"Yeah. I read it."

A couple walked down the hallway, hand-in-hand. They were older, in their sixties or early seventies by the looks of them. The woman spoke with a heavy Francophone accent. "Mr. Chip Hancock at the cinq-cinq-cinq Main, uh, sept heures. We come all the way out from Laval to see him. We miss him when he in Montreal. They didn't make us fill out form again, though."

"Chip Hancock. I know that name."

"He's de medium. Maybe there's tickets remain?"

***

The Centennial Concert Hall was an old place but was kept up to date. The ticket for entry wasn't cheap. Jody had never seen a medium and didn't put much stock in psychics. More it was something to do and a story to pocket for later.

By the entry into the theater space was a stand-up tray beneath a sign: *Sign-up to win tickets to a future show!* Jody took one of the postage-paid envelopes and held it in her lap once she got to her seat. Next to her were a pale-faced couple, somewhere in their thirties. Their eyes were red, and their cheeks were tear smeary. Jody nodded to them. The woman nodded back, but the man said, "Have you lost someone close?"

"What's that?" Jody said.

"Are you hoping for contact with a loved one?"

"Uh, no. I'm just in town and was..." Jody trailed. "You're hoping the psychic contacts someone for you?"

"Our son. He died of Leukemia... This is our second time seeing Mr. Hancock. He invited us out for this one. There's endless faces in the afterlife and it helps him if he can connect to a name. I'm so glad Jilly sent in that form. I guess Mr. Hancock understands that some spirits are worthwhile, and others are not. Timothy…oh god, I just know Mr. Hancock will reach him."

The woman leaned in and said, "I can already feel him here. A mother can, you know."

Jody nodded. "Oh, so you're not from Winnipeg?"

"No, no. We came all the way from Glace Bay—that's on Cape Breton. We saw his show in Sydney, two weeks after Timothy's fifth birthday…or what would've been," The husband said and gripped his wife's hand.

"That was almost four years ago."

Jody turned her eyes to the stage, anywhere but on the desperate couple.

***

The man was polished, and his beard was tight with a few patches of grey mixed into the deep brown. The suit he wore was the kind presented on wealthy TV courtroom battlers. Usually on the defense. His voice was crisp coming through a headset microphone with an earpiece. Nothing out of place and nothing left to chance, he spoke with certainty and every note hit. The show gave Jody goosebumps.

Until he called out to Timothy.

Jody watched the man and watched the willing parents feed into him. Suddenly the charade was a perversion. She clutched the envelope she'd grabbed on her way in, and when the spotlight drifted elsewhere, she got to her feet and made for the exit.

Night knocked the temperature down an additional five or six notches and made the hairs in her nostrils cling together on the moisture of her breaths. Rather than going straight back to the Howard Johnsons, she pulled her still frozen rental car into a diner parking lot. The place was comforting in its diner clichés: soft red benches, hard white floors and tables, stainless-steel framework holding the white and red together, a jukebox against the wall by the door, a pie display that spun four offerings and one vacancy, and the waitresses in red pinstripe shirts—though black slacks rather than skirts. Given the temperature outside, that made sense.

Jody fell into a booth and a waitress came over immediately. "Can I get you a drink while you look at the menu?"

Jody spied the pie display a half-room away. "I'll take hot chocolate and a piece of lemon meringue. You do have hot chocolate?"

"Yes, ma'am. Mini marshmallows, a jumbo marshmallow, or no marshmallows?" The waitress had slipped the pad into the pouch tied around her waist. The pouch camouflaged almost perfectly against the slacks.

"Mini, please."

Jody made a teepee of her fingers and rested her chin. Nine other patrons dotted the room. Each was single and six read the paper while the other three read from paperbacks: *Green Grass Running Water* by Thomas King, *His Woman* by Jessica Steele, and *Freedom in Exile* by the Dalai Lama. She locked around for a discarded paper and then felt into her pockets. She came up with the envelope and began unfolding it as the waitress reappeared with a steaming mug of hot chocolate and a piece of pie, fork resting against it. Jody said, "Thank you," and began reading.

The questions connected like cold finding a sore tooth. Of course, that shyster was so on point. Age? Sex? Address? Phone number? Family that might be attending? Have you lost a loved one? If so, what was his/her name and age? Under what circumstances did the loved one depart? What are you looking to get out of contacting this loved one?

The latter questions left room to write paragraphs of personal turmoil. On the backside was a plea for donations and a space to tell Chip Hancock all about yourself.

"Ooh, I so wanted to go see him tonight. Were you there?"

Jody looked up to the waitress. "Yes."

"He's incredible. I'll have to catch him next time. He seems to never stop touring."

Jody smiled politely, lips tight and curving only just. The waitress left off with her damp dish towel. Jody folded everything back together and pocketed the questionnaire. She took a sip of thick, very sweet chocolate and then dug into the pie. She pushed the so-called psychic from mind and tried to focus on the elderly people who'd disappeared in the day, or days, following the bloody scenes.

February 12, 1994 – Winnipeg, Manitoba, Canada

Things went differently on her second visit to the police station, but not in the way she'd hoped. Detective Todd and the chief corralled her into an office and explained all the ways she was an idiot for thinking they'd cooperate with some damned civilian and that she was wildly out of order, grasping at anything to make connections. When they let her out of the office, twenty-five men in uniforms and a handful in suits smirked at her. The few women in the building filed nails or pretended to focus on paperwork.

At the Free Press office, Buddy said, "Sometimes things work slow here," when she told him how everything played out as she slumped on a chair, hands cradling her head.

She lifted her face to him, didn't know what to say.

"The whole province is against change…equality and things like that. Know what I mean? Lots of sexism and old boys."

She had to laugh a little at this.

She let Buddy make copies of all her notes, and she made copies of the two sheets of scribbles he had on the disappearances. One thing, the locations were getting bolder.

She was out the door and, in her rental, when Buddy charged out in his shirtsleeves, waving his arms. Jody climbed halfway out of the running car.

"What?"

"You've got a phone call from a police officer in Gatineau."

"What?"

"Yeah, get in here!" Buddy cradled his arms and hurried back through the double doors.

February 13, 1994 – Gatineau, Quebec, Canada

Detective Dale Bourque's basement was very much like her basement, but only in one room. Most of the basement was finished, and children's toys littered the floor like soft and squeezable measles. That one room was on the opposite side of the staircase and had a lock on the flimsy door—a door designed to keep nosey family members out, but not those willing to throw a shoulder.

Next to the furnace, on a cinderblock wall, the detective put up the newspaper story of an event that had occurred the last night of a vacation in Orlando. He and his wife took their daughters—four and three at the time—to see Mickey Mouse, but a detective on vacation is still a detective, and he read the local papers and watched the news every morning of their stay at the resort before the rest of the family climbed from bed.

"Five bodies missing, bloodstains, a restaurant on the outskirts of a much larger center. It lingered because it was a little bit weird, I suppose." Dale pointed to the newspaper clipping. He knew that date and had it mailed to him after a similar story ran in the Papier Masson. "It's not in my jurisdiction, you see, but I know the guy on it. He's let me look. I told him the similarities, but he's not convinced." The man spoke perfect Canadian English, though French was most likely his first language.

He'd called the Free Press in Winnipeg because he heard a man mention the idiocy of the public and muddying up investigations by convincing scoop-hungry reporters of their conspiracies. The station was CBC Radio, and the man speaking was a politician. The wording of the sentence was forgotten, but the just of it suggested bodies missing from a bloody scene elsewhere did not mean bodies missing from a bloody scene in Winnipeg were at all connected.

"I've never been this close to it. This happened during the December's full moon." Jody spoke without ever hearing the date. "What about the missing elderly person or persons?"

"December twenty-eight, was that a full moon?" The detective sat on a fold-up chair at a card table, rifling through contents of what Jody brought along. "I don't know about any other missing persons. I should call. I'll call."

Jody folded her hands over her chest. She was tired and wired, wanted to get booting on this thing. Bourque looked up from the collection.

"Yeah, now. I'll do it now."

The detective told Dale he'd get back to him. Jody left to check into the Motel Adam and flopped on the bed. She rolled deep beneath the comforter blanket without changing her clothes and slept.

Chapter Thirteen

February 18, 1994 – Copper Falls, Ontario, Canada

Twenty-two inches of snow fell between three and seven in the morning. The call chain went from home to home to home: no buses, no classes. By eleven, the temperature was up near freezing and the roads were mostly clear. The snow had ceased falling around nine.

Alana Bader moved to Copper Falls with her mother in the summer. She was in Kit's class, but they hadn't become friends until middle-December. They bonded over a history assignment and a fortuitous seating change that put their desks side-by-side after a pack of boys needed separated.

Kit called her friend and Alana showed up an hour later, her mother waving from inside a Pontiac 6000LE as she hurried out the laneway. They got busy with shovels. Jake rolled up from behind the barn and shouted for the girls to get off the ice. He set the blower to it. Once cleared, he put away the tractor and brought over two wide contractor brooms and a corn broom.

After the shelter went up by the river, Jake cut back the help needed from Ben. There was just enough that one person couldn't do it comfortably, but not enough to trouble a second person all the time. Still, Ben followed Jake out of the shed. He had the skates they'd scored from the Johnny P's Sports for twelve bucks. They were ratty and one of the hard shells over the toes was almost completely barren, shining white amid the loose black strands.

Jake, Ben, and Kit swept while Alana sat on a snow-covered straw bale and pet a pair of juvenile cats who'd begun following human activity. They were both black and energetic and more than a little silly. Alana giggled as they chased little balls of snow swept along the ice while she tied her well-worn figure skates. The swish-swish-swish of the broom-play over the surface mostly drowned her out.

Kit set aside the corn broom and Ben snatched it up, swapping it for a big broom. He cleaned the ice like an umpire, small lightning slashes that sent the lingering build-up to the edges. Kit and Alana were already skating by the time Jake and Ben put down their brooms.

Ben sat on the bale and began tying his skates. He spied at Kit and closed one eye. She was looking at him and it was obvious she'd just finished whispering something to Alana, who also watched him.

Jake returned from the house with his skates in hand just as Ben stood from the bale. He took three ugly, forward leaning strides and then began wind-milling his arms before falling hard on his ass.

"Told ya!" Kit shouted and then the girls cackled.

"Hey now!" Jake said, but he was grinning as well.

Ben got to his knees. "Laugh it up." He climbed to his feet and took slow steps, gliding every now and then, his arms stretched like eagle wings.

Jake tied his skates and began at it. He was rusty and as much as Ben made him look like a pro, Alana made him look like an amateur. The way she skated was effortless music. Her strides carved and her spins had Kit asking all sorts of questions—of course Kit's skates let her off the competitive hook some, being a pair of Jake's hockey skates from when he was a little older than she was now. Still, she twirled and kicked when Alana salchowed and loop jumped.

"Ooogh!" Ben moaned from his ass. He got to his knees and Jake glided over to offer an arm up. "I keep thinking if I hit my head just right, I'll get my memory back." He climbed Jake's arm.

"Man, I can't imagine." Jake took a slow stride, keeping a pace that Ben could mimic. "I wish there was some way I could help."

"Shit, you're doing plenty. You've been so nice I keep wondering if you didn't know me before. Like that Goldie Hawn movie. Did you see it? She's this horrible bitch and falls off her yacht and hits her head? Then Patrick Swayze moves her into his house with his bratty kids."

Jake laughed. "Kurt Russell, not Patrick Swayze."

"No way. I don't remember much, but I remember that."

Jake laughed harder. "Who...who...who was in *Road House*?"

Ben stopped skating. "Kurt Russell."

Still laughing. "And who...who was in *Dirty Dancing*?"

"Patrick Swayze."

"Who was in *Overboard*?"

"That's what it was called! And that was Patrick Swayze!"

Jake pitched forward, laughing too hard to stand.

The girls skated around them. "Kurt Russell and Goldie Hawn are like married but not married," Kit said and then Alana said, "They did three movies together. *Swing Shift* and *Overboard* and a real old one. My Mom is nuts for them."

Ben squinted his eyes tight and looked up at the overcast sun hiding in the grey sky. "You sure?"

The girls shouted, "Yes!" from the far end of the rink.

Jake was rolling laughing.

***

Kit went home with Alana to stay over and Ben rode with Jake into Ruby's. The sun had been down for hours. Ruby's was hopping. The country shtick appeared to have the same effect Nash's business identity changes always had. Unfortunately, it almost always came in a single spurt and the patron head count went back to normal shortly after.

Alley Oates and Jake had been talking now and then on the telephone and went for two coffee dates. This would be their first interaction in a group, and with alcohol involved.

Dwight Yoakam came through the closed door, slow and sappy, singing about trying not to look so pretty. Jake swung open the door and stepped in. Even out front, smoke fogged a couple feet below the ceiling. One of Nash's sons was checking ID, but waved Jake and Ben by—the sons had been in attendance when Jake and Kit put up the decorative fence around Maurice the mechanical bull.

Alley seemed to pop from nowhere as Jake stood at the bar awaiting a Labatt's Blue. She leaned in and kissed his cheek, shouted, "Hey, you!"

"Hey, yourself! You probably haven't met Ben." Jake pointed to Ben and Alley waved a dainty, halfway drunk greeting.

"Is he single?" she asked, leaning in closer, so Jake could hear.

Jake got it and leaned away to answer, "Yeah!"

"Think he'd want to meet Sherry Robison? She's been clinging to us all night."

Jake smirked and shrugged. The beers came and he paid for his and Ben paid for his own. Together, the three of them made their way to an open space where tables usually sat, and began swaying to the music, chatting up the other Copper Falls twenty-somethings.

Every once in a while, a strong bout of cheering and hollering would commence, and heads would turn toward Maurice and the man just flung from his back.

***

At ten, Jake asked Ben if he could drive them home, meaning would Ben mind not drinking anymore so Jake could get drunk. Ben said, "Hey, these are your buddies."

Once midnight rolled around Ben was bored and Sherry Robison laughed at everything, he said to her like he was a comedian, but he hadn't said anything funny. She clung on his arm, perhaps afraid he'd fly away. He chain-smoked just to deal and drank free fountain Coke—Ruby's provided designated drivers free soda.

"I bet you twenty I can do it on top speed," Jake said into the face of another man about Jake's height. Everyone was smiling and nobody more than the man Jake had challenged.

"I bet you don't last five seconds," he said and pulled out his wallet.

Alley cheered a great whooping woo and the group headed over to the bull.

"I need a loonie," Jake called out.

It took a buck to get Nash to start it going. He had on a cowboy hat and a bolo tie. "How hard?" he asked the drunk man who handed over the money.

"Hardest. For science!" The drunk turned then and gave Jake the thumbs up.

All night patrons had requested the hardest and Nash ignored them. Nobody had ridden the eight seconds on medium.

"Tough as you got!" Jake shouted and then burped.

Nash bugged his eyes a bit and skewed his lips as he looked at the small panel of two switches and a dial. He hit the first switch and Jake straightened on Maurice's back. Electricity hummed. The thing was smooth leather beneath a faux cowhide. Two rubber horns jutted like it came bred from a highland lineage. In the center was a leather loop for grip.

"Do it, Jake!" Alley shouted.

Ben pushed in tight to the fence. His expression fell somewhere between cringing and smiling.

"He ain't gonna last five seconds," said the man who'd placed the wager. He wore a sneer, like he wanted Jake to fail for more reasons than money.

"Ready?" Nash said.

Jake slapped Maurice's mechanical ass.

Nash flipped the second switch and the bull dipped to the

floor while swinging right before jerking left and tilting back. Jake flew eight feet onto the padding. The crowd around the fence burst into laughter.

"That's it, fucking faggot!" The man who'd made the bet waved both twenties over his head. "Thanks for the easy money! Fucking pussy bitch!"

Ben looked at the man and then at Maurice and then over to Jake who had only just stood. He was wobbly and scowling. Alley reached out for him and the man who'd made the bet began yelling louder.

"That pussy faggot didn't last two seconds!"

"Double or nothing?" Ben nudged the guy. "Double or nothing?"

The man started laughing. "You? What? You're gonna ride the thing? You?"

"Double or nothing." Ben had his hand on the cedar rail fence, ready to hop over.

"Hand me the money?"

"Somebody else has to hold it. I don't feel like wrestling it from you after."

The man laughed and then stilled; he licked his lips. "You could try anyway." He had four inches on Ben and an easy fifty pounds.

"Don't want a bet then?"

"Don't do it," Sherry Robison said, popping up with a fresh vodka cranberry and hanging from his arm. "It's not worth it, baby."

"I'll hold it," an old guy with ashy skin and a long black ponytail said. He had a cigarette dangling from his mouth.

The angry man said, "George. Okay." He handed off the twenties and Ben pulled two twenties from his wallet and gave them to George as well.

Ben high-stepped sideways over the fence, like he was entering a ring. Jake came over and said, "What you doin', man?"

"Just riding," Ben said.

Nash had watched and listened to the entire thing. He'd pre-emptively dialed Maurice down to five. Loud mouths were bad for business.

Ben was on and Maurice did his thing, a little slower than before, and after the eight seconds was up and Ben had barely waved his free arm, he batted his hand toward the ceiling.

The angry man was shouting that it wasn't high enough. Nash stopped the ride and said, "Fine! Fine! Ready?"

Ben nodded gently. He had his left hand out and Maurice was bucking every electron to its max. Left. Right. Side. Back. Front. Side. Right. Left. Right. Back. Front. Then spinning three herky-jerky revolutions. The crowd went quiet, and Ben grabbed his toque from his head like it was a Stetson and rode with pure muscle memory. The music coming through the stereo switched to Garth Brooks for about the tenth time since they'd arrived. Eight seconds had come and gone, and nobody moved. Nash let it roll. Ben was in and going, anticipating the motion and moving like liquid.

Eventually he leapt off and landed on the pads. The patrons erupted and Jake ran over to him and picked him up in a bear hug.

"Eat shit, you cock—!" Jake spun, looking for the challenger, a local guy remembered only vaguely from high school. What Jake didn't know was that the guy had taken Alley Oates to prom when she was in the tenth grade.

Old George came over with the cash and said, "Guy left halfway through. Some ride."

***

The punch that flattened Ben came from behind, his chin nailed the ice on the sidewalk and split. Jake caught his punch when he turned around at the sound of approaching feet. His nose blew a big red raspberry on his face. The second punch split his upper lip. Alley began shouting. She'd left with them and was going to spend the night out at the farm.

"Think you're better than me?" It was the angry man who'd lost the bet and he was kicking Jake in the stomach and chest where he lay in the fetal position.

"What the fuck is this?" One of Nash's sons burst from the kitchen door. He wore a set of cook's whites, smeared with a night's work. He had a steel meat mallet in hand and swung it sideways.

The crunch was incredible. The angry man fell, clenching his arm. Down the street—Ruby's was exactly one block from the police station—a siren belted.

Ben got up and began tugging Jake. "Come on. Cops. Come on."

Jake got up with help on both sides, and Ben and Alley hurried him to the truck.

***

Alley was in her element when she took Jake to the washroom, stripped him down to his underwear, and began dressing his wounds. She kissed him, and he moaned into her mouth. She got them each a glass of water and put them on the nightstand next to Jake's bed. Her body—down to bra and underwear—spooned coolly against him.

The house was quiet but for the furnace rumble and the breeze outside finding a crack to exploit and whistle a tune through. Jake was too drunk, and Alley was too preoccupied to think about Ben who'd entered the home with them, grabbed a sleeve of soda crackers from the cupboard and a mostly empty jar of Skippy peanut butter, and then scooted out to the shed without a word.

Lying in his van, TV fuzzy but clear enough to see, Ben ate crackers, drank half-frozen beer, and watched a commercial-ridden presentation of *Rambo*. He touched his chin off and on between sips and bites, tender as it was. The gash felt like a gully, but it hardly bled.

Chapter Fourteen

February 19, 1994 – Copper Falls, Ontario, Canada

Eyes aflame against the crisp morning light, bloodshot and strained. The cattle mooed in the barn. Jake was about an hour later than normal getting out of bed, and it took him double the usual time to climb into his barn clothes and boots.

The man-door swung with a rusty scree, and the wind took it the rest of the way, thumping it flat against the wall. The manure scent made him gag, and he spat a pale green gob behind him into the snow. He paused there a moment, adjusting to the warmth, the scent, and the drastic dimming of light within the barn. The man-door opened next to the granary augur, which worked down a steel tube into the basement. From where he stood, Jake heard a bucket in action.

He cleared his throat. "Ben, you down there?"

"Yeah!" The sound came more from the opening to the stairs rather than from the augur hole, meaning Ben was probably heading down the feeder aisle with a bucket of chop.

Jake took his time getting to the stairs and stopped halfway down. He sat on a foot-worn step. Ben looked at him and grinned. Jake scratched beneath his toque and slow blinked.

"Man, go back to bed. No worries," Ben said.

Jake opened his mouth, closed it, and then opened it again to say, "Thanks." He stood, turned, and once at the top step, called down. "Come in for a hot breakfast once you're done."

"Sure thing."

***

Alana and her mother dropped Kit off just as Ben was shedding his barn gear in the garage. He sat on an ancient kitchen chair with steel banding strapped around the seat to keep it together.

Kit waved, and the truck drove off.

In the kitchen, Jake was over a pan of bacon, eyes vacant and pink. Alley wore a low-cut top and tight jeans—not the usual Gerber household attire—and fixed spots at the table. "Hello?" she said, smiling at Kit. Her makeup was a bit smeary, but mostly washed off.

"Oh, Kit. This is Alley Oates." Jake did not turn, instead kept staring into the greasy dance in the pan as if hypnotized.

"I know. She was on the homecoming float the year Dad made me do 4-H."

Alley barked a laugh. Obviously uncomfortable.

The door opened and Ben stepped into the kitchen, his right sock pulled way out in front of his foot the way Jake's always did when he yanked off his boots. Jake said to Ben, "Watch this for a second, would you? That's some gash." Ben touched the dry parting of flesh on his chin and then nodded. Jake turned around and put his hand on Kit's shoulder. "Come here for a minute." He pulled open the door to the basement that centered the wall that partially separated the kitchen and living room.

Their mother had stuff—steel cans, a ratty broom, bags of grocery bags, a couple old coats on hooks—lining the walls leading into the shadowy basement. Jake pulled the cord at the top of the steps and closed the door behind him. He began his descent.

"What do you think of Ben?" he said.

"You keep asking me. He's cool. I like him fine." Jake opened his mouth, but Kit cut him off. "And no, he doesn't do anything creepy. Doesn't look at me funny or anything."

"Okay." Jake reached the bottom step and flicked the light switch on the post leading up the stairs. "I'm thinking Ben could live down here instead of out in his van. Since we know he's safe."

It smelled like mildew and was about ten degrees cooler than the upstairs. The walls were uneven stone beneath green asbestos insulation held in by plastic vapor barrier that had yellowed with dampness mixing with dust. The floor was cement. There was a long-time unplugged deep freeze that stretched nearly the entire length of one wall. A closet-sized bathroom filled one corner.

Jake stepped to it and felt for a switch. His arm came back with a cob-webby hand. The bulb shined yellowly, and the cobwebs stretched most of the space on dozens of levels. Three grey spiders were immediately visible. The usual suspects: little ones with spindly legs and round abdomens.

"Fine by me."

"You sure?" Jake said, turning.

"Yeah. What happened to your face and did that girl sleepover?"

"Ben won a bet riding Maurice at Ruby's and the guy who lost the bet punched me. He's also an ex-boyfriend of Alley's, but from high school, like eight years ago. And she came home with us, so yeah, she slept-over."

"Did you do it with her?" Kit's eyes were huge and her head cocked down and forward.

"Get out of here."

Upstairs, there was a knock at the door and Ben shouted, "Jake, cop's here!"

***

"Who told you it was us?" Jake folded his arms across his chest, where he stood in the doorway facing the much larger Robert Mink—de facto chief of Copper Falls' tiny squad of lawmen.

"Sherry Robison called in the fight as it happened. Last night. And then called in this morning to say Henry Andrews should be charged for assaulting you and a fella named Ben, which is you, I suppose. Do you have any ID?" Robert Mink blinked too often as he spoke, as if something about the farm scent bothered sensitive eyes.

"Not in my pocket," Ben said.

"What's he need ID for? We're not pressing charges. I'm not even saying anybody hit us." Jake's voice raised a few notches by the time he finished.

"Looks like somebody hit you. What's your full name, Ben?"

Ben looked at the cop's moustache and said, "Lynch."

"Address?"

"Here."

"You live with Jake and his sister? In what capacity?" He pulled a pad of paper from the front pocket of his pants, maneuvering around a heavy gut.

"He works for me. Breakfast is getting cold, and I'd appreciate the next time that daffy bitch Sherry Robison calls you, you bother somebody else about it." Jake pushed back, bumping Ben.

"Have it your way," Robert said.

***

Ben sprayed air freshener before they piled into the van. Over breakfast, while Alley was in the can, Jake offered to let Ben have the basement. He'd popped from his seat and hurried down for a look. A step up, certainly.

Alley was back in her spot, the dregs of a second cup of coffee in one hand. The other hand played with the placemats that had sat on the table for about nine months straight. "These need washed," she said and then looked at Kit and Jake before covering her mouth to stifle a laugh.

"I hadn't even thought about washing them," Jake said.

"Me neither," Kit said.

Changing the subject, Alley asked about how Ben came to be in Copper Falls. The tale seemed to intrigue, and she made mooneyes at Jake. Like he was a real-life saint performing a miracle.

After that, Ben asked where he'd get some stuff for the basement. Used.

South of Copper Falls was a hamlet called Worrell. It had a big flea market, a variety store, a public use pond, a race car track, and a crummy restaurant where low lighting kept patrons from seeing filth.

They dropped Alley off in the driveway of a small rental bungalow with a backyard made almost entirely of the Saugeen River. It was quaint with pale blue shutters and a black front door. In the driveway was a white Ford Festiva.

"Bye," she said and then pulled open the van's sliding door but turned around quick and kissed Jake on the mouth. He'd sat in the second row and Kit sat up front. "Call me?"

"Yeah. For sure."

The door closed. Ben started rolling in reverse. Kit spun in her seat. "You did do it, didn't you!"

"Shut up!"

Ben looked in the rearview mirror wearing a grin. He carried on through town and southbound on Highway #6. Worrell came into view quickly and he had to slow to sixty. The flea market was at the bottom of a hill on the lefthand side. Streamers dangled limply from trees next to the highway, faded by the sun. There were a couple trucks in the lot and a row of bicycles under a blue tarp. The building itself was long, white, and windowless aside from the front section, like a poultry barn.

Inside smelled of burning dust from space heaters. Behind a register was a plump man with silver hair and pink cheeks. Behind him was a cubby shelf loaded with vintage pornography—only spines were visible. The proprietor nodded as they stepped inside. There was much more building to the right than to the left, so they naturally started right. The aisle was single-file wide. Junk piled on benches and on shelves. Rusty stuff. Grimy stuff. Cracked stuff. Collector plates. McDonald's toys. Picture frames. Sculptures. Ashtrays.

"Sure, they'll have—?"

Kit cut off Ben. "That's just the junk."

"I bet it's out there because people knock stuff over when they come through. Though those plates look real breakable," Jake said.

Kit hooked a left into a room without a door and the space was suddenly open. Ben walked over to rugs hanging on angle iron displays. A few of them were nice. One was furry and pure polyester, and only seven bucks. White shag with a coffee stain, or perhaps a dog shit stain.

"That's easy enough." Ben brushed his hand over the rug and then wiped the dust on his pant leg. "I'll come back for it. What else do you think? I can bring that space heater in from the shed, right?"

"Sure." Jake looked around; Kit had disappeared.

They continued and discussed how much power a little heater might burn through on a cold night, given the size of the basement, and then ways that could lessen the impact.

"'Spose we could frame out a room…" Jake trailed, "but that'd get pricey and…" he trailed again.

"And who knows how long I'll be around. I get ya. I could put up a partition around my bed. There an appliance store around here? Get a couple fridge boxes and staple them to two by twos, I could put it up when it's too cold and cordon myself in."

They walked further along the hall after finding only a rug in the big open room. The trinkets and oddities were less junky. They hooked another left into a room full of TVs, VCRs, Beta Max players, 8-track systems, record players, cassette decks, and shelves upon shelves of videos, cassettes, and records.

"Well, if it gets too cold, we'll bring you upstairs. You know, I'd let you sleep in my parents' room, but I don't know…" Jake trailed again. Over the weeks, he'd told Ben the whole story and about one hundred other stories. Most were good for a laugh or pertinent information, but the story of his parents was a sad one.

"Geez, I don't even want to get into this room. A man could blow a week's pay in no time. I knew this guy with a Columbia House addiction," Ben said. "Spent two hundred a month on videos and another fifty on cassettes. Crazy."

"Yeah, most times I'm fine with TV or just renting tapes. Music, whatever is on the radio works too. I wouldn't mind getting a Nintendo though."

Ben smirked. "I had a Nintendo, back in the late 'eighties. Sold it, I think... Shit that's funny. Some stuff is right there, but only halfways."

"It'll come back." Jake led them out of the entertainment room and back into the cluttered hall. "We should probably look for a hotplate or something, then you don't have to come upstairs every time you want something hot. I guess these dishes are the right price, maybe get a set of utensils and plates and bowls."

Very little matched in the boxes of silverware and ceramics. Ben bent over a box of mugs and cups. He picked up a hefty beer stein. He turned it and looked at the A&W insignia. Like hot glue, his eyes clung and burned.

"Do...you...smell...?" he mumbled and then swallowed.

"Hey, you all, right?" Jake put his hand on Ben's shoulder and rubbed it a little.

"I found just the thing for Ben!" Kit ran up from behind and bumped into them. Ben dropped the mug into the box where it broke a teacup. "Oh, darn," she said, seeing the aftermath. She held a pair of antique, double-bladed bob skates.

A tear slipped down Ben's cheek. He said, "I smelled French fries and blood. It was so strong."

Jake rubbed a final revolution and then patted the shoulder. "You need to go to the doctor?"

Ben shook his head and looked at the bob skates. The joke had blown its timing.

***

They sat around the table like a strange new family. Kit talked about school. Jake talked about movies he'd seen previews for on the television. Ben talked about the work he'd been doing at two other farms.

"Guess I'd never done chicken catching before," he said and laughed.

"Even doing the stuff doesn't make you remember?" Kit said, forkful of Green Giant yellow beans hanging limply a few inches below her chin.

Ben set down his fork and thought a moment, tapped his lip, and then shook his head. "No. Sometimes. It's like my body knows or it doesn't know. It doesn't know anything about catching chickens. That's bad work."

"You gonna quit that one?" Jake asked around a mouth of mashed potatoes and butter.

"It's piece work. Until you get good at it, it's not worth it. So, I think I'll just stay home. Not like I need the money, not if I'm sticking around here for a while," Ben said.

They'd picked up the rug, a couple books, a lamp, a hotplate, a kettle, cardboard from the appliance store in Sprucemont, and six 1x2s from the hardware and lumber store in Copper Falls. Ben had said while passing through the towns, "I guess I would've come this way, but none of this is familiar."

After supper, Jake helped Ben in the basement. The partition was simple, and the staple gun had it together and adjustable in only a few minutes. Earlier, they brought down a cot and five of Mother Gerber's throw pillows. The TV from the shed sat on a milk crate.

"Need to hook to the antenna," Ben said.

"I think your antenna in the shed works better than the one on the house. Now that you got it working right."

"Couple feet higher anyway. You know, Jake, I really appreciate this. I'd probably be dead out on the road someplace," Ben said and absently touched the spot where the gash on his side left a faint scar.

"If not me, somebody would've taken you in. You chanced on a bad road during some bad weather."

"Good road, bad weather. I don't think just anybody would've taken a chance on me."

Ben lifted his hands, palms up. "You kinda did us a favor too. It hadn't been going so well. I don't know how Dad and Mom did it."

Ben bent over his cot to plug the clock radio into the extension cord that ran from behind the old deep freezer. "I don't think farming's ever been the easiest way to make money. Figure more people do it because it's tradition and because aside from summer, they mostly get to make their own hours. Though all the snow you have to blow is some pain."

"Plus, that goddamned lynchpin breaks every second time."

Ben laughed. "Design flaw, or maybe too much snow."

Jake looked around the drab space and wiggled his toes within his socks. He stood on the floor rather than on the fake fur polyester rug. Silence mounted. They both began talking at once. Ben quieted again.

"Guess I'll go watch the tube, you can come, if you want," Jake said.

Ben leaned on the cot, back pinching pillows against the wall. "Nah. I think I'll start one of those books. Something about that one with the nailed hand jogs up here." He swirled a finger at his right temple.

"What's that one called?"

"*Savage Season.*"

"Never heard of it."

"Yeah."

Jake looked at his feet without talking for another twenty seconds before saying, "Okay. See you tomorrow."

"Goodnight."

"Goodnight."

Chapter Fifteen

February 21, 1994 – Sprucemont, Ontario, Canada

Detective Marc Foster twirled the peeled paper from the end of the Rolaids package around his index finger as he pinched the telephone between his shoulder and ear. He popped four Rolaids into his mouth. As he chewed, a voice came onto the line.

"I don't know where he's gone. You want me to have him call you?"

"I suppose."

Marc rattled off his number and underlined Vic's Camper and Scrap on his list of calls. He was floundering. Those bodies got to where they got somehow and the only clue was a very old RV. Starting with the smart move, he dialed around to other counties and the RCMP to ask about the vehicle. Turned out, campers did not speed, and cops didn't pull them over for suspicious doings. Meaning the drivers were probably either old or white or a mix of the pair.

The phone rang and flashed orange, banking off the picture of his wife and daughter. They, along with his son, had gone off to stay with Cheryl's mother until Marc got his shit together— her words. In retaliation, he'd told her it was all the stupid women at the nursing home, not a one of them were on a first marriage. They hated happiness, he'd tried to tell her, and when that didn't work, he called her a stupid bitch for not seeing it.

Cheryl's mother—divorcee—lived in town, but Marc wasn't about to go there. So far, he'd made Cheryl take the kids to the library or the arena and whenever she complained, he told her she could always take them home.

"I need a fucking win," he said and then picked up the ringing phone, "Detective Foster here."

"Just me," Paula on the switchboard said. "You have your

radio off. Tony Gibbons has a pair of suspect missing persons and went out to answer the call and the neighbors said they saw a great big Winnebago parked next to the barn for the last three weeks."

Marc tensed. "Is the camper there now?"

Paula made a moaning noise. "Winnebago, like a camper. I just said what he said, I didn't know what he was talking about, but now I get it. Ugh, dummy, huh? Anyway, you'll have to call him on the radio or head out to Fred Jalinski's farm. You know where that is?"

"Remind me."

"One road past the Six and Ten intersection, go east about four kilometers, it's on the right. If you drive across the bridge, you went too far."

"That bridge going over the Saugeen, do you know?"

"No idea. Probably though, right?"

"Thanks, Paula."

He hung up and turned the dial on his radio and lifted the microphone to his mouth.

***

Jalinski, the name, was familiar for a reason. Seeing the farm brought it back. They'd been on the news about a decade earlier, raising money for their son. An experimental procedure not covered by OHIP might save his life. The chief and detectives— back then Marc was still patrolling the highways—even sat in during a telethon put on by the local cable access station.

The lane had drifted over and been run through by at least two other heavy vehicles before Marc's Crown Victoria followed the route. Officer Tony Gibbons had his marked cruiser out, which accounted for one of the heavy vehicles. The barn loomed like a cold sore; the paint peeling and the grey boards looking sad and too weathered, as if the farm was inactive. According to the smell when Marc opened his door, that was not the case.

He stood and Tony started over to him. Tony was about thirty-five and as high in the station rankings as he was liable to get. Not overly smart or fit, and unable to keep his tendency toward racial profiling under thumb. Tony gave more tickets to Natives than the rest of the station combined, which was a talent given there wasn't any First Nation land for about fifty kilometers in any direction.

"Neighbors say the camper was parked down there by the side, at the fence. He only saw it, he said 'cause he was out walking his dog by the river."

"Anything disturbed in the house?"

"Not especially. It's lived in. Dishes washed in the sink. There's a note on the door says they decided to take a trip to Florida, but it was a cousin who'd moved to Florida that called it in. She says no way they'd go down and not tell her, so I asked the neighbors and got as far as the Bells there, and Eliot Bell told me about the camper, said the Jalinskis don't have a camper."

"Been in the barn yet?"

Tony shook his head.

"Okay. Go to the station and get the print kit and then you and me are going to try to not fuck up doing prints. Hopefully the Jalinskis didn't have friends over often."

Tony frowned and then turned.

"Just a sec'. Did the neighbor say how long the camper had been there?"

Tony answered without stopping walking. "First saw it two weeks ago. Last saw it last week."

Marc watched him until he got into the car and said, "You fuck." He went down to the barn basement. The rustling of large animals was audible from the main floor. There was one long pen. The cattle changed focus once they heard footfalls coming down the stairs. They'd been at a round bale feeder. The Jalinskis must've widened a hole for winter and dropped the big bales through, unfortunately…this offered plausibility to the note…though not much. Not really counting, there must've been at least twenty cattle. A bale wouldn't last long at all. No more than a few days most likely.

"Maybe they hired someone to come feed them," he said. "Maybe they bought a camper and are taking it nice and slow down to Florida, going to surprise the cousin." He stepped closer to the pen and said, "Hopefully." He scanned the dumb eyes of the big animals and then scanned the pen floor, studying the contours of the shit, until he saw the pile of bones and the rumpled and bloodied hides. "What in the fuck?"

***

"So, what do you think?" Marc was in Charles McCarthy's office. The door was closed, but the phone rang periodically. Inside, he'd never get the man's full attention.

"The scrapyards and park wardens didn't pan out?" he said and then answered the telephone. "McCarthy. Yes. No. Okay. Keep me posted." He hung up. "We've got a couple boys from the Patriots,"—the local Junior C squad— "who've apparently raped a passed out ninth grader. Dumbasses put it on camcorder. Hooting and laughing… So no to the wardens?"

Marc scratched at something he got on his pants on the outside of his pocket. Chocolate maybe, or manure. "Nothing. This is something. Could be it's beyond me."

"Thinking you'd like to call in for RCMP? They'll take it and turn you gopher, you know that?"

"Hell, we've got bodies and it's got nothing to do with drugs or anybody's wife, or ex-wife."

"Cheryl bring the kids home yet?"

Marc exhaled a heavy breath from his nose.

"That bad?"

Marc lifted his head and slammed his fist over the grime he'd been scratching at. "Yeah, goddammit and I'm going to get a win out of this fucking Winnebago. Maybe it takes a little time and maybe I have to get help."

"You put it on the wire?"

Marc guffawed. The wire sent out faxes to be pinned on boards and buried under the next nasty thing. If stations communicated how they did on TV, killers in enormous mobile homes wouldn't get around so damned easily. Finally, after a good pause, he said, "Yeah."

A knock landed on the door.

"Enter," Charles said.

The door opened and an officer named Larry Coombs poked his head in. "Newspaper dick is here to talk about that hockey video."

"Christ sakes. Marc, do you mind? Do whatever you like. You see it and you know it, so make it work. RCMP, no RCMP, whatever."

Marc got up. "Thanks for the chat," he said and stepped around Larry Coombs.

He had prints. He had a description of the vehicle. But he didn't have what unraveled something like this: motive. Understand why someone is somewhere, and all the rest becomes simple.

He went to his office and closed the door. He flicked the light switch and then fell into his chair. The seat squeaked and the castors sent him in reverse two feet before coming in contact with the drywall behind him. "Why take the bodies and dump them in the river? Why go to the Jalinskis to do it. Why stay there? Why the fuck is the sky blue and the ocean blue and trees green and godfuckingdammit!"

February 22, 1994 – Sprucemont, Ontario, Canada

The sniffer dogs went up and down the shore that touched the Jalinski property. Pointless. Days had come and gone, and snow did the investigation zero favors. The prints were there to match should there ever be a suspect, at least six different partial sets. Marc Foster read all this from the brief memo left on his desk by someone who'd worked later than he had. Of course, that someone wasn't in as early as he was. None of the day staff was there and the sun was still only a promise offered by places east of Sprucemont.

It had been that way since Cheryl left. Sleep difficult to grasp and just as tough to keep hold of once he had it. The coffee in his mug was hours old, but not bad. He pulled out a cigarette and lit it, rolled to the window to open it a crack. Winter was on the county heavy and any more than a crack would make the office uncomfortable.

He sipped and puffed while he leaned back. The chair creaked and he finally noticed the blinking red light on his phone. Cheryl hadn't initiated contact other than to accuse him of ruining their son, but hearing her voice was worth the risk.

Receiver in hand, he hit the voicemail button. It prompted for a password, and he gave it. A mechanical woman told him he had two messages. The quality of the hissing changed, and he winced pre-emptively. But it wasn't Cheryl.

"Hey, uh, hopefully I got the right line. That guy who put me through said I should talk to Detective Foster. Anyway, so I was shooting stock footage for—I'm Jeremy Grady, I do video and commercials and stuff for Billing Brothers. Anyhow, I was shooting for this commercial and I was rolling slow with the camera out the window and didn't think of it until this morning, but I got footage of when those people disappeared. From the A&W I mean. I wouldn't even thought of it if it weren't for the Cable Four station running with the story again. Just to say no updates or whatev—"

That was the end of the message. Marc wiped his eyes with the index and middle fingers of his left hand while the mechanical woman asked him what to do about the message. He pressed the nine button to save it. The next message started.

"Uh, so I got cut off. You can reach me at the Cardinal in

Worrell. Three-six-nine, nine-nine, eight-two, room eleven. I'm doing stuff in the area for a couple weeks. I brought the tape with me from Guelph when I left this morning. There's a van in next to the Winnebago, and a Toyota sedan leaving. Depends what time, like if any of it matters. It's time-stamped five-oh-four."

Marc saved the second message and looked at the clock on the wall to his right. Just after six in the morning was too early to call someone. The amber of his cigarette warmed his fingers and he snubbed it out in the tray. His hands went behind his head and he looked at the cork drop ceiling—a leaky roof had a mild yellow line running across three panels.

***

Killing time. Readying for the eventual. Marc stepped into the Becker's Milk Co. convenience store and pulled four rolls of Rolaids from a box and asked the woman behind the till for a carton of Player's Light regular size. Still early, he took a stab at the woman. "Anybody saying anything interesting about the A&W thing?"

"People are saying all kinds of crap. Best one was that the people who washed up in the lake learned the recipe for the root beer, and the bear himself had them killed. Two people told me that one."

"Right. Nobody half-bragging or suggesting they know something? Sometimes people clam up and don't come forward, even if they want to." Marc pulled two twenties from his wallet to pay for the cigarettes and the antacids.

"Not about that." The woman ran her hands through greasy black hair. "Sometimes guys come in and tell me who they beat up. When people are drunk, they tell me all kinds of things. They come out of Sleepy's or the Kent and they go on and on."

"Worth a shot."

"Too big to brag about. Beating somebody up, okay, but killing people and dumping bodies, that's life in prison stuff, right? Nobody's going to be easy-peasy with that."

"No. You're right."

The bell above the door jingled and Marc headed off with his purchases, stuffing the Rolaids into his pocket. "Thanks again," he said once his shoulder pressed against the door.

The woman saluted him.

***

At a quarter to eight, Marc picked up the phone in his office, dialed to the Cardinal Motel, and asked for room eleven. Jeremy Grady picked up and said hello around a toothbrush.

Fourteen minutes later, Marc was inside the motel room, standing as Jeremy played the video, while making a dub copy. The time stamp was about right and the Toyota leaving might not remember anything, but the driver of that van—a dark blue Ford Econoline, mid-eighties, maybe earlier—might know something.

"Well?" Jeremy said. They'd stood in silence looking at the paused screen for about a minute. "Any help?"

"Sure. That's all you've got? Shoot any other video around town that day?"

"Plenty."

"The van in any of it?"

Jeremy turned back to look at the TV. His thinking face reflected from the screen. "Maybe. That's possible. I was rolling up and down, just recording traffic. You know, for b-roll, like when a reporter's talking or voiceover on a commercial. I've sold b-roll to movies too. I have about seven hours of it from that day."

"Now how do we—?"

"We nothing. I have stuff to do. You can hang here and watch it. I have the tapes in the van. I don't have time to watch the stuff with you. But look. This wheel speeds it up and—"

"How about I just take the tapes to the station?"

"Got an SVHS player? I doubt it."

Marc shrugged.

"Nah, you don't, but look. The tapes are numbered. That wheel will speed it up. I have to film a farm just west of here, be gone for a few hours, minimum, but you can stay. I mean, I know where you work, right?"

Marc scratched his ear and looked around the room. There were three ashtrays. "Can I smoke near the machines?"

"I do," Jeremy said. "I'll go get the tapes. Door automatically locks, so don't leave unless you mean it. Did you watch how I dubbed the tape? It's already set-up, if you see your van again. Just scroll back with the super video and hit record on the VHS. Easy as hell."

"Yeah, okay," Marc said.

Jeremy stepped out and returned to find Marc had lifted the telephone receiver. He set the plastic Pepsi crate of cassettes on the floor and turned to leave. "No long distance," was the last thing he said before the door closed.

***

"Newspaper dick is here again," Larry Coombs said, half out the back door to the station. Marc was with Charles McCarthy, smoking cigarettes while they sat at the picnic table. The deep chill made the cigarettes taste crisper but cooled their coffees quickly. A trade worth making.

"You want me to tell it? Might be better if you do. In not too long from now I'll retire and you're the logical next step. Won't hurt to be out front of things sooner than later," Charles said and snubbed out his butt.

"Yeah. Okay."

In the boardroom, the Cable 4's reporter and cameraman, plus one reporter from the paper, stood facing the wooden podium. The overhead lights turned the winter pale skin of the already pale men green. The single woman sat on a tabletop, her face beneath a layer of almond-toned foundation—the light brought out the pastel brown hues of the makeup like sun to flesh. She wore a fine pantsuit and had a faux fur coat draped over a chair. Sasha Lane, Cable 4. All the men in the room wore parkas and blue jeans. Huge boots that came up to their knees.

Marc cleared his throat, then said, "Welcome. So, we've called you here today with a request. On the day the murder victims disappeared from the A&W, January twenty-seventh, this van," he pointed to a picture that he'd pinned to the wall prior to going out for a quiet smoke with the chief, "was seen at the A&W in line with the time of the incident."

Sasha Lane said, "Instead of the Winnebago camper or in addition to?"

"Addition to," Marc said. "We have a partial shot of what appears to be the back of the van. This was taken eighteen minutes earlier than the last known whereabouts of the van. Which, of course, was the A&W parking lot."

"How do you know times?" the newspaper reporter asked. His name was Ernie Humphrey, and he chewed a pen lid while he spoke and wrote on a pad. He had a tape recorder rolling on a desk in front of him.

"From the shots."

"Stills? Can I get access?" Ernie Humphrey asked, words made sloppy by the pen lid.

"Video."

"Can I get access?" Sasha Lane asked.

"Yeah, to both. We need this van, not because we think it's involved in the crime, but that the driver probably saw something and doesn't know it. Unfort—"

"How do you know?" Sasha Lane asked, her cameraman didn't move. He kept the lens on Marc and the chief standing silently next to him.

"We're working under the theory that the Winnebago

spotted at the Jalinski farm is the same Winnebago that was at the A&W. The van was never spotted at the farm." He paused for any possible questions, when none arose, he continued. "As I was saying, unfortunately, the van was visiting. We cannot make out the digits on the rear plate, but the coloring is green on white. We're thinking likely it's a Saskatchewan plate."

"What are you going to do if you can't locate the van? Do you have other leads? Are there fingerprints from the Jalinski farm?" The newspaper reporter swayed little, whether it was peewee hockey or murders, he asked with a negative lead.

"The van is a breakthrough. It's how this kind of thing works."

"But you wouldn't know. I mean, how many multiple murders have you worked? Wouldn't it be wise to involve someone more experienced?" The pen fell from Ernie Humphrey's lips. He scooped it up and popped the tip back between his teeth.

Marc took a breath, and then said, "That's a—"

The chief stepped forward. "Once we feel this has passed our capabilities, we'll gladly involve the RCMP. As it stands, they know what we're doing and they're assisting where possible, but sometimes you can have too many cooks in the kitchen. Now, Grace, we've got a copy of a VHS with video to run. This is coming courtesy of Billing Brothers Supply and Advertising, please be sure to note that. And Tim, the stills are cut from the same. Remember, we want to speak to this individual or someone who knows them. They are not a suspect at this time. Thank you."

The chief nudged Marc and then started out of the room.

"Such a prick," Marc whispered once clear of the ears in the boardroom.

"Absolutely," Charles said.

Chapter Sixteen

October 13, 1987 – Toledo, Ohio, United States

The house stereo thumped Guns N' Roses, chasing down something a few years older from Boston. The bar was lively enough, though the dance floor was empty yet. The band wasn't due to take the stage for another five minutes.

Nobody turned to see when the doors swung open and a young woman in white jean shorts—cut so high the pockets wagged like dog tongues and her ass cheeks peeked below the frayed edges—a button-up blouse tied just above her midriff, and cowboy boots staggered in. She bumped a table and took up the half-empty mug of beer. She chugged it back, gagging on the cigarette that had been floating, but kept it down without vomiting. She had raccoon eyes from makeup meeting tears, and some puke on the collar of her shirt and in her long blonde hair.

A few seconds later, the door swung open again, and the woman's ex-boyfriend stepped in, steady as can be. Work boots. Blue jeans. Leather jacket over a tight, white t-shirt. His hair was shoulder length and greasy enough for easy management.

The man in leather was Homer Ryder, but nobody had called him Homer since his mother and she'd died of emphysema six years earlier, three days after Ryder's twenty-first birthday. Her death was a hard one, even for a hard man. The day after burying her, Ryder killed three men and two women with a pair of pistols he'd stolen from a neighbor's basement. He'd settled down some after that, got a job lugging sheet metal and got drunk four nights a week at Logan's, a tavern not far from home. He'd then started in with Juney.

Juney was his most recent ex. The woman who'd just stepped in before him.

That old feeling came upon him after the sheet metal plant

decided to amalgamate with another business and layoff a quarter of the staff. Ryder took those pistols out of the shoebox buried deep in his closet and slipped one inside his jacket and left one under the seat of his 1978 Dodge Aspen coupe—done in all black but for the whitewall accents on the Goodyears. He had shown Juney the pistol from inside his jacket, asked her if she'd die for him. She'd laughed and tilted the Jim Beam bottle against her lips. He told her he meant it and she slugged again before telling him that of course she would. "I want you to suck it then," he'd said, and she reached into his lap, but he pressed the muzzle of the pistol into her pursed lips and hard teeth. "Open your mouth and suck it," he'd said. She opened her mouth and the cold, greasy barrel slid along her tongue, back and forth until it gagged her, and she jerked her head away. "You motherfucker," she'd said, and tipped that bottle against her lips as tears streamed down her cheeks. "You talk about my mama again and I'll knock your teeth through the back of your head," he'd said. She took another drink and tried to apologize. "We're done, Juney. Get out of the car alive or get out of the car dead," he'd said. She'd climbed out and began crossing the huge, dusty parking lot. She tossed the bottle without finishing it, but with each step, the booze hit her a little more. She leaned against a Harley with a sidecar and started gagging before puking into the gravel. Ryder watched this from the car. He put his jacket piece away and followed Juney into Kelley Joe's, a roadhouse she'd talked him into.

Inside, he went up to the woman tending bar. She wore a V-neck tuxedo t-shirt that barely covered her breasts, her tummy was flat and tanned. "Get me a Budweiser."

"Yeah. Two and a quarter."

"Get me a shot of some Canadian whiskey. You got Canadian whiskey?" He had his hand on the pistol. Everything was Russian roulette.

"Yeah. Three for import shots."

His hand lowered to his back pocket, and he withdrew six

singles from his sparse wallet. He took the shot and walked away with the beer, savoring the smooth burn. The music stopped just as he saw Juney. She was leaning on a flabby man in a leather jacket, much like his. The man had a long salt and pepper beard. Juney was saying something to him, and he turned to look at Ryder. It was almost funny.

"All right, back by popular demand, Kelley Joe's regulars, Blue Moments Red," a small man said into a microphone before stepping offstage. He harbored a big belly and was wearing a cheap suit and a gold chain.

A guitar strummed and the baseline thumped. The lights came up a touch and a woman with long blonde hair, curly and full-bodied, centered one man on guitar and another on the drums. To the side, up to nothing at the moment, another man sat at a stained and well-worn upright piano. The woman opened her mouth and lifted her chin. Her face was beautiful music on its own. Her voice was roadhouse deadly. The song was *The Chain*, a Fleetwood Mack oldie.

Ryder let both hands fall to the beer bottle as he sank into a heavy wooden chair.

***

"B-M-R will be back next Saturday," the man on piano said into the microphone as he carried the music into closing.

The stereo booted again, and Poison was on the air, though quieter than the band had been. The first row of lights above the dance floor lit. Ryder had three empties on the table when a fist rocked him to his feet, sending them tink-tinking onto their sides. He looked up at the chunky man in leather Juney had latched onto.

Without thinking, he lifted his right foot and drove it into the side of the man's left knee. He buckled, and on the way down, Ryder's fist planted a kiss on his chin. It was the shortest fight he'd ever been in. The man was out on the floor, shaking, arms stiff at his sides like a one-punched boxer.

Juney threw a beer bottle at Ryder and a bouncer appeared out of nowhere and corralled her. Another bouncer stood behind Ryder.

"Time to go, Pal."

He was a huge man, made of hard-packed fat. Probably inching somewhere near three bills. Ryder started his hand toward the pistol when he saw the singer of Blue Moments Red head out the side door, the man in the suit and gold chain shoving her along.

"You got that right, *Pal.*" Ryder didn't let the bouncer dictate exit and he followed the singer and the manager of Kelley Joe's through the secondary exit.

***

Talia Grey stumbled a little as Stan Podubny gave her a shove. "Come on, come on. We're late."

Stan used Kelley Joe's to launder heroin income. Blue Moments Red became regulars thanks to a deal with Mugo—the drummer—to move heroin on through several different restaurants all over Ohio. It changed things. Chip on piano and Gusto on guitar were both hooked on brown. Talia dabbled in the past but hadn't touched it in a while.

The guys who flew the stuff in from Columbia by way of Mexico were in town to discuss bigger plans. The band idea was good cover. They wanted to hear the music. Stan had two bands, the first of which opened the late-night rendezvous at Stan's compound in farm country across the Maumee River.

Talia only knew this because Stan's mouth got big when he filled his nose with cocaine. His eyes were like saucers as he prodded her into the back of the cargo van. They had their gear. They had a cooler. They had a promise that they could ride as high as they liked after they played the second set.

A month earlier, Talia brought up recording an album of

originals; she wanted to try the demo route again. Mugo looked at her with eyes that told all the truths and then his lips told her if she screwed up this deal he had going, he'd have a party, all his good buds, and they'd use her up and leave her for dead. He closed with a line about how cops believing some roadhouse singer, one step up from a prostitute, was laughable: so good luck. She didn't try him, did not test his resolve. She was twenty-seven and getting old. Too old for fairy tale dreams of demos. Besides, the heroin money was more than quadruple what she'd earn playing regular gigs. All she had to do was be quiet and sometimes use her face whenever a cop pulled them over, and not make a stink when uniformed hands roved her curves and under her bra, not even when those hands went down her pants.

The van peeled out of the lot, once space opened to do so. Kelley Joe's did good business and when the lights started coming on, the drunks departed en masse. Chip was at the wheel of the cargo van, which was how it always went. He could drive stone drunk, even explained how it was done. Overthinking and oversteering was the trouble with mixing booze and the road, he'd said. Next to him in the shotgun seat was Mugo. On one bench in the back, across from Talia, reaching into the beer cooler, was Gusto. Sitting beside her, chain-smoking, was Stan in his suit. Sweat ran and matted his sparse hair to his pale head.

They were into the county when Stan got to his feet and pointed out the back window. "Somebody's following us!" he shouted. "Lose him! Lose him!"

Chip said, "It's not even a cop. It's just some car. An old Dodge, I think. It ain't no cop."

"Undercover! You fool, undercover pigs drive undercover pig cars! Step on that fucking gas and you'll see!"

Chip did. Pick-up was slow with the big van, but they started to make distance. The car rocketed up behind them just as soon as they did.

"Shit! Shit!" Stan turned and stumbled along between the

in-facing back seats. He grabbed Chip's shoulder and began screaming. Chip broke his rule and oversteered. The van hooked across the lane into the shoulder on the other side. Gravel pinged the undercarriage like automatic BB fire. He yanked hard right. Talia flew across the aisle and landed sideways on Gusto. Her hand snaked under the seat, her elbow bent, fingers wrapping around steel framework.

"Shit!" Stan tumbled back and then hit the ceiling as the van began rolling. The steel crunch and the glass shattering happened in something like slow motion. The van slid on its roof, the weight scrunching the shape down a couple feet, and then tipped into the ditch. The running lights remained aglow, and the horn sang steadily.

Talia looked around and let go of the seat. The guys were mangled. Gusto's head nodded and jerked on his neck, his eyes were vacant, and his arms were raised to chest high, hands like monkey's paws. He exhaled a great bubble of blood and his movements ceased. Stan began blubbering about his leg, groaning in long breathless whines. Up front, Mugo grabbed Chip and pulled him back from the horn. He said, "Fuck. Fuck, think he's de—" The shot rang out through the van a half-second after the pistol entered the space. A second shot reverberated. Then a third.

"Shit. Shit." Stan began sliding forward on the wall of the van, toward Talia where she'd rolled onto her back on the seat she'd clung to. "It's a assassination. A takeover."

The van's rear doors creaked four times before opening wide enough to reveal a man in jeans and boots and a leather jacket, bathed in the red of the running lights. He pointed a pistol inside.

"No man! No man!" Stan shouted, waving his arms. Three shots blasted and echoed a jarring report off the hollow steel.

"Girl. Singer girl," a voice said. "You hurt, singer girl?"

Talia didn't say anything, staring at the silhouette.

"Answer me if you can. If you can't I'll leave you here with them."

Talia mumbled, "Yes."

"What's that?"

"Yes. I'm here…but no, I'm not hurt."

"Singer girl, you're real pretty and I want to take you somewhere new, and we can do anything you want. It's destiny I came to see you tonight."

"Are you a heroin man?" Talia said.

"What's that?"

"The drugs are probably at Stan's."

"I don't want drugs. I want you, singer girl. Come with me and we'll go wherever you want."

"Why?"

"I told you. It's fate and I don't leave fate to chance. I take it. You want to live, singer girl? I told you how I feel and if you turn me down, I might be able to let you be, but I don't know. You're real pretty and destiny called me out to that roadhouse just like destiny forced that boy at the wheel to flip this van."

Talia sat quiet for close to a minute before she crawled out.

December 29, 1987 – Studio City, California, United States

The Christmas tree a few feet from the raging fireplace was the biggest Christmas tree Talia had ever seen inside a house. The ceiling had to be fifteen feet high, and the spike of the golden star topper was only thirty or so inches short of that. Fifty-three and flabby with man tits and big purple nipples and a hairy abdomen, the producer named Desmond Shute sat at a mirrored table and leaned over a fresh-cut line of cocaine. He had a fifty-dollar bill rolled in his hand. Talia played hard to get, but the man went to the bathroom a few minutes earlier and came back in his robe and boxers, meaning time was short.

"Why don't you come take a bump and then lose that top?" Desmond said in between snorts and wiggling his nose like a rabbit.

No harm. She lost her shirt. She didn't wear a bra and her smallish breasts were right about where tits on a girl trying to make it in the music business ought to be. She accepted the bill and did not flinch when Desmond's Vienna sausage fingers pinched and rolled her left nipple.

She jerked back with the coke punch and hopped to her feet. "Let's put on the tree." She bent and pushed aside some of the fake gifts to find the power cord paddle. She plunged the extension cord button off and on five times, stopping once she felt Desmond's arms around her waist and his stiff prick rubbing against the seat of her pants.

"I say we forget about the tree, and I slide my cock in you."

The game was up. "How come you turned down my audition so quick?"

"Huh?" he said, kissing her bare back.

"You turned me down."

"When's that, baby?"

"I came to try for the lead of the band you were doing, and you turned me down before I even got to the hook."

Desmond straightened to slip the zipper down the back of Talia's pants. "I fucking love a T-bar, baby, how'd you know I love a T-bar?" Her baby blue thong was on display.

Talia squirmed away and pressed her back to the wall. "Tell me before we do anything?"

Desmond sighed. "When?"

"Three weeks ago?"

He squinted. "Oh, yeah. I knew I recognized you. Another girl had exactly what I wanted but it seems like I was wrong about you. Maybe you have what I want, too. There's always more spots." He stepped forward.

A pane of glass fell, but the alarm remained silent—when they'd first arrived, Talia rammed her tongue in his mouth as he was about to set it, though he'd managed to turn the deadbolt.

"What the fuck was that?"

Talia reached around and zipped her pants. She then

walked to the couch to retrieve her shirt. She pulled it down and buttoned to the top for a bit of emphasis. Desmond stood in the middle of the room—his boxers on the floor next to him—with his dick wilting and his mouth agape.

Ryder wore the same leather jacket and boots he'd worn the day he rescued Talia from the swirling drain. He carried the same pistol as well. "Let's go see the safe," he said.

Desmond sneered and said, "You fucking know who I a..?"

The shot exploded the man's right foot and he fell to the marble floor and began screaming. He hit all the high notes.

"Where's the safe? I know you nasty fucks keep safes. Your heroin money. Your bribe cops when you kill a whore money. Your motherfucking home invasion money."

"Bedroom. Upstairs."

Ryder nodded. "Honey, take this and shoot his dick off if he tries anything."

"My pleasure." Talia accepted the pistol and pointed it at the producer. His teary eyes took on a hurt expression. Like they really had something going.

Ryder stepped behind Desmond and Desmond covered his head as if to thwart blows. Hands in armpits, Ryder pulled the man across the waxy floor. His feet made little squeaks as he kicked out haplessly, whining over his foot the whole way to the staircase—a winding setup and with more steps than necessary. Ryder looked up and then down at the fat man. He looked up again.

"How about you tell me where to go and how to open the thing. You're too big to carry and if I get irritated, I won't get my money because I'll have killed you. Got it? So where?"

Sixth door on the left. Rug in the middle of the room. The combination: three-nine-two-three-four-nine. Ryder took two stairs at a time and Talia stayed behind with the pistol pointed.

"I can make you a star."

"I bet you can. You can make me a whore, too, my bet."

"No, really. I know desperation and that's the only reason

you'd be with a man like that. You work with me, and you become a star. But we have to kill the boyfriend first."

"Star my ass."

"You think Expose and Heart and Stacy Q have deals because they're the best? They played the game and got to be stars. You can too. It's simple. You give me the gun and call that chump down here."

"Shut up."

Desmond closed his eyes. Sweat ran off him in waves. "Look, you'll end up nowhere doing these stupid things for him. Drop that loser and come with a winner. I can make you a star, baby."

"A star." Talia stared at the carpet a few feet over the producer's head.

"That's right. Big as Whitney and Madonna, and Gloria, yeah, I see you like a Gloria Estefan. Big as big gets. Just give me the gun and call him down. I'll make you a star."

Talia licked her lips, then shouted, "Ryder, come here!"

"Give me the gun," Desmond hissed.

"Ryder!"

"Give it to me, now."

"Ryd—!"

"What?" he said from the top of the stairs.

"Did it open?"

"Sure."

"Money."

"Sure."

"Do we need him?" Talia pointed the pistol at the sweaty, bloody, mostly naked man.

"Nah."

She lowered the aim and sang, "*I know the time has come to set you free. But the words get in the way.*"

The shots echoed through the otherwise quiet mansion. Two holes smoked from Desmond's chest and grey tendrils climbed from his slightly parted lips. Talia grinned up the stairs.

She was already a star to the man who took her where she needed to be, saved her from bad decisions, the only man who mattered.

July 6, 1988 – Boulder City, Nevada, United States

"Call me a cab, eh Rita?" The man who sat at a counter stool had only one leg and a pair of crutches. His blue jeans had safety pins to keep the excess material from dangling. A coffee cup with brown lip prints and brown trickles marring the white porcelain sat before him. He wore a green tank top and had a tattoo on his shoulder. It had faded very little since inking. The papers came and he was to be deployed to Panama, only to be involved in a car accident two nights prior. A blood clot in the leg ended his service before he ever saw violence.

Rita turned and rolled her eyes. The man came in everyday, ate supper, drank two Budweisers, and told her to call him a cab. While he was in, he made sure each new face saw his tattoo and his dog tags. That he lacked a leg, nobody missed that.

Rita lifted the telephone from the receiver and hit the paddle five times in quick succession when the sound coming back at her was only the blood rushing in her ear. She turned and said, "Phone's out?" She looked around the diner, as if the nine heads in attendance might have an answer as to why.

It was a usual Friday evening. Most of the people lived in the area, but a few weren't recognizable as locals.

"Phone's out," Rita said again and turned to look into the cook's window. "Phone's—" She didn't finish because the cook wasn't where he ought to be. "What in the heck is going on?"

"Want me to have a look?" a man said. He was older and had money well beyond his appearance, and money beyond what most patrons of the Lucky Dog Diner had ever seen. He was in three or four nights a week and watched the horse races on the TV mounted above the dead jukebox.

"I don't know. Maybe Joe's done something." Rita stepped

through the swinging half-door into the kitchen. "Joe? Where you at? Joe?"

"Move and you're dead as dead ever gets," a voice said, low and serious.

Rita side-eyed a man in a hard plastic Porky Pig mask. He pointed a pistol at her. She looked at the knife on the counter.

In the dining area, the bell jingled above the door and Rita turned partway around to shout for help only to find Daffy Duck holding an identical pistol. Daffy was a woman and she said, "Everybody, hands over your heads."

The ancient woman with grey hair down past the small of her back wearing a long dress and a loose sleeveless tee whistled between cracked lips. Her eyes seemed to shine, and a grin itched to play on her mouth. She did not lift her hands.

Porky nudged Rita with the pistol and whispered, "That fella Joe is dead, so let's keep our eyes off sharp things and our minds focused on not getting lit up."

"I'm a veteran of the United States—"

"Shut your hole, gimp," Daffy said.

Porky worked Rita in behind the counter and she punched the button to open the till. About seventy bucks and change.

"Now the safe," Porky said.

"Safe's empty. I go to the bank on Thursdays to—"

"You go Friday nights. Had you gone last night, I would've popped you on the street and walked away with the bag," Porky said.

Rita sighed and dropped to her knees, began spinning the lock. Across the counter, Daffy had the wallets of every patron but the veteran and the old lady who sat with her hands on her thighs.

The veteran pulled a knife and threatened. "I bet you don't know nothing about shooting. It takes will and strength, nothing some coward in a mask like you would know about."

Porky said from across the counter where he bent down to see everything Rita's hands touched, "How you doing, baby?"

"Peachy." Daffy's smirk from behind the stiff plastic played out on the rhythm of her words. "Nothing about shooting, huh?" She spun the pistol on her finger by the trigger guard seven consecutive back and forth revolutions. "Now give me your wallet."

"Fuck you, so you can do tricks—"

The shot rang and the one-legged man fell from his stool, hands to his throat. Blood rushed from between his clamped fingers. His mouth yawned and closed, yawned and closed. The wealthy old man fainted.

Behind the counter, Porky stood. "Up you get." Rita stood. "Now run along, stand by the rest at the wall." As she went, she passed the woman still sat at the counter. Porky stumbled backward and swallowed something heavy and invisible.

"You're up, grandma," Daffy said and touched the pistol to some thick grey hair. "Give me your money or show me your blood."

"Baby," Porky whispered. "Baby."

The old woman said, "You're real fine with that gun. Good to see a lady able to protect herself in these strange times."

"Yeah-huh, money."

Porky smacked his lips behind the mask. "Leave her. She's good. She's…we can't take what's hers. Let's mosey before the next customer shows."

"Okay," Daffy said, and returned to find the veteran's wallet.

Porky grabbed the plastic bag Rita had filled and put it on the counter. His eyes remained glued to the old woman. Absently with his free hand, he began gathering wallets. Daffy stood and popped a wallet into the bag.

"Shall we?" she asked.

Porky lifted the bag from the counter and followed his girl from the scene. Once outside, they began running the mapped route around a block and then down an alley to the Dodge. They dropped the masks along the way.

Once in the passenger's seat, Talia said, "What was that all about?"

Ryder swallowed that same heavy something he had before and then said, "That's my mom, I mean if she didn't die and got to be real' old. That's my mom. I swear, unfuckingcanny."

"Oh. Wow. Wild," Talia said as Ryder wheeled two blocks south and then into the lot of the motel they'd booked four nights prior.

The car parked around back; the pair scurried to their door: 109. When they checked in, they wore their dork clothes—a Hawaiian shirt for him with khaki shorts, a fishing hat, and neon green flip-flops, and for her, a pair of loose red jeans, a Disneyland t-shirt, a Reebok visor, and a fanny pack—as it wouldn't pay for someone to spot them in their regular duds.

They'd learned to take it easy after robberies. Racing down the freeway or into the desert was a quick way to get noticed. Better to play it cool.

Once cleaned of cash, the wallets went back into the bag and Ryder walked to the snack machine. Next to the machine was a garbage. He dropped the bag in and used stolen change to buy a Butterfinger bar.

July 7, 1988 – Las Vegas, Nevada, United States

Talia had a gig at the Davey Lounge, a Vegas outskirts casino that switched owners every few years. To make things seem authentic, Ryder sat behind an upright piano. Nothing much was real in Vegas, so the manager of the casino had no trouble with Ryder slotting the piano solo cassette into the system and setting it to the single speaker behind the piano. The microphone ran through every speaker. Talia sang to the small group of drunks taking a break from handing off their cash and the couple of pimps who liked the joint to do some business— no competition, one ran girls and the other ran boys, all gathered up from the hard streets of Hollywood.

Talia sang like she was on her own record, like she'd sold out Madison Square Garden, like her whole life teetered on hitting the notes of each of the songs. She wore a sequined dress and silver stilettos. Her hair and makeup done just that evening for a price more than she'd get for performing the gig.

Some places were better than others. Didn't matter. Talia was a real-life singer and she wasn't running drugs and she wasn't burnt out. Most days she lazed by a pool in a different city, designer shades over her eyes. Dependent on the score, they could usually go a couple weeks without putting anybody else out. Not that robberies weren't a thrill.

People came and went from the lounge and Ryder and Talia took breaks after every fourth song—had to flip or change the tape. They drank copped beer and martinis and mixes with funny names and even funnier looks.

Before the final leg of the show, Ryder took a tall glass of water and a dirty martini that a waitress had dropped off by the piano up to Talia. The waitress had cocked her head and then laughed once she got a look at Ryder's still hands while the piano music came from the speaker behind him.

"Really cooking," he said.

"You see that one guy? I think he's from TV, but I can't remember from where."

Ryder turned from the shadowy wings and looked out onto the small crowd. "Which table?"

"Second row, one left of center."

Ryder squinted. At the table sat two men and three women. The women snuggled in close to the man familiar to Talia. "I don't recognize him. You think he's a producer, here to listen to you?"

"No. No. Nah."

"My singer girl is better than all this, so you never know."

"Yeah, but you said it. How's someone better than this place going to see me in this place?"

Ryder frowned.

Talia said, "Oh, not like that. You know this life is a million, gazillion times better than where I was. I ain't complaining. I'm just saying, I've sang nicer places, so those places had better chances, you know?"

Ryder nodded. "You want me to go say hi to him? If he's somebody important he might want you and if he's important and doesn't want you, I can gut him and empty his safe...be nice to hit another Hollywood guy, huh?"

Desmond Shute was the reason they were no longer in Hollywood. The cops cared about his death and it was almost six months before they pinned the crime on two Mexicans. The Mexicans resisted arrest and never got their day in court, according to the report. The autopsy suggested something closer to execution.

"No, best not. If you like, we can try to follow him after."

Ryder mulled it, his head bouncing left to right on firm shoulders. "Probably too much risk. Seems like maybe we got away with something with Shute."

"Worked out though."

"Not for those poor Mexicans."

"We didn't kill them."

"True." Ryder slugged back the second half of a Heineken. "Ahh. Ready?"

"Kiss."

He kissed her and then flipped the tape. He had seventy-five seconds to get from the wing of the stage to the piano. No trouble at all.

***

"Do you believe it? Chip Hancock? Do you believe it?" Talia asked for the ninth time between the casino and their motel rental.

"I knew it." Ryder rubbed her thigh as he turned the wheel. His hand popped off her leg and onto the shifter. "You gotta show me this guy on the TV. I don't think I ever heard of him. Is he for real?"

"Seems pretty real to me...but I saw a thing on the news someplace about how he gets all the facts beforehand."

Ryder parked around back of the motel and killed the engine. "Yeah, but he said like big theaters. Think he'll pay for shit?"

"Not likely." Talia laughed then. "I think like twenty singers make a good living and the rest of us fight for their spots."

"Yeah, well." Ryder kicked open the door.

Talia followed him out. She'd changed out of the dress and into practical clothes and practical shoes. The sequins were always trying to fall off the dress and keeping it nice was a total pain in the ass.

They got to the side of the building. It was dead quiet, and the moon was nearly like the early morning sun it was so bright. Ryder opened his mouth to say something when he started turning at the sound of lightning footfalls crunching gravel. A huge beast landed on him and bit into his shoulder. Talia had her hand in her purse, reaching for the derringer she'd kept on her since scoring it from a woman at a steakhouse down in Yuma. Before she had her hand out, a second beast leapt onto her. This one took a nibble from her elbow.

In a blink, the beasts departed the scene. Ryder helped Talia to her feet and they hurried into their rented room.

Chapter Seventeen

February 24, 1994 – Copper Falls, Ontario, Canada

Jake and Ben leaned against the rusty, shit-speckled bars that separated the feeder and one of the two pens.

Jake said, "Man, you don't look so hot."

Ben shook his head, cleared his throat, and spat a yellow gob onto the straw bedding laid over the frozen cow shit.

"Maybe you ought to take the day off, or maybe go take a bath."

Ben nodded but did not move from where he stood.

"I'm going into town. You want me to grab you something from the pharmacy? Like maybe some—" Jake began.

Ben balled his body tight to the bars, moaned from deep down, and let fly a pink deluge. He clenched, moaned, and out shot another. "Christ. Oh, Christ." It happened again and his eyes went deep red with burst capillaries.

Jake grabbed his shoulders. "Come on. Let's get you inside."

A couple heifers stood a few feet back while a cow stepped gingerly to the vomit to smell it before bucking away like a bronco.

"What'd you eat?"

They got to the stairs and Ben took them on his hands and knees. Jake stepped behind him, making sure he didn't teeter backward. At the top, Ben said, "Saltines and strawberry jam."

"Never heard of Smucker's and crackers making someone sick. Must have the bug. Can you walk?"

Ben climbed to his feet with helping hands beneath his armpits. Once outside, he paused in the incredible whiteness and clenched five times in a row before letting a small, much darker, serving fly from his mouth.

"Christ," he mumbled as he walked at a grandmotherly

pace across the yard toward the house.

It hadn't snowed in two days and the temperatures remained well into the negative double digits even at the height of the afternoons. It crunched and packed beneath their shuffling steps.

"Wait out here a minute, okay?" Jake said once they got to the door to the garage that led into the home. "I'm gonna grab a wash bucket for you to carry."

Ben only nodded as he clenched off and on, but he managed to avoid anything else coming up. Jake ran to the driving shed and grabbed one of his mother's mop buckets—plastic, red, and cheap; she'd bought it to replace the heavy one that she'd rolled around forever. Since, Jake had used it in the shed to clean out vehicles and wash windows.

In through the garage and to the door. Ben held the bucket underneath his chin. It was dusty, and a tired cobweb stringed a network at the bottom, but the resident was obviously long elsewhere.

"Let me get your boots off out here." Jake was already in his socks and bent beneath the bucket to untie Ben's boots. "Lift your right foot." Ben did and tipped against a wall for support. "Left now." Ben put down his right and lifted his left.

Inside, Jake stripped Ben's jacket and ben fumbled with the zipper of his heavy overall pants. His thumbs went into the suspenders, and he nearly pitched backward. Jake put a hand up and pulled at one of the suspenders. Ben got the other and let the pants fall then. Jake stepped on the legs behind Ben—they piled like a wedding train—as Ben shuffled in his socks and long underwear. The bucket was back under his face.

In the bathroom, Ben stumbled sideways to the toilet and flopped onto the closed lid. Jake stood a few feet away and said, "Can you take it from here?" Ben nodded. "You want me to get you something? There's a couple cans of ginger ale. I can—" Ben's insides revolted, and a red string shot into the bucket and remained dangling under his face. "Shit," Jake said and began rifling through the stuff behind the mirror in the medicine cabinet. Gravol, Imodium, and Pepto Bismol. "Take some of these." The Pepto was old, but brand new and he peeled the plastic wrapper from the cap with his jackknife.

Ben looked and said, "Which?"

"A little bit of each probably won't hurt. I'll be back with the ginger ale." Jake hurried out and was back in seconds. He put the can on the counter as Ben fumbled with the Imodium packaging. He started the water running and once hot, put the plug in. "You need me to help, or do you got it?"

"You're always taking care of me," Ben whispered.

"Somebody's got to."

Ben managed to get three pills down with a Canada Dry chaser. He tipped the pink Pepto Bismol jug, squinted, and then left it be. He set the bucket down and then stood. He got his shirt up over his head and off without tipping over.

"Looks like you're good," Jake said.

"Not good, but not dying."

Jake stepped back and closed the door behind him. He stood outside, listening to the water and the gentle movements of the sick man, waiting for a disaster. Two minutes or so ticked away and he guessed the worst had passed. He left off. From the kitchen's everything drawer, he grabbed a cheap flashlight and hurried downstairs. He checked everywhere for black mold, found a little, but not enough to hurt someone that quickly.

From a box already down there, he used a spray bottle with masking tape over the original Lestoil label. The word on the tape was *Clorox*. He used rags and wiped the walls and vapor barrier around Ben's sleeping area.

"I'm going to town for a bit. You need anything before I go?" Jake asked through the closed door. The squeegee noise of a foot moving against the slick tub surface sounded before Ben answered that he didn't need anything.

***

"Holy, what's wrong with him?" Kit was home from school. Ben was on the living room couch, bucket next to him, sweaty and sleeping beneath a quilt.

"Think he's got the flu. What say we give him some space and we go out for supper?"

"Yes, okay."

"How about Mickey D's and we see what's playing?"

"Cool. Movie probably doesn't start until seven or eight though, right?"

It was only four.

"Yeah, but you got homework or something, or you'll wanna talk on the phone or whatever."

"Okay, so what time?"

"We'll leave at five-thirty. Go do a lap at Zellers if we have to."

"Okay."

***

In the truck, Kit asked if she could spend the night at Alana's tomorrow. Jake didn't question it and told her that was fine. Alley Oates had already suggested that maybe he crash at her place and that sounded all right, even better if he wasn't leaving Kit at home alone—or with Ben, even as much as he'd come to trust him.

The highway was bare. Crystals banked the early moonshine back into the truck's headlights. The farm was almost a half-hour from Andover, between the two spots on the map were homes and fields and forests. They passed a hitchhiker bundled up against the elements and Jake shook his head. Too cold, but the truck wasn't exactly roomy.

"I bet we wouldn't be going to the movies if Ben didn't move in, huh?" Kit said.

"What do you mean?"

"His rent."

"Oh, yeah, probably not. I don't know how Mom and Dad did it."

"Funerals were expensive," Kit said. She hardly cried over them anymore, but sometimes…

"So was the lawyer's fee, and the bank transfer fee. Crazy how much people make doing paperwork versus how much people make breaking their backs doing farm work."

The lights of Andover breached the dark horizon. "Let's eat first."

"Yeah. Sure."

"Think Ben'll want something?"

Jake grinned. "I've never seen someone who'd want greasy McDonald's food less than Ben right now. If he didn't talk to me when I asked questions, I would've took him into emerge', just to be sure he wasn't going to die."

"How do you know he's okay though?"

"He hasn't puked since this morning. Probably be feeling like shit for a week, but it'll pass. It's just the flu."

***

Ben left the couch to sit in the tub again after he found another can of ginger ale. His insides were on fire. As the water ran, his bowels demanded evacuation and even being a couple feet from the toilet already didn't make it any less of a close call. Like lava, he moaned until it sounded almost like howling, which was strangely soothing.

***

Jurassic Park was on its third week—it had been out months already in some places, but folks in small towns with single screens had to be patient. Kit and Jake both came out absolutely buzzing.

They stopped back into McDonald's for a second helping

but took the drive-thru instead. They both ordered burger meals—having had McPizzas prior—and had to park and wait about three minutes for a manager to scoot out and knock on the window.

"Should have got another pizza," Kit said. "Alana's cousin lives in Kentucky, and she said they stopped doing the pizzas down there."

"Oh, no way. I hope they don't stop it here too."

"I'd say." Kit spoke around a mashing of dough, fixins, cheese, and beef. Part of her face glowed yellow from the Golden Arches and the rest glowed pale blue thanks to the nearly full moon and clear skies.

At home, they found Ben wrapped up on the couch with the fireplace going next to him. Jake set down the twelve-pack of Canada Dry and the bottle of Aspirin he'd picked up at Zellers—the old woman working in the drug section suggested there wasn't much a body could do but take some Aspirin and hope for the best.

***

Ben heard them but could not move. The fire inside him burned like nothing he'd known before. His slitted eyes remained hard on the bay window, past a tall oak tree, and to the moon. There was no looking away and time moved aside from his existence until the burning changed and a hunger so deep it seemed to come from his heels ground the muscles of his core.

He kicked out from beneath the blankets. The home was dark, but there was a scent, something incredible. It came from two directions at once. He stumbled barefoot into the garage. Slobber trailed from the corners of his mouth, and he swiped a forearm after slipping through the door and closing it in his wake. His feet crunched over the cold snow. Behind him on a wall, a Pioneer Feed thermometer read -29° centigrade. He licked his lips. The slobber was coming faster, trailing great sticky streams over his chin.

The scent was closer and when he opened the door of Jake's truck, the scent redoubled. The yellow interior light lit, but the world lost color aside from those two white bags with red and yellow writing that lay on the floor. He swallowed and scooped up the first bag, dug in, found two French fries. He swallowed them and moaned, eyes closed, bag pressed to his chest.

He opened the second bag then and found only burger wrappers. He grabbed the first bag and nuzzled his nose into the paper. He inhaled deeply and then exhaled. He inhaled another partial breath before forcing the McDonald's garbage into his mouth. Grunts left his chest as he chewed and tore. In seconds, the first bag was gone. The second smelled so good, it went down just as quickly.

He turned, heavy breathing, saliva so thick it dangled long enough to become ice and only broke when he kicked the door of the truck closed behind him and sprinted into the home. That smell had been two places before and he'd find the second, even hidden amongst so many other strong smells.

The door wheezed shut and he pushed his back against it to close it the rest of the way. Nose to the air, eyes closed, he sniffed. The scent was there, inside. He fell to his knees and hands, started across the kitchen in a silent crawl. Down the hall, he stopped and sniffed again. The smell branched, but to his right was stronger. He nudged open a door and started into a room he'd never been inside of, following his nose. He crawled over dirty clothes. Homework books. A backpack. Shoes. He got to the bed and rose to his knees, sniffed over Kit's sleeping form.

Close.

He lifted a corner of the blanket and stuck his head beneath. There. Right there. He rooted like a pig, up her thighs, sniffing all her smells. He found her right hand.

She rolled to her side, and he jerked away.

Back down to his fours, he crawled around the bed. Both her hands dangled outside the covers. He licked his lips.

The index entered first, and he tongued beneath her fingernail, gentle, but needing. He sucked and bathed. Moved onto the next finger and the next.

Kit's breath hitched and she yanked her hand from his mouth, scratched absently, dreamily at her ear. He moved onto the still dangling left. His tongue ran the grooves of her fingerprints, of the lines of her palm, collecting and savoring the salty crud hidden beneath her nails.

She rolled and took her hand with her.

Ben leaned up on the bed and stared at Kit. Something about her throat. The pulse, it flashed like an open sign. He licked his lips.

That flesh looked almost as delicious—

A door opened and a swatch of light played over the hallway. Ben fell back and raced, running on his fours, past the glow left from the open bathroom door. He got to the coffee table in the living room, the sound of piss hitting porcelain behind him. He lay, waiting, and then the fire resumed and tore deep into his organs and guts. He moaned.

"Oh shit," Jake said after flipping the switch. Ben was in the fetal position on the floor, legs and feet sopping from his adventure outside. Jake bent over him and touched his shoulder. "You all right?" he said.

Ben shivered and whined. "I think I sleep-walked," he said.

"That's okay. You want me to stay up with you?"

Still shivering, Ben said, "N-n-no."

"Let's get you to bed. You want to stay on the couch or go to bed?"

"Base-basement co-cold."

"That's okay. You can sleep in my parents' room." Jake started to pull Ben upright, his hands on Ben's shoulders.

Ben smelled the lingering cheeseburger scent, but also urine. As they walked, Ben let his face fall closer to Jake's hand.

The moment before Jake let go, Ben licked.

Jake didn't react and let Ben fall onto the dark bed. The sick man rolled and cocooned into the duvet.

"You gonna be all right?" Jake asked.

Ben whispered, "I'm hot and cold."

"At least you stopped shivering. If you're still real sick tomorrow, I think maybe we ought to take you to emerge' and have a doctor look at you."

To this, Ben did not reply.

February 24, 1994 – Copper Falls, Ontario, Canada

"I need a note that says I can go home with Alana, remember?" Kit had her lunch packed, her coat on, and was about to slip into her boots.

Jake had just come in from the barn. "Oh, right." He moved quickly, taking that Kit was in a rush to get down the lane. In his socks, he went to the kitchen table where Kit had out a pad of paper from Home Hardware and a pen from the local credit union. As he wrote, he said, "Ben was sleepwalking last night. Made it outside in his long johns and t-shirt."

"Holy."

"Yeah."

***

"So has that guy done anything weird yet?" Alana asked. She was stretched out on a black rug in her basement. At the end of the room was a huge 36" TV built into a wooden wall unit made of cherry. The shelves were loaded with VHS movies, hundreds of them. There was also a Super Nintendo Entertainment System with nine games stacked neatly next to it.

"No. Well, yes. Last night he was sleepwalking, but he was very sick. Like barfing and looking green." Kit was used to the open spread of the farm, the trees, the fields, the animals, the aged amenities. The drafty house that was in the middle between old and ancient when it came down to the structures and fixtures. It was nothing like Alana's.

"Think he was out there naked?" Alana rolled over and twitched her eyebrows up and down.

"Gross."

Alana lived with her mother. After the divorce, the court order, and the insurance money, she had enough to buy the nice house, stock the entertainment shelves, fix Alana with everything she'd need to fit in and feel normal, and buy a new Pontiac. Alana's father became abusive right before his father finally died and handed down a miser's fortune. Unfortunately for him, that money went into limbo during the divorce proceedings and in a fit, he burned down their home and his soon to be ex-wife's car. Alana didn't so much as ask after him.

"You ever see his wiener?"

"Gross. No."

"You ever see any man's wiener?" Alana sat up.

"No," Kit whispered.

"If you want, my mom has movies hidden down in the drawers."

"What kind of movies?"

"Pornos. The men on the movies have huge wieners."

"Okay."

"You wanna see?"

"Yes."

"After Mom goes to bed, but we have to turn the volume all the way off."

Kit gulped a swallow down.

Alana rolled back over and grabbed the TV remote. They had cable and she was flipping between a movie with the Coreys in it and a *Friday the 13th* movie. It was a little after ten and Alana's mother was still moving around upstairs.

***

"Where's your friend?" Sherry Robison stumbled over to where Jake sat with Alley and a few of her friends, plus a couple guys from his graduating class.

Jake took a breath. Drunk as he was, sometimes rude things slipped out and that wasn't nice. "He's resting up." It was also important to avoid giving Sherry Robison too much information. She obviously wasn't above house calls.

"Oh."

"Sorry."

Corey Hart was on the stereo. Nash was on vacation and he forbade any of his kids or employees from operating Maurice out of his supervision, so the bull was still. Most of the usual locals between nineteen and forty were there, the ones without kids or with babysitters. There were a few faces that didn't look nineteen. It wasn't so hard to get a good fake. It was only hard to have the body working the door not recognize a minor from around town.

Alley had her hand on Jake's thigh and the plan was to spend the night at her place, finally consummate whatever it was they had going on. She'd told him she liked that he was playing slow, and he told her that he hadn't known he was. She'd laughed at that.

"You know Henry was saying he was gonna get you back," Sherry said.

"Henry?"

Alley leaned in. "Henry, my ex. The one who jumped you and Ben."

"Oh fuck. Assholes are always talking."

"He had to spend a week in lockup because he's not supposed to be drinking in public," Sherry said. She held an empty glass, like she was waiting for the knight of shining refills. "His brother's here tonight, though, just so you know."

"Where?" Jake perked up a touch.

"Over with Toby Bernhard. Remember his little cousin tried to run away and died?" Sherry pointed over her shoulder.

"So, you're sure Ben ain't coming out tonight?"

Absently, Jake said, "He's got the flu." He shook his head and looked away from where Sherry pointed and then said, "But he's doing better. Told me he didn't want to get anybody sick and didn't feel much like bothering with people tonight."

Sherry bobbed her head around to CCR. "Okay. See ya later."

"That woman has no self-awareness," Alley said into Jake's neck where she leaned. Her breath smelled of rum and sugar.

"No. Strange 'cause it's not like she's stupid... Usually it's guys who can't see themselves all the way around. You know? Like a big fat guy going around calling chicks fat and talking 'bout how he'd like to get with some prime babe, like he has any chance."

"It's different though. Guys and girls. Most girls don't first look at what a guy looks like, more they worry about if he'd be a good provider or protector. I learned that in first-year sociology."

Jake kissed to top of Alley's forehead. "What do you look for?"

"I like the opposite. I like when a guy will need me and if he's kind, and if I think he's sexy." She moved her hand some, though not a lewd amount, certainly not by Friday night bar standards.

"You think I'm sexy?"

"Yeah. And I think you need a woman to take care of you and I think you're kind and I want you to get us a cab and then we can go back to my place. I'm getting tired and if I have another drink it'll be a wasted night like last time."

Jake blinked. Then he got it and stumbled over to the direct line to Laroux's Taxi. Standing had the room going a bit swimmy. "Hey, I need a cab from Ruby's." The voice on the far end asked where to and Jake told him it was in town a bit behind the grocery store, but didn't remember the street name, but his girlfriend would. The man on the other end told him five minutes.

Back at the table, he leaned in and said to Alley, "I told the cabbie you were my girlfriend."

"So romantic," she said.

***

The toilet seat clattered down as Ben launched himself forward. He'd felt a bit better during the day, but the sun disappeared, and his guts began swimming anew. His skin itched. Tears spilled. His eyes were sensitive to light. His nose sensitive to scents. From eight to nine, he bounced from the bathtub to the toilet, back to the bathtub. The bathroom floor was slick. His clothes and two towels sopped underfoot.

"Come on. Please," he moaned. The discomfort was surreal. His skin wasn't his, it belonged to someone else, and his under-tissues were in revolt. "Godfuckingdammit!" He let it out, screaming obscenities until a howl cancelled all else. Like salve on a burn. He howled again.

Stumbling, he turned the doorknob and spilled into the hallway. His hands moved with the dexterity of floppy oven mitts. Slobber poured from his jaws and his back end curled in on itself. The rest of him balled, coiling like a snake. A howl banked from his knees where his lips touched chilled flesh.

Hair became fur and tickled into his nose. His bleary eyes remained pinned on his legs as they thinned. A grey and black coat seeped from his pores. He howled again. His mouth puckered...his lips gone. Wet nose sniffling. Legs kicking and sliding on the linoleum. Ben's bottom half was no longer his, nor was his face. His abdomen was changing quickly. He scrambled on his fours to the door and fumbled numbly at the knob until it turned. He spilled into the garage and carried on. One more knob. He howled. Abdomen a scruffy coat, arms shortening, fingers stubbing into claws.

The knob turned as Ben pressed a beast's face into the cool

door. The door was open a crack and he dug with claws.

Freedom was pleasure and he bucked and ran, leaping and rolling in the fresh powder. The bushy tail swung beneath his ass, and he tilted his head and called to the moon.

A smell hit him then.

The chicken coop's door had a hook and eye. It was loose otherwise. Ben pounded sideways into the door, over and over and over until the magic tink-tink sound of hook and eye un-mating played beneath the soundtrack of his steady, panting breaths. Heat hit him and the sweet scent. The chickens began squawking. Like breathing, like blinking, he tore into the birds with ravenous instinct. Bloody and frantic, he paused in the doorway of the coop and fell sideways. The pain was back, and vomit rose up his throat. Fingers tried to grow, and toes tried to sprout. The tail tried to suck back into his body.

And then it stopped, and he was up and running again. Into the barn. One cat. Two cats. Three cats. Four. He howled and then sucked at the blood and meat and fur. The cattle below mooed, and he raced to the stairs and…the pain was back, and he rolled against the hard steps. He groaned with his human sounds, rubbed at his legs with stubby human fingers…Up, and fine…wary, he raced toward the house.

Pain.

He rolled.

The cold burned his flesh.

"Ah, fucking motherfucking," he said through a grimace and clenched teeth.

Onto his bare knees, up to his bare feet. The house was twenty yards away and each step was a dagger in his soles.

Chapter Eighteen

February 26, 1994 – Gatineau, Quebec, Canada

Jody Penrose woke from a fitful sleep, hit the bedside lamp, kicked out from beneath the heavy hotel bedding, and stepped to the wall of photographs. The full moon was one day gone, and that meant, almost surely, the killer or killers had moved on and left more bodies in their wake. Detective Bourque got her inside the home of the deceased elderly couple, ones she encouraged the officers to search for, and she tried to imagine the life. Old and lonely was about as far as she got. Making sense of everything was impossible, but the situation demanded her attempts. She'd been into desks, saw receipts, flipped photo albums, and rooted through the fridge. Detective Bourque even managed to score copies of the last year's bank statements. On the first read, nothing hit her, but something nagged.

In those numbers was the one thing that would crack the case…if only she could see the statements of all others. She had six months back of two additional sets of victims, but nothing stuck out; time and perhaps leeway had escaped her. Eventually, an investigator became the person on the far end of the line that ruined days, who grated the once helpful and who aggravated typically forthcoming.

Minutes to three, she hit the lamp and rolled beneath the covers. She stared into the dark, blinked, blinked, blinked, and the phone was ringing. She swatted out an arm to answer—the clock read 8:05.

"Shit. Hello?"

"Jody, the January incident happened in a little town called Sprucemont. That's in Ontario. The killers dumped bodies into whichever Great Lake is nearby, I think Huron, but they got stuck in the ice. The old couple are still missing. There's another kick, a dead cow. Looks like they killed it and used a dog on it.

So those hairs and paw prints found don't seem so random anymore."

"Holy god, that's fantastic. Not fantastic, but you know."

Detective Bourque had a smile in his words. "I called ahead. Marc Foster is eager to speak with you. I told him your background…might have suggested that you were once FBI but left most of it to his imagination. These guys, well, you know guys."

"Especially cops," Jody said, smiling right back.

"Exactly. Now, you'll keep me in the loop?"

"Of course."

"Good luck, Miss Penrose."

"Thank you, Detective Bourque."

***

Pearson International in Toronto was busy and poorly structured. Getting down to the car rental area meant navigating a set of stairs and a detour thanks to a busted escalator and contractors fixing a water leak behind a wall. The only vehicles left were small sedans and she accepted a Reliant K with a big scratch and a chipped windshield because that's what was available.

Sprucemont itself existed in an inconvenient area. There was a small airport an hour north and one an hour south, but no flights were stopping there when Jody needed to be there. So the plan was Ottawa International to Pearson to the highway in a rental car. The drifts were dalmatianed with road crud from regular snowplow use, and the highway was slick where it wasn't crunchy with salt. After about an hour, the tall buildings disappeared, and the homes became sparse. Beneath a long lean-to, at least thirty horses stood in the snow munching on hay and Jody took an extra pause at a stop sign to look at them. She never understood the fascination with horses. A Toyota truck beeped its horn and she moved along.

"Fill'er?" a boy said from behind a scarf at an Esso station.

"Please," she said through the cracked window.

She listened to the nozzle and then the splashing liquid. The Reliant K was a tin can. The vinyl seats squeaked, and the ashtray needed emptying. The boy came back to the window, and she handed out a credit card. He huffed and hurried away. Her window squeaked as she rolled it up. The chill invaded, but she waited to start the car. The boy came back and the cold bit at the hairs in her nostrils as she rolled the window down far enough to get the clipboard inside. She signed. The boy handed off a slip and turned to hurry back to the warmth of the station building.

The radio spoke of small, country things and she scrolled impatiently, bumping along the airwaves until she found talking. She listened for ten seconds and scrolled again. News was the hope, but only music and evangelical offerings found her.

The sky was grey, and her eyes were heavy when she finally rolled into Sprucemont a little after four in the afternoon. The police station was as easy to find as the detective had suggested over the telephone, and she parked in the visitor's lot. A big man was walking up from behind the car to the front entrance, tilted his head as he passed the bumper, and then stopped a handful of feet from the door.

"Are you Marc Foster?"

The big man shook his head. "I'm Charles McCarthy. The chief. Marc briefed me on you. I sure as hell hope you've got something that helps figure this out...you're no longer in public law enforcement?"

"P.I."

"Yeah, fine. Don't talk to any reporters, please."

"No worries."

She'd called Buddy Marron before getting on the plane in Ottawa. She told him what she knew, and he asked her to marry him. When she said no, he asked about a romp next time she was in town. She hung up, but with a grin. It had become a game. If she told him sure, he wouldn't know what to do with himself.

"Good. Marc's set up in the boardroom. A few patrolmen have been helping, but mostly with busy work. We have nothing to go on. I'll tell you; I'm not surprised this is part of a serial pattern."

Inside, the scents of body odor, stale cigarette smoke, and coffee met her like an old friend. Charles got her a cup from the pot and then led the way into the small boardroom. Her eyes settled on the dead cow. That was new as far as she'd heard, but it was also an avenue she hadn't really explored. Two dogs were dead on properties, but that made sense from an invasion perspective. Dogs are protectors. Dogs needed to be dispatched.

"Marc, I found Jody Penrose in the parking lot. Enterprise tried to kill her with a K car."

Marc turned his head from a stack of pages he had out on the desk before him. "Hello. Hello." He rose and put forward a hand. Jody accepted it and gave the firm shake that men liked. "Please tell me everything."

"Right to it. Okay," she said, sipped her coffee, and then got into what she knew and what she suspected: the camper, the full-moons, the additional dead linked away from the scene, and so on. "I just don't know how the victims are chosen. Once we know that, we know why, and things start to fall into place."

"Hopefully," Charles said and puffed a cigarette.

Marc stabbed a butt into a tin ashtray and picked up the copies of the financials Jody had from the Quebec case. "Full-moons, huh? The Rintouls. Normal. Average. Nothing special." He flipped through like his fingers could read and consume. "Maybe if I compare the Jalinski's stuff."

"What about the Saskatchewan plate on the van? Is there a van or a Saskatchewan connection?" Charles said, he stood over Jody and Marc who sat at the table behind a clutter of paper.

"What, because of the color?"

"Yeah. It's green."

"If it is connected it could be from anywhere. I might be wrong, but I think New Hampshire has green plates, and if it's actually connected, like I said, it could be from anywhere. These people bounce all over." Jody tipped her mug at her lips to find it empty. "Look, I've had a long day. I need some food and I need to find a hotel and I need to sleep. Can I take copies of these financials and see if anything rings familiar?"

Marc nodded. The information available on the Jalinskis was minimal by comparison to what Jody brought.

A knock landed at the door and all three heads turned. A face popped in. It belonged to Officer Richie Hawkes.

"Sorry to interrupt, but you said if anything funny comes up…and I was thinking about that cow…the one that got all tore up?"

Charles swirled his hand in a go on gesture.

"Right, well I was in Andover at Zellars and I saw Petey King, he's an officer over there, and I asked him what's going on and he told me about this Schenk guy's sheep. Tore to shit last night. Real mess, I guess. It's probably got nothing to do with this," he waved at the room, "but maybe?"

"Likely coyotes, but probably worth a call. Good stuff, Hawkes," Charles said.

Hawkes turned on heel to leave the boardroom without a word. Charles followed him.

"Where you staying?" Marc began organizing paper.

"Don't know yet. How many options do I have?"

"Two in town."

"Either any good?"

"Both are clean."

"Give me your number at home in case I think of anything," she said, also shuffling paper.

February 27, 1994 – Sprucemont, Ontario, Canada

Drunk on sleep, Jody sat up in bed and then hurried over to the room's desk and began flipping the pages of financials. She'd been through quickly, once, but nothing clicked. In sleep, her subconscious brought forth an idea and in a hair beyond drowsing, she understood that the key was right there, somewhere.

The words and numbers were stark even under only the dim yellow from the lamplight. "Come on," she whispered and then groaned, closed her eyes and tipped her head back. "Come on." She shook her head and breathed a deflating breath. She dropped the pages to the desk.

It was gone.

Chapter Nineteen

March 5, 1994 – Copper Falls, Ontario, Canada

Jake had his father's .22 rifle out. He had an eye closed and peered down the dark barrel. He hadn't fired the thing in years. When he was a kid, he used to shoot pigeons in the barn and the occasional tomcat that came over, got too neighborly with the cat's in heat, and then beat all the males mercilessly—a weak local tom in a barn meant there was always room for an interloper.

He was in the shed and had screws hooking out next to the rifle and the old Crown Royal sack—purple cotton with a gold drawstring—where he'd dumped the rounds. The plan was to put the rifle up in the chicken coop for easy access. Kit showed no interest in learning how to shoot. She'd leave it well enough alone.

Ben was back to work on Monday, he'd told Jake that Jake didn't even want to know about the mess he'd made with bodily functions and that it was good that he'd had time to mop and sponge the bathroom. He'd then asked how was the night with Alley, which was much nicer than how Kit prodded him: "Did you do it?" Getting into it with Ben was normal by comparison, he'd told him it was fine and then admitted that he'd only ever had sex sober about five times, it just rarely came up because he'd never had a long-term girlfriend. Ben simply shrugged and Jake told him that Sherry Robison was still hot for him and he rolled his eyes. They both laughed then. Ben suggested she might need a therapist instead of a man and they laughed some more.

Jake crossed the yard with the loaded rifle. It had an undercarriage magazine: a simple tube that held eight extra shots. The tool was more than twice his age and his father got it from another farmer, one who'd suggested a farm can't do without a gun of some fashion. He'd also suggested they get a dog, and they'd had, a bitch forever in heat but too scared to interact with other dogs. Sheba. Enough of a pain in the ass that she was the first and last dog they'd ever had on the farm.

"Maybe a dog would keep the coyotes away," he said as he pushed open the door.

Kit had been mad at herself. She was the last one in and that meant she hadn't latched it well enough. She felt so bad she got down the old cookbook from the shelf and read about plucking feathers. She cleaned the two chickens that were mostly whole. One went in the freezer and the other was on the table that night.

The hook screws were big and sturdy U-loops with yellow rubber coating. The old wood of the wall behind the door had a soft enough exterior that Jake hand cranked them in without any difficulty. Three of them up, he hung the sack and then the rifle. It cradled a bit sloppily and he moved it so the trigger guard hooked over one of the loops. He turned then, his hand crawling up beneath his toque to rub and scratch his head and drank in the scene. He'd go to the next auction and pick up another six, maybe a dozen, chickens for Kit.

He took the pitchfork from where it leaned against a wall and turned over all the bloody bedding. The lighting was dim at best and that helped to keep anything offensive a little less offensive. It was short work, and he was about to leave when he decided better and took the rifle.

He stepped into the barn and searched the rafters. Pigeons nestled together. The trick was to shoot them without firing into the roof, the old walls didn't matter, busy with cracks and holes as they were. He lined the near sight with the sight at the muzzle and fired. The birds took off and one fluttered into the snowy bales. Jake hurried toward it, but one of the barn cats—a mangy old girl that Kit called Dorothy—took off with the kicking and twitching bird.

"Want another?" he said.

A couple more cats had come out to see what was happening. Jake located the pigeons. They no longer clustered together. He sighted the first and the second. He took a deep breath and then let the rifle fall. His father had complained a hurricane about pigeon shit. Jake didn't see it the same. Everything was covered in shit in the barn, always.

"Sorry," he said to the curious cats.

He picked up their water dish. The overnight cold had it frozen solid, and Kit was at Alana's until the next morning. Jake had asked why Alana didn't visit the farm and all Kit had to do by way of explanation was to describe all the cool stuff at Alana's house. The cool stuff on a farm was mostly boy stuff, at that age anyway.

The rifle returned to the chicken coop. The nitroglycerin smell of the blast lingering and clinging some to his jacket. He swung the hook into the eye of the door, despite its lack of chickens, and headed to the spigot with the cats' water dish. He clanked and banged as the cold water ran and the thick ice hunk fell out. It wasn't nearly as cold as it had been even just a couple days prior, but his hands still ached while he messed with the dish. He filled it up and walked quickly but carefully back to the barn.

***

"I don't remember ever being on a snowmobile," Ben said.

Kit stood next to him wearing her mother's apron and holding the ready-made lasagna dish. She dropped a corner onto his plate.

"I remember there was this hill when I was a kid, and my grandfather gave me one of those great big wooden sleds. I was so embarrassed when my dad made me take it out to meet with the others. I mean, it was huge and ancient and rusty, but holy did it fly. By the end of that day everybody was piling on, we must've had eight kids on at once," Ben said.

Jake was grinning, he held garlic toast on a cookie sheet in one hand and a steel flipper in the other. "That's always the way, eh?"

Kit said, "Watch you don't scratch that pan all up. Everything gets stuck in scratches."

"Yes, dear." Jake dropped two pieces of toast on each plate. "The trip's at the end of the month. Last Friday, Saturday, Sunday, come home Monday. Dad used to go, and the old guys asked me to come. I don't know, it's pretty cool. Get to see some animals usually. Caribou and stuff. It's up by Timmins. You know where that is?"

Ben shook his head.

"Guess not, well it's up past there, pretty much winter until June in some of those places." Jake put the tray on the coiled stovetop and joined Kit and Ben at the table.

"Sounds fun, but how much?" Ben said and dabbed his bread against sauce.

"See, that's the thing. I would've said no because who has the money, but the old guys said they'd cover my rental and gas to get up there. They want me to drive a truck because they've got their trucks packed. They all have their own Ski-Doos. They want me to pack the food in back, I figure."

"What about me?" Kit said. She hadn't yet touched her food, wore how she felt about being left out on her face.

"It's men only...sorry."

Kit began pouting.

Ben kept mopping sauce with bread, eyes low. "That isn't very fair, is it?"

Jake looked down the table to Ben. "I got an idea. You and me, we go out and find ourselves a hundred good cedar rails, dry'm, sell'm, and send Kit on a shopping spree. What do you think?"

"Sounds like a mess of work, but for Kit..." Ben said and then finally began forking pasta.

"Wait. How much is that?" Kit wore goggle eyes and

bounced her attention back and forth between Jake and Ben.

"If we can find the right buyer, they usually go for at least a buck each. Remember, we had this conversation?"

"Oh. Yes, but before, you also said something about ones that weren't so good, like the ones we put in at Ruby's." Kit held her bread a few inches from the plate, and just let it hover.

"I guess I did. I think me and Ben'll just go for big ones this time and you don't even have to come out to help."

"I could ask if Harold knows anybody," Ben said between bites. Harold was the retired father of the hog farmer Ben worked a couple days a week for and knew everything about everybody, so it seemed.

The conversation shifted and Kit began talking about the Sears catalog. Her mood spun one-eighty and she almost bounced on the seat. Jake said it was a bit sad that she should be so excited about new stuff, and when she frowned, he clarified that she should get new stuff more than she did. He even went on to suggest a new truck for himself someday—though not brand new.

March 6, 1994 – Copper Falls, Ontario, Canada

The sun had the temperature a couple notches above freezing. The heavy snow crunched, and melt dripped from the trees. Jake and Ben were almost instantly soaked. Jake took Ben out to a spot where someone had obviously made plans for the rails sometime in the past and stacked them to keep dry. The stack no longer remained in any intentional shape, but the cluster of rails was welcome. The only issue was that they were about fifty feet past anywhere the tractor could go with that much snow on the path.

They wore the heavy canvas pants, which left shit smears in the crystalline white snow, their work boots, and flannel button-ups. Their coats were on the tractor seat, it had gotten too hot to wear the coats or gloves and lug soggy wood. The work itself was slow. Each man entered and exited the bush dragging a rail and then tossed it with a bit of care over the pallet fork loader attachment they'd dug out of the shed.

They'd been at it about forty minutes and had close to a full load when Jake dropped his rail by the tractor and shouted, "Sonofabitch!"

Ben followed behind him, dragging his own rail and said, "What did you do?"

"Oh, Christ that's tough. Jesus that's tough." Jake had his right hand squeezed tight in his left and blood dripped into the snow.

"Holy, better let me have a see." Ben grabbed Jake's hands and peeled back the protective grip to look at the surfaced end of a sliver a quarter of an inch in diameter, which had lodged beneath the fingernail of his middle finger. "Wow. Look at that."

Jake was wincing and half-dancing like he had to piss. "Think you can get it out? Needle nose pliers in the toolbox there."

Ben took a step to his left and flipped open the steel lid of the toolbox mounted on the side of the tractor. He felt around for pliers. They were rusty and stiff. "Can you keep still?"

Jake exhaled, closed his eyes, and stiffened up. Ben had to use both hands on the pliers. They were clumsy. Jake danced a little all over every time they missed getting onto the sliver.

Ben said, "Not going to work," and tossed the pliers back into the little toolbox. "Be a brave boy for me now." He grabbed Jake's hand.

"No. Wait." Jake winced as Ben planted his mouth over the finger and positioned his teeth around the wood. "Ouch!" Jake said, pulling his hand downward at the same moment Ben jerked his head back.

He pulled the sliver, about an inch and three quarters long, from his teeth and turned around. He held out the wood like a gift. "Look at that bitch," he said, lips red.

Jake did and then let his eyes fall onto Ben. "You got blood all over your mouth. Looks like lipstick."

Ben lifted his arm to wipe but stopped himself and said, "Does the brave boy need a smooch from his nurse?" He then made kissy sounds.

"Get outta here… I better put some iodine and a Band-Aid on this before I do much else.

"Full load anyhow," Ben said after wiping his lips and chasing his sleeve with a handful of crunchy snow.

They loaded the last two rails, and Jake fell into the seat while Ben sat on the left fender as they rode up to the barn. Jake told Ben where he thought would be a good spot for the rails, and then Ben hurried inside. He cleared some drift snow with a broom and tossed errant wood from the floor toward the wall, and then Jake pulled close and shut down the machine. Jake started to the house as Ben began stacking. He'd laid the bottom level and turned back toward the tractor to find a scruffy grey cat sitting on the hood—not unusual, tractor hoods were often the warmest thing in the barn.

"Hey, kitty-kitty," Ben said and reached up a hand. The cat hissed and reared back, its hackles raised and its pupils huge. "Screw you too, buddy."

At the front of the tractor was another cat, one he'd seen Kit petting a few times. It bolted, terrified. He watched it run and scoot between two bales. When Jake and Kit came home to discover dead chickens and cats, Ben never mentioned that he'd had a fever dream, only partway remembered, but completely strange and sickening. He couldn't tell them because maybe it wasn't a dream at all. The fur and the tail and becoming a dog, that was obviously the fever playing games, but he'd been out, had blood on him, and puked chicken feet and a piece of a cat's tail into the toilet.

He picked up another rail and got busy working double time, counting as he went. He was up to thirty by the time Jake returned with a bandaged hand. Only three remained on the tongs.

"Look at you go," Jake said.

"Faster we get done…well, the faster we get done."

Jake laughed. "We'll do another load and take a break. Kit's so excited about these rails that she's baking us cookies."

"My friend, you should feel pretty lucky. I've never seen a little girl who acts like your sister. Sure, does take all this in stride, huh?"

Jake dropped the second to last rail onto Ben's pile and then rubbed his face, his hand trailing beneath his toque. "Probably would've had to sell or send her to an orphanage or something if she wasn't. It was hard on her at first, but you're right; she's a good one."

"Hard on you too, I'd guess."

Jake shrugged.

Ben held the last rail to his right as he walked to the pile. "You know, if you ever need someone to talk to, I can listen."

Jake pursed his lips and was silent for a ten count before offering an artificial grin. "Nurse then therapist, what's next?"

Ben batted back a similar grin. "Just an offer, man."

"I think I'll be okay," Jake said and climbed onto the tractor. The cat on the hood accepted a few good strokes, lifting its back and butt to meet his palm, before hopping down.

"That bugger was hissing at me." Ben took his spot on the left fender and Jake turned the key. "I don't remember anything about cats in my life, must be a dog person."

"Blasphemy."

Jake backed out of the barn and took a different route out by the creek. It was bumpier and slicker thanks to the shade of the treeline, come midday it would pit and run like the other side, but they had more than an hour until lunch hit.

They stopped every ten feet to grab one, two, three, or four rails. Ben quickly took to walking on the crunchy shoulder of the path rather than climbing back up between stops. It wasn't much effort to keep pace.

"Must be twenty in here!" he called from just inside the strip of bush.

Jake killed the engine and let the loader attachment fall. "You know, Dad said all the time he'd bring me out to get these rails. Mostly when I was young. I could've come out and got them myself anytime. I was lazy as hell when they were still around."

Ben worked quietly, casting a look over his shoulder or between his legs when bent over to dig out a rail.

"It's not the same when you're a kid, even when you're eighteen, nineteen, twenty. You work, but it's for stuff and for beer money. It's not for life. Working for your own life... I don't know. I didn't really much think about farming before they were gone. I figured I'd get a factory job or get on as a janitor or maintenance guy at the hospital. Money's good at a hospital, doesn't matter what you do. Then they died and the farm was real' important. Does that make any sense?"

Ben said, "Sure."

"I don't know. We'd be better off living in town and me working, wherever, but it really feels like I gotta make this work. Like if I make this work...oh, I don't know."

Ben stepped by with a snow-covered rail during the conversation break as Jake worked at digging up one of his own. When Ben came back with empty arms, Jake passed him by. He meandered by a rail sunk in the mud some, but mostly uncovered.

"I think, maybe, if I can make it work, I get to hold onto a bit of them. You know?"

"That makes sense, and it's noble. Sounded like you had good parents and good parents are probably worth trying to hold onto."

"Remember anything yet about your parents?" Jake said, turning his red eyes down to get a closer look at rotten rail. To keep those budding tears to himself.

"No. But I've been thinking that if I just came to Canada in a van with nothing else, probably what was in the States wasn't doing a good job of making me want to stick around. I know I harp on it, but it's the damndest thing."

"Yeah, I'd bet," Jake said.

Chapter Twenty

"What?" Ryder was on his side, clutching his testicles; the same thing he'd done when he was a small boy and sick to his stomach. He wore only his boxer shorts and an undershirt that had yellowed with sweat. The light from the ceiling fixture seemed to sear into his eyes. He'd only woken an hour earlier. The scratch he'd suffered announced its presence, but was simply part of a choir, singing his pain. He said it again to the old woman who reminded him of his mother. "What?"

She'd knocked on the door incessantly until Talia flopped from bed and turned the knob far enough to make the noise stop. The old woman had been gracious enough to swing the door closed behind her, immediately. She pulled up a chair and said, "You've begun a change. One I went through ninety years ago."

"Get the fuck outta here," Ryder said and removed his hand from his genitals to reach for the nightstand.

The woman rose and opened the drawer. She took out two pistols. She carried them over to the table and sat back down. Talia's purse was next to the woman, meaning the derringer was out of Talia's reach, not that she was up for much; she been dry-heaving and slobbering bile onto the carpet where she lay off and on since staggering into the room after the attack.

"It only gets better from here. Every moment from now until a month from now, you'll feel a little bit more like your new self. Could be longer." The old woman knelt from her seat to pet Talia's hair. It was damp with sweat.

"I…I…think…I'm dy…ing," Talia said through sobs and gags.

"Come now. We'll get you in the tub. I've seen it help." The old woman lifted at Talia's ribs and she got her feet beneath her. The door had to close partway to allow access of the bath. Water running, Polly came out to Ryder sitting where she'd sat, the pistols in his laps. "This is going to be a lot harder on you two if you don't listen to me. Not that Cynthia and Gary would give you another tomorrow if I don't come out of this room before you."

Ryder took a deep breath and lifted his right hand. It shook, but the barrel pointed, more or less, at the old woman. "Then why don't you get out while you can."

"No getting out now. You're with me, and the pack is mine." The old woman stepped up to Ryder, snatched the pistols, and used the one in her right hand to knock Ryder from the chair.

July 9, 1988 – Las Vegas, Nevada, United States

"He'll be normal again though, right?" Talia sat with Ryder, holding him tight. He'd become like a crazed animal, terrified and lost.

"I've turned four others over the years, a few times the memory was gone, or a goodly sum of it, for a few months. It's not permanent." The old woman had told them her name was Polly Harp and come first thing in the morning, they'd all climb in the camper and meet the other members of the small pack— the others, aside from Cynthia and Gary, Polly had turned since 1899 were test runs in a sense; in a more accurate sense, she didn't recognize what was missing from her life. Making a wolf opens a space inside and keeping her wolves around filled that space.

"We can't go nowhere. I got the gig of a lifetime coming up. I'm 'sposed to call Chip Hancock and do openings or something for his show."

Polly tilted her head, interested. "The medium?"

"Yeah, he saw me do a gig and came up after and I'm finally getting' to where I'm 'sposed to be."

"A singer. That's risky…but perhaps there's a reward. The pack only does what's good for the pack. A test run."

Talia frowned. "You really expect us to believe what all you said about werewolves?"

Polly tutted. "If I were younger, I'd show you right now. Something about getting old, I can only do it when the moon calls me."

Talia scrunched her eyebrows tight. She was pale and sweaty. She hadn't puked in a few hours, but her guts burned like brimstone. "So, what? You sayin' you didn't need a full moon before? Werewolves always turn at full moons, everybody knows that."

"That's true and before you understand the change, you'll only turn on the full moon, give or take. We *have* to turn under the Mother Moon, but we can become wolf any old time we please."

"Except you're too old, huh?"

"You'll see."

"She poisoned me. I know it," Ryder said into the loose sweatshirt sleeve Talia wore.

Talia petted his head much like Polly had petted her head while she was sick.

July 10, 1988 – Goodsprings, Nevada, United States

"Jesus! Jesus!"

Talia backed tight against a wall of the Winnebago. The one named Gary stripped down naked and began a quick transformation. The woman, Cynthia, looked on, breathing heavy and licking her lips.

"Jesus fucking Christ!" Talia shook her head as Cynthia began yanking off her clothes, just as quick as she could.

Gary prattled close to Talia and Ryder. Ryder's head bounced, looking for a weapon maybe, or an exit. Gary ignored Ryder and popped up onto his hind legs, his forelegs resting on

Talia's shoulders. He licked her face and then fell back as Ryder took a great swing and nailed his belly. In a flash, Gary had Ryder pinned and his jaw around Ryder's throat, putting pressure on, but not quite enough to draw blood. It was always possible to go too far once blood started leaking.

"Run it off, Gary," Polly said. Gary didn't question it and broke away, bolting through the Winnebago's door. "You too. Say hi and then go do your thing."

Cynthia took slow, swaying steps over to Ryder. He remained stiff and scooted back against Talia's legs. Cynthia licked his face and then popped up like a circus animal, her fore legs bent before her. She leaned in some, bending at the hind knees, and sloshed out a thin tongue, bathing Talia's face.

Talia squeaked and pressed as flat as she could get. Suddenly there was a vacancy in front of her, before she could open her eyes, and only the trio in human form remained within the Winnebago.

The night was long, and they moved outside. Polly had a good fire going with wood from a cargo compartment underneath the camper. They sat in folding lawn chairs with blue ribbon seats and backs. They drank cans of Old Milwaukee and ate roasted hot dogs and beef jerky from a bag. In the distance, howling and screeching sounds carried over the desert. Behind them, the lights of Goodsprings told them they weren't all that far from the normal people.

Polly talked about her life and the chance that made her into what she was—bitten but escaped alive thanks to a sturdy horse still able to run on three good legs and one going soft. "I know forever it's been custom to shoot a horse with a bad leg, but I didn't even consider it. Charm was my girl and even when she got a little squirrely after I started smelling different to her, she managed. I nursed her for three months up in that cold hell. I never got the bastard who done it to me and hurt Charm's leg. I didn't really want to give him the chance to finish the job."

"I never rode a horse," Talia said.

"Nothing special to riding a horse," Ryder said, sullen and better than most of the way to drunk. A pile of empty cans sat next to his chair, as did an empty jerky pack and an Oscar Meyer wrapper.

From the darkness, Cynthia came forward. Blood ran down her face and onto her chest. Ryder stared at her breasts. She carried a dead jackrabbit.

"Brought you a gift," she said and showed Polly. "I'll put it in the sink." She stepped into the Winnebago.

Close to an hour later, Gary moved from the shadows. He was muddy and bloody. Cynthia laughed at him, and Talia took three strong glances at his penis.

"Want to hose me down some?" he said to Cynthia.

"Tank's only a quarter full. Forgot to fill it," Polly said. "Have to do it in the morning, fill it I mean. Use the sponge to bathe."

Gary did not argue, and Cynthia helped him wash under the bright shine of the moon better than three quarters full.

July 17, 1988 – Las Vegas, Nevada, United States

It wasn't to open for Chip Hancock, but to close. Talia had to sit Ryder in one of the two tiny bedroom spaces and explain what he should've already known: they were together because he saw her dream and moved her toward it, and she loved him for it.

"So, you have to sit here and wait for me, okay?" He hadn't yet adjusted to Cynthia and Gary's ability, and the loss of much of his memory had him frustrated and scared.

Polly took Talia inside. Neither met the usual dress requirements for the test show, wearing jeans and t-shirts. For Polly it mattered only as far as the disbelieving eyes let her remain backstage when appearances suggested she should've been elsewhere. Like the kitchen. For Talia it meant a quick fitting in a dress from a rental store that was willing to deliver.

She wasn't in the outfit until Chip had already spoken with three dead parents and a dead child.

Polly and Talia sat in a small room in the back. All night assistants came in and out with questionnaires and spoke into mics with earpieces, the kind rock stars and televangelists wore when they needed range of motion. They'd find pages and add pages. They had information on dozens in that particular audience and after the initial collection of filled in sheets, had information on everybody willing to offer.

When Polly asked the young man about it, he said, "We do Vegas like twenty times a year. Can't leave anything to chance."

"So, he's a fraud?" Polly said.

The young man frowned. "He's an entertainer. It's not his fault people believe in ghosts and goblins and vampires."

"And werewolves," Polly said.

"Exactly. It's pure fun and gives people hope." The young man lifted his arms and deepened his voice. "The end is not the end."

After he left, Polly said, "I'd like to eat him."

The young woman came in shortly after and asked Talia if she knew the lyrics to *Wild Horses*. Talia nodded. "That's almost always the one lately. I think it was on a TV commercial or something. Could be it was on some movie."

"One what?" Talia asked.

"People say it's their dead loved one's favorite song. Page after page. Neil Young used to get it more, but this one's the one lately." The woman began digging through a box of cassettes. "Acoustic piano stuff, just like you're used to."

"How much is the pay to sing one song?" Polly had her head tilted and her hands in her pockets, flexing her chest, looking big as she could.

"One hundred, if it goes well tonight. These are recorded, not every show airs, but the best ones air. You have no residual rights to any portion of your voice appearing on air and we stop the run-time for television just short of paying for use of songs while still getting people to associate popular songs with the show." The woman hadn't even turned around, said all of it as if it was a smart but obvious situation.

"For one song?" Talia said.

"Yeah, but not tonight. Tonight's a test. You pass, you get the money for next time. It's because you've got to come on the road. You sign a contract, and you follow Chip from show to show. He does five shows a week in the summer and three a week the rest of the year. He likes you; you sign a contract for a year. How you get to shows, that's on you. Pay is withheld a month in case you decide to breach your contract."

"Why don't you put a call out in cities before you get there, and pay them per night?" Polly said.

The woman turned around. She had pages and the Rolling Stones acoustic cassette in hand. "Bad for business when too many people see how the cook makes the meal, you dig?"

"Sure, we dig."

Talia just shrugged. She was going to be on TV, a little bit anyway.

August 1, 1988 – Spokane, Washington, United States

Talia told Chip and his assistants that she needed some of her pay. Chip told her absolutely and then walked away. The assistants informed her that he meant absolutely once she'd spent enough days doing her job, as the contract stipulated.

Ryder had robbed a high-end liquor store that night, killing the man behind the counter and two customers in the process. He came away with nine hundred. The police did not look for his car or the Winnebago, and Polly informed Ryder that robberies were great, but his car had to go. He'd tried to argue, but Gary and Cynthia put a stop to it with a growl beyond human.

The car went into a dealership the next morning and Ryder came away with another five hundred dollars for the pack pot.

August 6, 1988 – Great Falls, Montana, United States

Talia tried to argue with the others—Ryder was quiet on the subject, he'd fallen ill and only opened his mouth to vomit—that she had to work, but they promised her, she wouldn't be working. The show was in the local hockey arena and Talia snuck inside. She was suddenly ill and writhing on the floor.

Minutes later, Chip's male assistant came through the door. Talia leapt, pushing him to the wall and tearing out his throat. Through the wall, the applause of Chip stepping on-stage was terrifying. Talia ran on her fours, bits of torn clothing dragging behind her and blood dripping from her jaws. Away from everything, she barged through a door—parts of her back to human—and was in the snack area. There was a deep fryer, a greasy grill, hot chocolate machines, and a wall of candy. Unable to stop herself, she made for the cold fryer and began lapping at the grease. Once she transformed back to human, again, she broke from the scene and made it to the camper in time to open the door to a transformed Ryder. He prattled past her, and her body revolted against its humanity, and she trailed behind him, on her fours.

Talia gave a report to the police in the morning: a great dog, maybe a wolf or huskie, attacked the man and she bolted and hid in a closet, and then simply ran out of the arena, too scared to think. She used the word hysterical, and the cops nodded, questioned her no further. Within the hour, Talia was in Chip's hotel suite. Aside from size and a Jacuzzi tub, there was nothing special about the room. Two women were there with Chip: one the original assistant, the other a quick replacement for the deceased.

"Something's off with your personal life and your performances have suffered."

Talia blinked at Chip. Her performances had been simple, and the standards were scads beneath the effort she'd employed. Every stage was the big stage and every performance deserved her all.

"What?" she said, a scowl burning her cheeks and forehead with creases.

"Carey will catch you up. Last night, the performance you missed, was your last," Chip said. "I'm sorry it has to be this way, but I expect more."

Talia looked at the assistant who was bent over a desk and was writing out a check. She stepped back and Chip rose from his seat and signed his name. He couldn't be bothered to hand off the check himself. The assistant walked it over and Talia accepted it. She turned to leave.

"I trust you'll keep everything related to the show to yourself. It was in your contract, and if you don't want me to sue you…"

Talia barked a single laugh and opened the door. "You're lucky I don't tear out your phony throat," she said to the empty hallway.

She rode the elevator to the lobby and told Polly. Polly told her to meet the others in the bar for a drink, she had something to do quickly before they headed off to someplace new.

"What did you take all these for?" Cynthia asked, back in the Winnebago. There were six file folder boxes piled by the little stove.

"There's a wealth of information in these questionnaires." Polly patted one of the boxes. "We won't have to do much guessing, might even settle down now and then. In spurts. We kill the right people and everything's easy."

Feeling better, though not totally himself yet, Ryder said, "But we keep Talia on stage as much as we can."

Polly shook her head. "I can't see how that's wise. Her singing days are through. We need to think for the good of the pack."

Chapter Twenty-One

March 7, 1994 – Sprucemont, Ontario, Canada

"You can hang around if you like, but a call came in from an old fella named Harold Washington. He lives outside Copper Falls a ways. Says he knows the van we had the paper mention." Marc Foster slipped his arms into his coat as he spoke.

Jody Penrose stood in the doorway of Marc's office with two cups of Tim Hortons' coffee and a brown donut box. "Can't I come with you?"

Marc puckered his face and shook his head gently. "Not this time. I want to keep things as easy as I can in case this guy doesn't like talking to cops. The fewer the better, you know? I really need a win with this."

"All right… Everything's still in the boardroom I guess?" Jody had her files in the car if she needed them but using the department's copies would save her hassle.

"Yeah." Marc stepped out past her and stopped. "You were right, you know. The plates weren't even from Canada. New Hampshire. Is that what you said?"

"Uh huh."

She sat at the big table and began flipping back through the finances again. Somewhere deep down, a burr poked at her grey matter. She flipped the bank statements from the Copper Falls couple, and she flipped the bank statements from the Masson-Angers couple—trying to recall the blips of French she knew—and finally spotted something. Each had a big purchase in the last year for a trip. It wasn't much to go on, but maybe it was something.

She rolled her chair to the phone, dialed the number from the top of the statement, and bit from a chocolate glazed donut as she listened to the ring. A feminine voice greeted her, and she said, "I'll need to talk to a manager or supervisor, so save time and put them on now."

"I'm sure I can be of assistance."

"I'm working a case. This is in reference to a dead person. You're not going to feel comfortable giving me the information I need."

After a tick, the woman on the far end of the line said, "Please hold."

***

"Can I help you?" Jake was in his winter barn gear, full outfit. In the night, the weather had turned bitter, and the world was a block of ice by morning. He and Ben had been in the barn for a couple hours, addressing the regular chores as well as laying down fresh bedding. Jake had left the barn to fetch a shovel from the shed when the unmarked cop car pulled in the driveway.

"I'm Detective Marc Foster and I got a call about a fella named Ben, drives a blue van with New Hampshire plates." He pointed across the lot, over by the cut snowbank in front of the driving shed. "That van."

"Why?"

"I take it you're Ben?"

"No, I'm Jake Gerber and this is my farm."

"Where's Ben?"

"Ben who?"

Marc sighed and withdrew a notepad from his interior breast pocket. "Ben Lynch."

"What do you want him for?" Jake leaned his forearms on the handle of the shovel, his breaths came out in great grey puffs.

"On January twenty-seventh, a blue van was seen around Sprucemont with green letters on the plate, and also in the lot of the A&W, right around the time of a violent crime. I'm sure you heard about it."

"Yeah. Holy. The murders. So, what, you think Ben killed people? Guy's gentle as it gets."

"No. I think he might've seen the people who did kill people and he got out of there in time to save himself. Now where is he?"

It was Jake's turn to sigh. "Follow me." He started over toward the barn door. "I don't know if he'll be much use. He's got amnesia or whatever it's called. Like his memory is real' spotty. My sister and me found him in his van. He was sick and hurt."

"Is that so?"

They entered the dim barn and a cat popped from a shadow and began rubbing and figure eight-ing Jake's legs. Ben was clearing icy snow from bales.

"Ben. This cop says you were at the A&W right before those people got murdered. The ones in Sprucemont."

Ben turned, wide-eyed. "I was?"

A cow mooed and the cat that had been circling Jake skittered away.

Marc said, "Video puts your van there. You live here and just got to town recently, correct? How did you lose your—is there a time when your memory stops?"

Ben looked to Jake, expression open and readable. He shook his head as his shoulders raised.

Jake said, "He got here probably the next day or the day after that whole mess at A&W. It was right around when that Mormon girl died. I think she was Mormon."

"I heard about that. Might've been the same twenty-four hours," Marc said. "So what happened that you can't remember?"

"I don't remember!" Ben was visibly agitated. "I might've been there, you tell me? You have the video, right? You tell me, I don't remember hardly anything. I remember riding bulls and America and liking John Hughes movies and other meaningless crap. I only know my name because of my ID. I don't remember hardly anything!"

"Do you have your ID?"

Ben reached into his pocket and withdrew his wallet. He tossed it the short gap between himself and the detective.

Marc held it and withdrew a pen to write on his pad. "How long you planning on staying in Canada?"

Ben looked at Jake and Jake tilted his head slightly, quickly. Ben said, "Once I get my head back, I'll know why I came, and if that doesn't happen soon, well I guess I better go on home to New Hampshire. Sooner than later, I mean."

"Right. Well don't go far for a bit here. You sure you don't remember anything about A&W?"

Ben took a glove off and rubbed his cheek and then beneath his hat, unknowingly adopting Jake's mannerism. "Do they have big mugs?"

Marc looked up. "That's right. Root beer steins. What about them?"

"I don't know. I held one at the flea market, remember?" Ben said this to Jake and Jake nodded. "I thought for a minute I was remembering something new, but it went away, but maybe that was the flea market, like a smell or the dust or the way the light hit the silverware in the box. I don't know."

Marc chewed a sliver of dead skin from his lip and then asked for the number where Ben could be reached. Jake gave the house number. The last thing Marc said before he left was, "I'll be seeing you again."

***

Charles had to help Jody in the boardroom as her presence didn't carry the necessary weight, this despite the fibbing about official capacities. The man in Montreal was not interested in what she said. Within two sentences, the man cooperated with Charles and explained the large charge in question was to a travel agency—the initials on the printout were VIS LAP.

"Need me to stick around some more?"

"No. I think I've got it."

Charles offered a soft smile. "You should become a real cop."

"Maybe," Jody said and dialed the operator. Charles left and she quietly told off the man in Montreal for being a prick. The line connected and she put on her people friendly voice. "Hi, can you get me the number to Visiter LaPointe. That's probably in Gatineau, I think."

"One moment." The phone beeped and the number read out in a robotic voice before connecting.

"Bonjour."

"Hello. Do you speak English?"

"Oui. Yes."

"My name is Jody Penrose, I'm here in the Sprucemont police station, working on a case and I need some information."

"This for crime?" The voice carried a heavy French lilt.

"Yeah, multiple murder."

The voice on the other gasped and Jody could almost hear the woman's gossip-greedy expression forming on her face. Still, she offered up a juicy morsel and then asked the question. Once finished, she heard a filing cabinet slide open and then closed, and then typing.

"Fly to Toronto and then Hamilton. Stay in Hampton for deux nuits. Fly to Chicago. Stay in Motel quatre nuits. Fly to Montreal."

"No tickets or anything like that?"

"We book none."

"Okay, thank you."

"I cannot believe they are dead. They were nice old, talk about no children now and easy flight. Sad this happen."

"Did they say anything else?"

"No, only children pass, and easy flight."

"Pass as in deceased?"

"Oui."

"Hmm. Okay. Thank you. Goodbye"

"Au revoir."

Jody hung up and cradled her head in her palms, staring at the hard, damp carpet beneath her boots. Grey blue, the kind of shade that took traffic and dirt well. The design was a tight jagged weave, short and forgiving. Standard issue stuff.

"You both took trips that started in Canada. You both stayed out a week. You're both elderly. You..." She rolled her chair over to the file. The Jalinski information wasn't thorough and did not answer her question. She got up and jogged to Charles' office. He wasn't there. She found him out back, looking at clouds and smoking. "The Jalinskis, did they have any kids?"

Charles startled from his reverie and blinked at her a few times, computing, and then said, "Dead. They died in a drunk driving collision in...uh...I want to say eighty-one."

"Hmm. Okay."

Charles turned his eyes back to the sky and said, "I hear gears moving in your head. I won't even ask but tell if you need to bounce an idea."

"Right." Jody stepped inside, shivered in the thin sweater she wore and went back to the boardroom. The tines left behind from a burr in her head touched on ones left by a different burr. "Dead kids. Dead kids. Old parents. Dead kids." She picked up the phone and called the operator.

She asked hapless questions of hotel employees and then began asking about the dates on file. The records existed, but there wasn't much going on inside the registry to jog memories. She'd reached a dead end when Marc stepped into the boardroom with a pizza box in hand.

"What kind of pop do you want, I'll get it from the machine?" he said after setting the pizza on the table.

Jody looked at the clock before answering. It had been a productive morning. "Iced tea or Sprite or Seven-Up."

***

The operator found the number for the police station in Littleton, New Hampshire and connected it a couple minutes after Marc finished a post-meal cigarette. A dispatcher answered and sent his call through to a rookie officer. "Uh, give me a minute and I'll check the files for him. Ben Lynch, right?"

Marc told him that was correct and then waited. Jody watched him with her eyes, but it was obvious her head was elsewhere. He recognized the expression: a dog who knew a bone existed but couldn't quite get at it.

The man came back on the line. "Born in sixty-five, right?"

"Yeah."

"He's got a sealed juvie record, but nothing as an adult. Not in our files beyond a couple paid parking tickets. Really no information on him. He causing shit up there?"

"No. Don't think so. He was on the scene of a murder only minutes before we think it happened, was hoping he saw something. I'm just being diligent."

"Ah, smart. I know—" The officer turned and spoke away from the phone; Marc heard the name Ben Lynch said and then brother. "Okay. So, a fella here went to school with Ben, known him for years. His brother is a known thief and Ben not so long ago lost his job at the plant and started at a job painting houses for realtors. Took off just after the New Year, so it seems. Had his brother calling around looking for him."

"I see. Can't fault a guy for what his brother does, and I guess you can pass the message on to Mr. Lynch's brother that he's all right. If he calls again. Though he had some kind of accident and hit his head, has a bit of amnesia, which I'm only starting to buy now that I know he doesn't have a rap sheet."

The officer huffed. "I had a woman claimed she had amnesia, didn't know how the twelve grams of coke got up her ass. Tried to say someone must've knocked her out and put it up there and she didn't notice. This despite that I pulled her over not a mile from a crack den. You get many of those up there? We've been getting more and more drugs lately, enough that we've got dens. Used to be only yuppies did coke."

"I reckon, but I've got to get moving on this. Thanks for the information."

"Yeah."

The line went dead. Marc looked to Jody. She yawned. He said, "Average guy and lost his job. If what he said is true about forgetting, he might've been driving just to blow off steam and then misplaced himself."

"Awfully inconvenient for us. His not remembering."

Marc lifted limp hands and let them drop to his lap. "How often is a regular person thinking about everybody they see someplace? Guy gets his supper, eats, leaves, and what happens after that... It doesn't do us any favors, but he was either a grade-A actor or he's lost some memory. He has one of those faces you'd love to sit across from at a poker table."

Jody tapped a fingernail on the pizza box and moved her face around and tapped some more. She then stopped and said, "Wait a minute, maybe the Jalinskis have stuff on this trip. I mean papers. Nobody's cleaned out the house yet, have they?"

Marc lifted the telephone receiver again and called a familiar number at the bank. "Ross, Marc Foster here." He paused. "Yeah, cold as hell again. Canada, what do you expect?" He paused and laughed politely. "The Jalinski place, you do anything with it yet?" He paused. "Not destroyed yet, though?" Pause. "Right. I'm gonna head over there and pick up the paperwork stuff." Pause. "Holy, that much. Well, it has to be done." Pause. "Thanks, Ross."

"How many boxes?" Jody asked once the phone receiver fell into its cradle.

"Twenty-nine banker's boxes. Unlabeled."

Jody snapped her jaw shut. "It's doable. Can we get some help?"

"You're like a dog on every bone we get." Marc stretched

his arms over his head, danced his fingers at the stained drop ceiling. "This a personal vendetta? You lose a family member to it?"

"Just work," she said. "Seventeen days until the next full moon. Let's get those boxes."

Chapter Twenty-Two

March 10, 1994 – Copper Falls, Ontario, Canada

The call came as Kit was eating toast with strawberry jam. The buses were cancelled again. She hissed a yes before finishing up and donning her coat, hat, and boots. The sun was up, but it was still dim. She crossed the yard into the chicken coup, pushed open the door, and closed it behind her. She took the lid from the garbage pail in the corner behind the door, scooped out the mixed feed, and fed the chickens. Once through, she stood a moment, looking at the small rifle before taking it down and aiming through the sights.

The first time she'd taken it down, she'd entered the coop and was killing time, psyching herself up to go back into the cold. The chilled steel had a comforting impression, and yet turned her insides some.

Now, the .22 returned to its hooks and she departed the coop. In the barn, she heard Jake downstairs talking to the cattle. Ben had to work that morning at the pig farm, so she had Jake to herself. Three cats circled her feet up to the top of the stairs and they let her be to ascend.

"School's cancelled again," she said.

Jake leaned on the rails of the feeder bars up the left side of the pen. "Yeah, thermometer said minus thirty. I don't remember it ever getting this cold so much in one season."

Kit blew steam, imitating smoking a cigarette. "You were late getting in last night, huh?"

"Not so late."

"I was in bed and Ben was downstairs."

"So what?"

The juvenile cats had followed Kit to the basement, and she picked up an orange one and scratched its head. "So, are you going to marry Alley Oates?" The cat began purring and she set it down and picked up a black and white tuxedo cat.

"You're nuts."

"Are you doing it with her?"

Jake started back. He carried the empty feed pail. "Why are you so worried about it?"

"Because."

"Because why?"

The next cat began purring and she set it down and picked up the third, another orange one, but lighter in shade. "What if you get married and then she comes and lives with us."

Jake had set the pail down and leaned against a whitewashed foundation wall. "Probably if that happened, it would be like Ben, but she can cook better."

"Okay."

"You like Ben living here fine, don't ya?"

"Yes, but what if Alley turns out to be a crazy person and she gets you sex blind or something?"

Jake shook his head. "What are they teaching you at school?"

"It's Alana. She has *every* movie."

"Ah. I don't know what to tell ya. I like Alley plenty, and yes, we've done *it*, but that shouldn't really have anything to do with you."

"You're my brother."

"So."

Kit opened her mouth, and it was a few seconds before the words came out. "You're my guardian. You have to do things thinking about me."

Jake stood up straight. "Yeah, I suppose that's true. Okay. I don't think Alley will want to move in any time soon and I don't think I'll go sex blind. I know guys like that. I've never been a slobbering fool after a girl."

Kit set the third cat down so it could brush her shins with the other two. She waited and then said, "You aren't going to sex parties, right?"

Jake's eyes popped and then he laughed. "Sex parties? Hell you know about sex parties?"

The heat rose in Kit's cheeks as she blushed. "Alana's mom."

"What do you mean, Alana's mom? She doesn't have a bunch of guys over when—"

Kit shook her head. "No! But Alana showed me a movie her mom hides."

"Ah. That's probably just for her, you know…"

"Yes."

"Yeah."

"But are you going to sex parties?"

"Kit, I've never even heard of a sex party happening in real life. I think people did them in the 'seventies and then in pornos. That's about it."

"Good. They're gross."

Jake gestured for Kit to lead the way upstairs. "Should I be worried about Alana?"

"Like how?"

"She isn't giving you booze or drugs."

"No. She just has all the movies. Her mom is in with Columbia House and insurance bought them or something."

"That's good. No drinking yet."

"When did you first drink?"

They were outside and the cold bit into them. They picked up their pace without mention. Jake said, "First time, I was thirteen and puked all over. Then I got drunk most weekends once I was in high school. But you got to be more careful."

"How come?" Kit said this through a gasp as a gust of wind hit her.

Jake had his head downturned and didn't answer until they were in the garage. "Boys want sex parties to happen for real, so they get girls drunk. Bad guys screw the too drunk girls. Got to watch it."

"Yes, I understand." Kit kicked the snow from her boots

and opened the door.

***

The winds continued pushing through the morning. Kit had a few borrowed videos and she and Jake watched them until Ben came home in the late afternoon. He was filthy and shivering.

"I gotta take a shower," he said through chattering teeth.

Jake stood up and looked at the clock. Behind him, a great snap seemed to shake the house. Dim outside, but he could see well enough that a big old maple in the front yard had cracked and was halfway to toppled.

Ben rushed out with a towel around his waist, the shower playing background percussion through the open door. "What was that?"

"Great big tree cracked." Jake turned then and looked at Ben. Ben stepped over to the window to Jake's right. Kit stood at his left and he said, "See?"

March 11, 1994 – Copper Falls, Ontario, Canada

"You know anything about cutting down a big tree?" Jake stood in the shop over the oiled and fueled Stihl chainsaw.

"I don't know." Ben bent and picked up the chainsaw and held it, rotated the blade and then got into a Leatherface pose. Still holding it, he said, "Doesn't feel familiar."

"Guess I'm up then. Think I'll go where the crack is and then I can do the rest of the stump later. I can hardly believe that sucker went."

"Maybe the cold messed with its give or something. Too stiff against the wind." Ben set the chainsaw down. "Then what'll we do? Got enough wood that it doesn't need chopped right away. Right?"

The question came on a foundation built by the weather. The thermometer on the wall had read -27° that morning.

School was on, but that didn't mean working outside or even in the shed or the barn would be much fun. At least until the sun was high.

The chainsaw buzzed and smoked. The scent of burning oil was heavy on the frigid air. Everything was stiff, not only the frozen tree. The limbs thwumped into the snow on the lawn and Jake began buzzing with the chainsaw as quickly as he could. Ben swung an axe against smallish limbs. It wasn't exactly a fair deal.

Within half an hour, Ben was bringing the tractor around while Jake finished cutting. The cold sank into their feet and fingers. Running once the tractor was parked and still purring, they loaded the tongs with the big hunks and limbs—come warmer weather it could be cut into stove lengths and then split.

Jake whistled and shook. "Jesus, I'm freezing."

"You want these in the shed?"

Jake was nodding, blowing onto his gloved hands, and said, "Yeah. Maybe in that corner where you had your van before."

Ben reversed and Jake got to stacking the sticks. He made a slapdash pile and waved to Ben as Ben pulled the secondary driving shed door closed.

"House!"

***

The pot on the stove was boiling. Both men were in their long underwear and sweaters, wool socks pulled inches past their toes. Jake had suggested they watch a movie to kill the afternoon and Ben didn't argue. The selection was a bit girly as the newest stuff came borrowed from Alana, but they decided on *Buffy the Vampire Slayer*.

The kettle squealed and Jake fixed two overlarge mugs of Carnation hot chocolate while Ben stoked the fireplace to blazing. Ben sat on the loveseat and Jake stretched out on the couch after pushing the movie into the VCR.

"Goddamned glare," he said.

The screen was a pale swatch over whatever was happening during the opening credits.

"No glare here," Ben said.

"Lucky bastard."

"No, I mean you can sit next to me," Ben said.

Jake got up and took his mug over to the loveseat. He then pulled the coffee table close so they could put their feet up. It was cramped, their legs made contact often, as did their arms. Ben shivered. Jake pulled the quilt from the back of the loveseat and put it over Ben.

"There you go."

"You're always taking such good care of me, Mommy," Ben whined.

Jake elbowed him and he laughed. Jake shivered then and the blanket stretched and covered both their laps as the movie made quick work of introducing all the important cast and establishing what would need to be broken and then fixed later in the film.

Chapter Twenty-Three

November 7, 1992 – Bend, Oregon, United States

The Domino Room in Bend, Oregon was the smallest of the three-part venue offerings called Rock Rink & Roll. Ryder pushed through one door marked "Employees Only," with Talia trailing close behind him, and then stopped at a door with the word "Manager" written on a piece of masking tape—not off-putting, as masking tape lined the walls for the entire hallway. The fresh paint absolutely stank when mingled with the morning-after beer scent of a rock show.

Through the door, Ryder heard a file cabinet slide closed. He knocked and then pushed inside. A short, sweaty, sickly-looking man turned and frowned.

"Fuck are you?" he said.

Ryder stiffened, fought off a growl. His hackles were already agitated knowing that once this tactic worked, he'd have to answer to Polly and by extension, Gary and Cynthia. "I hear you need someone to open for a chick named Liz Phair."

The man sank into his seat and looked around Ryder to Talia. She wore tight blue jeans and a cropped top that revealed a firm midriff. Her face was damned near symmetrical and her blonde hair fell with little curls. The color was a dye job. Talia was all put together and in all the right ways.

"Who told you that?"

Ryder moved closer and propped his right thigh and ass cheek onto the corner of the man's cluttered desk. "A little birdy."

In reality, Jesse P. had a show the night before and Ryder met her outside the club, turned wolf, and tore out her throat. Two security guards saw him loping away on all fours, dripping a blood trail for close to a block.

"Oh yeah. And what, you two are a duet?"

Ryder sneered. "I can't fucking sing or nothing. Talia Grey, she's the talent, my singer girl. Used to open for Chip Hancock before she got sick of doing it just for the money."

The man straightened up some then. "Chip Hancock, yeah, I remember, like during the credits. He did the big room, the Ballroom, back then he didn't have any music. Packed house for that guy. Can he really talk to dead people?" The man was looking at Talia.

"No. It's all research and vague shit."

The man laughed. "Entertainment, baby."

"You wanna hear her sing or what?" Ryder leaned in close, eyeballing hard.

The man looked over at his phone and then to Ryder. Ryder was closer than security, closer than the phone in fact.

"Sure, I do."

Talia got up and surveyed the desk. She picked up a pen and then sat back down. She closed her eyes and began tapping the steel of the pen against the wood of the chair's arm. She hummed into, "*Sometimes I feel, like I don't have a purpose. Sometimes I feel, like my only friend…*" Once she finished her nearly acapella version of the Red Hot Chili Peppers *Under the Bridge*, she tapped out the pace for six extra beats and then opened her eyes.

"Got a band?"

Talia shook her head.

"Gig pays for a band, so if I gotta hire a band, your cut is just about diddly. You aren't doing it for the money, anyway, are ya?" The man grinned.

"She'll take fifty." Ryder had leaned away some. This was already a win.

"She can take forty in bar tab or twenty cash. I gotta pay someone to play guitar. I only need her for two songs. I got this Bryan Murphy guy's band, just called him, but I like a chick before a chick, keeps the crowd good. Not right away, you do the Chili Peppers song and, you got one of your own?"

"Yeah."

"Acoustic?"

"Yeah, I wrote it to the instrumental of *Don't Dream it's Over*. You know, *hey now, hey now, don't dre*—"

"Simple enough. So, you can do your original and the other one. Get here by six-thirty. Come in through the backdoor, just tell Ricky your name. You go by Talia Green?"

"Grey," Ryder said.

"Grey. Okay. See you tonight."

Ryder got up and Talia skipped in front of him, letting out a short hoot. Behind him, he heard the manager ask himself what he was thinking.

***

The camper was parked behind a motel. They rented a room with money they'd earned devouring four on-duty police officers receiving blow jobs from too young working girls down in Redding, California. The cops had been leaned against a chain-link fence outside a rundown housing complex. Between them, they had more than six hundred bucks in wallets and Gary kept an antique gold watch to pawn later, carting it to the Winnebago in his mouth while Polly worked fast over the bodies.

Cynthia was in the office asking about a laundromat when Ryder burst through the door bearing something between a snarl and a smile.

"Polly, guess who's gonna sing at the club by the roller rink?"

Polly wore a bathrobe, her hair wet. The room smelled like cigarettes and carried the dampness from the recent shower.

"If it's Talia, you better think again, because—hey!"

Ryder shoved down his pants and dropped to his knees, kicking out of them as fur sprouted and his bones began transforming.

Polly said, "Get Cynthia," to Gary, but Talia lifted a pistol from her purse. Gary pulled down his pants and began transforming before he even fell into a squat.

There were moans and whines, as there always would be. As used to any of them got to becoming a wolf, it never came without discomfort. Ryder was in form and waiting, snarling and growling, watching Gary shift. Once he'd changed, Ryder launched his lithe frame across the room, sending Gary rolling. Teeth planted and yips rebounded from the walls. More growls and much snapping. Behind Talia, Cynthia knocked on the door. Talia stepped aside and swung it wide.

"Get in and shut up."

Cynthia saw the action and unbuttoned her pants. Talia licked her lips at this, her breaths hitching, a whine coming up from her chest. Ryder wanted this just as bad as she wanted to be a real singer. In only her pink underwear, Cynthia was on her fours, changing, in time to see Gary cower in the corner next to the heater. She leapt a second too soon and Ryder sank teeth into a hairy arm rather than a leg. Limbo had her and she wailed in woman and huffed in dog.

Ryder put his teeth on her throat, and she flattened herself, stretching over the stiff carpet. A tear slid from her eye. She was all woman and she had failed. Ryder left her with indents in her neck and all the shame she'd handle. He prattled slowly to Polly on the bed. She'd gotten naked and had her eyes closed. She'd gone thirteen full moons in a row without change and before that, it was spotty. Her dog days were behind her.

Ryder stretched his jaw over the top of her downturned head. She stopped breathing and waited. Ryder did not bite. Cynthia and Gary curled together against the wall, watching, terror written behind their stone faces. Talia was wide-eyed and showing her teeth.

"Tell him, you bossy bitch. Tell him this is his pack. He's the alpha, tell him!" Talia was livid, bouncing.

Polly finally breathed and said, "It's his pack."

Ryder let go of her head and backed away, slowly, and then

began the comparatively easy change into man.

***

Polly had a cigarette lit and resting in the white, ceramic ashtray at the table she'd chosen. She wasn't long at the chow line because she'd grabbed two pieces of lemon meringue pie and a cup of coffee. Cynthia and Gary were loading up. Transformation was hungry business. They'd left the motel on foot and entered a busy cafeteria. Hungover young men and women made up about half of the Saturday morning crowd. The rest were a sampling from the general population. It was loud, smoky, and smelled like deep fried food.

Cynthia and Gary got to the table after Polly finished her first piece of pie. She sucked back on a fresh cigarette and avoided eye-contact. She said, "That wasn't entirely unexpected. I wanted them because of who they were. I simply wasn't ready...I wanted to make you ready." She finally looked up to Gary.

"What's it matter? We'll just go our own way, let them do whatever. It has nothing to do with us," Gary said and then snapped a fry into his mouth. He and Cynthia both had double orders: burgers and fries on big white plates. Coffee in mugs and sodas in tall plastic cups.

"I think he's right. When they go to Talia's thing, we take the Winnebago and—What?" Cynthia said to Polly shaking her head.

"I spent many years on the road and in the woods alone and I had a longing. I never understood it. It ate at me, and I went crazy at times. Then I finally figured it out. I was part of something bigger. We all are. We are a pack, and a pack needs to be together. I need it while I'm still here. I need you all with me."

"But what about what just happened?" Gary's voice rose high. "How can we live like this?"

Polly carved into the second piece of pie. "We adapt. It's the way of the wolf, it's the way of survival. Ryder has been the alpha since he understood the change and we made him. All three of us. He's a part of us and you'll ache with his absence. He's in charge and that's not so bad."

"How?" Cynthia spoke around a mouthful of burger.

"He wants to give Talia the stage and he will. We follow him and we follow our research. I've seen you when you come back to the camper from the nights with Ryder in the lead. You're alive all over. I haven't been that way in a long, long time. I've been turning you old before your years. As wild as Ryder seems, he's only getting started. It's in our nature to live to the height of our desires and will."

"This is crazy," Cynthia said, gazing at the blank wall across the table.

"For every wolf I've made, I've felt a crack in my heart that couldn't be filled, not without the pack or their demise." Polly slid the plate away on the tray and brought her cup and pack of Marlboros closer.

"You mean we should kill them?" Gary said and then snapped six fries at once. His plate was down to a few burger bits and another handful of stringy, yellow fries.

"Never. They're our pack and that's how we survive. I'll stay around as long as you'll have me, but I haven't been a fit leader for a couple years, at least. Everywhere but in my heart and spaces in my head, I'm just a woman."

Cynthia reached over and rubbed Polly's hand.

***

The crowd mostly milled around the bar while Talia readied to take the stage a few minutes after the sound check man came out. The lights dimmed, and an old man with curly grey hair, yellow teeth, and long fingers sat on a stool, swaying, and began playing the melody to *Under the Bridge*. A blue spotlight shined on

Talia where she stood behind a microphone. She wore the same top she had earlier but slipped into a denim skirt and cowboy boots. She wore two slim braids that tied a halo around her head.

She breathed into the microphone and said, "I'm Talia Grey, and I hope you dig my sound."

From the shadows to the left of the stage, Ryder whistled around fingers, gripping a Heineken bottle as he did so. His enthusiasm brought a handful of men over. More came to consider the sex appeal of the singer. At the mid-point of the Chili Peppers song, most of the crowd had relocated to near the stage. A trio of women in Nirvana tees lifted lighters. A chain reaction started, and Talia and the guitarist stretched the song, did the whole thing twice without missing a beat.

"This next one is one I wrote for my man. *Moon Shaped Love.*"

The pace was a little quicker than the original Crowded House instrumental, but the man on guitar was a pro. He'd played shows in his own bands, filled in on stage and on records for others, taught lessons, and warmed up instruments for stars.

"*My skin is your skin, your touch is my touch, free-dom's running...*"

Chapter Twenty-Four

January 30, 1994 – Port Hampton, Ontario, Canada

The salesman at Pierson RV made eyes at Talia. Her coat was open, and she wore a push-up bra beneath a low-cut V-neck. She asked about the specs of a Palomino Pop trailer. Asked about tire life and demanded a demonstration, then began asking about financing. Only the manager and that particular salesman were on-duty at the time, neither noticed Ryder slink in to pull the ground wire from the back of the security pad just inside the second locking door. He broke across the showroom, and dove behind the parts desk. Once there, he dug himself into the shadows, amid the telephone, computer, fax machine, and printer wires. Then he listened.

The clock on the far wall was dim but readable, until the lights in the dealership went out at a little after four. Talia laughed the loud laugh they'd agreed to mark her exit. He closed his eyes and turned his right ear, honing a sense beyond human.

"Damn beeper's broken," a man said.

"Maybe it needs a new battery," another man said.

"Hmm."

"Maybe we ought to call now?"

"It's Sunday, they'll probably just tell us they'll send someone in the morning. The yard line runs directly to the electricity, so to hell with it…though I kind of thought this one did too… Ah, to hell with it."

"Yeah, sure. See you…" The voices floated beyond earshot and Ryder relaxed his body. He remained where he was until close to five, when the sun had disappeared. He got busy then.

Down a hall and into the second office he tried, he found a locked case hanging on the wall. He continued through the hall then and entered the shop. He found a flathead screwdriver in a red Snap-On Tools chest and took it to the steel key case. The flathead slid into place, and he tapped his palm against the handle a few times before he muscled the lock open.

What he wanted was new and on the shop floor. He'd seen it when he went looking for a screwdriver. 33.6 feet of rolling home. He read keys and found two sets for 94 Fleetwood Pace Arrows. The first set he tried slid into the ignition and lit the engine.

He flicked the shop lights and got busy with the second act. Big plastic containers full of oil stacked by a wall and ten feet left of that, were a fire hose and a fire axe. He broke the safety glass. The light ax went over his head and he slammed it into the nozzle of one of the oil containers. Sludgy brown-grey fluid billowed out like hot molasses. Bolted along the cinderblock wall next to the containers were covered electrical wires. He swung the axe again, low to the ground. A spark flashed, but nothing came of it. Ryder looked around and his first idea was to put an oil drain pan against the live wires, but it didn't even smoke. He looked around some more and went to the front of the shop and picked up an ancient hand grinder from a cubby stall and set it down so that the cut wire touched inside the steel housing of the grinder. Still nothing.

"Well, shit," he said and dumped a garbage can into the oil. He took a discarded box from a set of brake pads and lit it with his lighter. The fire was slow and not guaranteed, but time was already too long. He picked up the axe and climbed into his new home.

The camper backed up to the huge roll-up door. He got out, and without thinking, hit the button to lift the door. It jerked an inch and a huge spark flared and lit the oil. Smoke puffed in a heavy, hanging cloud. The chain pulley lifted the door, and he wheeled the RV out. He then unhooked the pulley chain and let the door drop behind him. The fire flashed off windshields and windowpanes all around him. He hurried to the chain-link gate and got out. He swung the axe twice and the Master Lock snapped and rolled.

He was on the highway and then off the highway. He made it to where the pack was shacked up in less than ten minutes.

February 25, 1994 – Sprucemont, Ontario, Canada

Mary Gould was the middle child and she walked with ginger steps, her feet smacking gently against waxy hardwood, as she made her way under the pale blue of the moon to the washroom. A noise had awoken her, though understanding what, was beyond her comprehension. She pushed the door closed and hit the light switch. She squinted against the glow emitted by the six bulbs above the vanity as she dropped her pajama pants and sat on the toilet. Once through, she had awakened wholly and recognized that someone was moving around on the main floor. She heard them talking, and more than just her parents.

She left the light on behind her, and crept to the stairs. She went partway down. Leaned forward, she looked onto the kitchen to see strangers. In fact, it appeared her parents were not in the room at all, which was weird for two reasons. One, adults in the home were always accompanied by at least one of her parents, and two, they were leaving bright and early for their trip down to Disney World and said they were going to bed right after Mary and Samantha and Pete had.

She listened hard and heard a woman say, "Sheet says there's three kids somewhere." Mary popped up and hurried on. Samantha was oldest, and she'd know what to do.

Mary passed through the light cast by the bulbs in the washroom and pushed open Samantha's door. She hurried over the spotless floor—everywhere had to be clean before the trip, according to their mother—and began shaking a lump on the bed.

"Wake up, wake up," she hissed.

Samantha rolled over and said, "We going?" and sat up.

"No, there's people downstairs and Mom and Dad aren't

with them."

Samantha argued none and took the very route her sister had and stopped on the very step her sister had. She peeked down and saw nobody, heard nobody. She took another step closer to the ground floor, still leaning to see. Nothing. Nobody.

She turned to Mary and whispered, "Were you dreaming?"

"No. How come the light's on? Mom and Dad wouldn't leave a light on."

This was true and both sisters took another step down before hearing the metal clank of the screen door of the boot room rattling closed and hightailed back to the top floor.

Mary said, "Let's check Mom and Dad's room."

Samantha grabbed her sister and they walked like conjoined twins, through the dim hallway to the door at the end. The master bedroom was bigger than the other bedrooms and their parents shared a queen size bed. It appeared empty under only the moonlight and Samantha felt the wall for the switch. The room lit.

It was empty.

"What about Pete?" Mary said, small as a mouse burp.

They left their parents' room in a shuffle, that light adding to the light emitted by the bulb cast from the washroom. They opened the door and immediately flicked the switch. Pete was a lump on his bed, blanket pulled up to his ear.

Samantha took the lead and began shaking at his shoulder while Mary said, "Wake up, wake up."

He turned and the smiling eyes looking back at them was not Pete but was a woman. She said, "Sorry. No Pete here."

The girls screamed and turned to run, but an old woman stood in the doorway.

"I don't see what's funny about that," Polly Harp said.

Across the room, clothing rattled on metal hangers in the closet and laughter spilled forth, as well as the man laughing.

"You got no sense of humor," Ryder said, gasping.

Talia was smiling on the bed and the little girls were

shivering at the center of it all. Mary began crying and Samantha held her. Since it was their *turn*, Gary and Cynthia prattled along outside, waiting. They weren't hungry, but dogs always had room for the choicest cuts. When it came to humans that meant the throat, and the younger the better.

Polly walked the girls down the stairs and whispered if they had a god, it was probably time to pray and Samantha said they stopped doing church and Polly said that was fine, so had she. Polly told them they didn't need their boots and that their parents were out in the car waiting for them, but they had to run or the scary people upstairs would get them. They ran despite the snow underfoot. They ran despite that the car appeared frozen and without a driver. They ran despite the instant ache the atmosphere stung deep into their chests.

They ran unknowing that it was always better when the prey ran.

February 26, 1994 – Sprucemont, Ontario, Canada

Bacon sizzled in a cast iron pan. Cynthia hummed a tune from her youth by Little Richard. Gary cut cheese from an enormous brick that he'd found in the fruit cellar downstairs. There was no bread, but Polly had been up before the others, and had dough rising on the counter beneath a damp tea towel. She'd also put the coffee on and was two cups deep by the time even Cynthia arose.

In the living room, Talia was up, but stretched out on the couch. For a few weeks, she hadn't felt well, and it was getting worse. Unheard of after the change, she'd always felt well once settling in as a wolf. Ryder stepped into the kitchen in his boxer shorts and an undershirt tank top after asking Talia about her stomach. He got a cup of coffee, put in a spoonful of sugar from the bowl on the counter, stirred it, and took a seat at the veneer table.

"Any idea what's wrong with Talia?" he said to Polly.

They didn't talk much, in fact, Polly mostly only spoke when spoken to since losing her spot as leader of the pack.

Polly lowered the newspaper and said, "Yes. I know exactly what's wrong with her."

Cynthia and Gary both turned from what they were doing.

Ryder eyed the old woman hard and said, "How come you didn't say before?"

"You didn't ask."

Ryder leaned back and puffed his cheeks on a heavy exhale. "So what's wrong with her then?"

"That man who cut her. She must've scratched him deep enough to change him, but not deep enough to kill him." Polly lifted the paper.

"Meaning what?" Ryder said.

Polly lowered the paper to make eye contact. "Means we got one more in our pack and she's not going to feel good until we bring him in…or kill him. Trust me, she won't want that once she sees him. Like how at hospitals nurses take babies from mothers who're giving them up for adoption before they can form a bond. Changing someone, that's a hard bond." Polly turned her eyes on Cynthia and Gary at the counter. "You two didn't have to get sick, we brought them in right away."

Ryder sipped at his coffee. Cynthia and Gary both stalled in a half-turn. Talia shuffled into the kitchen.

"So, what, I'm like a mother all of a sudden?"

"Close enough," Polly said and got to reading the paper again. After a few seconds of silence, she slammed the paper down and ran her finger along the story as she read aloud: "Police are looking for a blue, Ford Econovan, mid-nineties, in relation to the murders of three A&W employees and two customers. Detective Marc Foster stated the van was at the scene, had green lettering on the license plate, and was at A&W just before the atrocious acts were committed. The driver is wanted for questioning, but at this time is not considered a suspect. If anyone has information, they are…" Polly trailed.

"Huh. Speak of the devil," Cynthia said.

"Indeed," Polly said. "Turns out your idea to stick around wasn't such a bad one, given Talia's insides. Maybe this Marc Foster or this Ernie Humphrey can lead us to where this man is."

Ryder drained his cup and set it clumsily on the table, the base slid and bumped. "We'd be gone if that manager who runs that theater wasn't in Mexico. Some strange luck, if we want the van guy. If he ain't good, my singer girl won't say a word to me ending him, will ya, hun?"

"That's right," she said and left the kitchen to flop back onto the couch.

March 14, 1994 – Sprucemont, Ontario, Canada

The tall, lanky man at the Roxy looked nervous and abnormally tanned, given that it was grey winter outside. The pair in his office called ahead, he assumed. Someone had called and asked if the manager was in, and he said that was he and the caller hung up. That was only an hour earlier. He glanced out the window at the beat-up old farm truck they'd come in and wondered if he'd have time to call the police if things got hairy. The whole scene was downright unorthodox.

"Talia Grey's done shows all over and since we're here, she'd like to do one at your theater," Ryder said, sitting how he always sat during these conversations: looking down at a man while he leaned one thigh and ass cheek on a cluttered desk—this desk was cleaner than typical. "She can give you a performance here or on stage and then we can work out a date."

"Uh." The manager looked at Talia, eyes like high beams.

"Go ahead, babe."

Talia picked up her guitar. She'd learned the basics and strummed tunes that mostly sounded the same until she let loose her voice. For the manager of the Roxy, she sang Pearl Jam's *Dissident* and chased it with Donna Summer's *Hot Stuff*, no break between the songs.

The manager said after a dozen silent seconds, "You know, I can afford only a couple really good gigs a year and then the advertising budget and the show don't match...but this really fits with what I like to... How much?"

Ryder straightened up. "Hey, we don't want to put you on the spot. Fifty percent of the tickets and you've got to do ads in the paper and on the radio." He dug into a pocket of his leather jacket and handed over a Memorex cassette tape. "That's got a live show on it, probably you can make some copies and go to the stations around here."

The manager said, "Only one station... I can do fifty percent of the tickets, after I hit even with the radio and newspaper ads. That needs to get paid up front."

Ryder pouted a lip and slow nodded. They'd found a respectable sum in traveler's checks in Archie Gould's suitcase and an additional two hundred in cash. The booking deal was just for show.

"You drive a hard bargain," he said and held out a hand.

The manager took it and didn't relax until the pair were out of his office. Something was very strange about them, but he'd probably make a few bucks. Talia Grey had talent and a fun gimmick.

March 20, 1994 – Aystadt, Ontario, Canada

In the new camper—parked at a small campground in a village about twenty minutes west of Sprucemont—Polly lifted and snapped the Sprucemont Confederate to the continuation of the A&W situation. Of course, this Ernie Humphrey called it a tragedy or atrocity or some variation of one or the other with each new update. Talia was in the mounted recliner with a heating pad on her stomach. She was listening to the radio, hoping to hear her voice again. She'd heard part of herself singing a Rolling Stones cover the day before the show and it drove all the bad stuff from her guts, if only for a while. Same went for the performance to a nearly sold-out crowd.

Ryder was stretched on the sofa, his eyes closed, listening, too. Polly shouted for one of them to turn it off for a minute and listen to this. She ran her finger beneath the words as she read aloud: "Police are no longer looking for the blue, Ford Econovan in relation to the murders of three A&W employees and two customers. Detective Marc Foster stated that the van belonged to a man residing in Copper Falls but wouldn't elaborate further."

"Huh," Talia said.

Ryder had been going on about tracking down the reporter or the detective and forcing information from them. Gary and Cynthia talked him out of it; the reporter was too quickly high profile and a cop would be dangerous. If they waited, maybe things might come together naturally.

In the quiet trailing the update, the camper door opened, letting in a good chill, and Gary and Cynthia returned from an afternoon walk. Polly immediately read the bit from the paper aloud once more.

Chapter Twenty-Five

March 17, 1994 – Sprucemont, Ontario, Canada

Jody couldn't tag along, as there was no certainty that it was connected, the trademarks were there, but the killers had hit twice in one county. That alone had Marc holding off spilling everything to her. He'd visit the scene, assess, and decide then if it was anything to the case.

"Been dead at least a couple weeks, far as I can tell. See the coloration? You've got some greenish hues around the throat wounds, in with the black of it. See if it was just this week, you'd have almost perfectly preserved bodies. The warm spell hit up here too, yeah?"

Marc nodded at the broad-shouldered woman in the puffy parka and yellowy rubber gloves, pointing and prodding at the five corpses beneath the firewood lean-to.

"See, these bodies froze quickly, my estimate at least a week before the warm spell based on the way the ice built around their heads and necks. See?"

Marc leaned closer. Two adults, husband and wife, and three kids, two girls and a boy: the Goulds. A mailman had resumed delivery after a scheduled break. He'd had a bundle of mail and brought it around back to set inside the door—an arrangement they'd made before, concerning parcels—and discovered the bodies. The ice around their necks and heads was thick and that the doctor from Guelph pointed it out made it interesting.

"Yeah," he said.

"Okay, so the wind blows the snow in and then it settles on the frozen flesh. The warm weather comes, melts the snow, much of it sinks into the skin, but enough of it runs off. Without blood moving beneath flesh, it freezes quickly, and water can settle and grow soggy and discolored."

"Huh."

"Though you'll never know for sure, not with frozen bodies, I'd say this family was killed right around the end of February."

"Early as the twenty-fifth?"

"Sure, easy. Might even be older, but the mail was cut off for the twenty-fourth?"

Marc nodded, that's what the mailman had said in his statement.

"So probably not much before that or people would've been coming around more. Why was the mail cut off?"

"Don't know yet." Marc stood up straight, looking that closely at the bodies had his guts in a swirl.

"Somebody knew they were leaving. My estimate. See, they even tried to dig a hole but gave up when the ground was too hard. See?" She pointed to the shovels and the indents in the dirt floor.

"My guess is that's about it."

***

"Here, take a look. It's connected, right?"

Marc tossed photos and a summation report on the table in the boardroom in front of Jody. She had red eyes and a cup of coffee steaming next to a stack of bills from the Jalinski boxes. It appeared she'd only recently climbed from bed.

"I'm almost certain. But they knew. Whoever's doing this knew the family was leaving."

"Could be a copycat." Jody looked at the photos and they were so close it ached. She'd never been on the trail up to the most recent. Butterflies lit her belly with action and her tired eyes were wide awake. "Too close though. But for the bodies…oh, they were digging?"

"Theory is the ground was too hard and they just left them. I've got to get a hold of the rest of the family. They didn't have anybody listed outside themselves at the hospital, but the old doctor on file…have to call him."

Jody began nodding as she read. "We're close. We're so fucking close I could kiss you."

Marc smirked. "I might hold you to that."

***

"This is Doctor Keenan."

Marc scratched his ear beneath the phone receiver and settled it back tight as he spoke. "I need next of kin information on Diana and Archie Gould, uh, their kids were Pete, Samantha, and Mary."

"No in-depth medical though, right? I can't just hand that stuff out."

"No, only next of kin."

"Okay." The face had turned from the microphone for the next piece. "Shannon, get me the file on Archie and Diana Gould." The face turned back. "They're dead?"

"Yeah, unfortunately."

The doctor sighed. "I thought they'd do all right after they got away from the church."

"Oh?"

"Yeah, they had twin girls. Got infections, liver, bad. They needed blood and that damned Archie told me, almost smiling, that God would protect his girls. He took them home. They were Jehovah's Witnesses and it killed them."

"When was that?"

"Thanks, Shannon," the doctor said away from the receiver. "What's that?"

"When did they die?"

"Eighty-six, I think. Yep, right here. September nineteen eighty-six."

"So they were estranged from their next of kin?" Marc began rubbing his forehead.

"Yeah, but you never know. People leave churches all the time. Especially the ones where they go with wishing for miracles instead of seeking medicine." The tone was there, anger and disgust. "Anyhow, you have a pen? I've got a name and a phone number."

"Shoot."

The doctor gave the name and number, exchanged pleasant goodbyes with Marc and then hung up. Marc didn't cradle the receiver, instead tapped the paddle to disconnect and began dialing out. The phone rang in his ear and he took a deep breath, wholly uncertain how the information of the deaths was apt to go.

"Hello?"

"Is this Abagail Gould?"

"Yes. Who is this I'm speaking to?"

Marc reached into his pocket for Rolaids while he gave his name and affiliation. "I'm sorry to say that Archie and Diana, and the kids, have passed."

There was a pause and breathing and then, "That would be sad if I had a brother named Archie, but under God, I have no brother named Archie."

Marc listened to the click and then the disconnect pulse. "Jesus fuck," he said and set the phone down. He rubbed his head and then face before pulling his bottom lip while he unrolled two chalky tablets. He got up as he popped them into his mouth, grabbed his coat, and stopped into Charles' open office. "You didn't happen to know the Goulds personally, did you?"

"No. Next of kin not pan out?"

"Estranged and then some. A religious thing."

"This one's close, what are you thinking?" Charles had a pen in hand, floating an inch from a report on his desk.

"Can't wait. I'm gonna ask the mailman if they had any friends and then maybe I'll go over to Tim Hortons and ask a few of the old heads hanging arou—"

"Harold Washington. Before you bother with putting yourself out, call up Harold Washington. He called us about the van, and according to Smith—she took the call—the guy rambled off about thirty names of people who had vans that weren't the van after he mentioned the American."

"Linda isn't in today. You have her number?"

The chief dropped his pen and picked up the telephone to call Linda Smith. She worked reception and some radio dispatching three afternoons a week.

He didn't dial and instead said, "I know how this'll go, she'll just tell me to check the damned file." He grinned at Marc.

Marc tapped his temple three times and then hurried away. Six minutes later, he was back in his office. He called the mailman at home, but he'd returned to his route, so he dialed the man named Harold Washington. Feeding gossip to a gossip mill might be counterproductive most times, but they were so damned close to a breakthrough.

***

Jody sat in the mess of unboxed paperwork, seeing nothing useful. She lifted her face as Marc entered and gave him a hopeful expression.

"This mean anything to you? The Goulds were driving down to Orlando to do all the tourist stuff and on the way back, going to a Chip Hancock show." Jody stiffened at the mention and Marc said, "What?"

"Chip Hancock. I've seen him. It's just a… I was following the case in Winnipeg and ended up at one of his shows. My brain just glitched at it, connected something by default. Go on."

"Well, speaking of the Hancock thing, the mother, Diana had told her friend they'd gone before, after their twins died."

"Twins?"

"Shit, right." Marc explained what the doctor had told him

and then about the sister and the church, what he knew of it anyway. "So after the twins died, I guess they tried to talk to them through the medium, but they weren't picked. I guess someone in the crowd told them the spirit makes a better connection after a second time and if Chip knows the spirit's name, sometimes it's lingering."

"The friend said all this?"

"Yeah, she was broken. Kept calling them dopes. Chip didn't call at first so Diana called Chip's people and asked why and they mailed her a questionnaire, told her it was possible the girls were there, but Chip didn't know how to connect the dots, so could you please fill out the questionnaire and send it back."

Jody slumped. "I kept mine. You're supposed to hand it in. It's wild. They ask a ton of personal questions and then you see it, Chip fogs it up and delivers the same kind of stuff right back to the people. Like he's just pulled it from the air...or the spirit world. I'm surprised they didn't fill out one at the first show they went to."

"She says Diana said they did, filled out two, like to double their chances."

"So what happened to the first ones?"

"No idea."

Jody ran a hand over the back of her neck and closed her eyes. "It's probably a false positive, but maybe we call Chip Hancock and ask about the questionnaires."

"Don't be let down. This is something. This is a crack and we're peeking through. You're only one step behind. How long you been trailing this thing?"

Jody shook her head at that.

"Maybe you need to relax. Look, I haven't been out of my house besides work, and I'm stressing over my shithead son and my soon to be ex-wife and how my daughter's doing. Let's say you and me have a non-work dinner and go to the show at the Roxy. There's some folk singer there tonight. I read about it in the paper. She does rocker's songs, but to just an acoustic guitar."

Jody opened her eyes and looked the man up and down. She said, "Okay, but I'll probably thinking and talking about this all night, don't get your hopes up for my undivided attention."

"Good. Can you call around, find Chip Hancock's contact?"

"Don't need to. Like I said, I have my questionnaire in my stuff at the hotel. Almost certainly there's a number on it. I'll grab it, call from my room, probably he's got an answering service, being as he's on the road pretty well all year, but if I can talk to him, I will. I'll come back if he's available. If not, you'll pick me up at what time?" Jody stood and began gathering her things, eyes on Marc.

"Show's at eight, so how about six-thirty. I'll book us a table at the Chinese joint in Arthur. You like Chinese?"

"Sure."

***

The dim lighting and constant clang of buffet elements kept any chances for romantic ambiance at a minimum. They'd rode together and got most of the business conversation out of the way: Chip Hancock did indeed have an answering service, to which Jody gave her name and Marc's name, her number and the number at the station. Marc explained that Ernie Humphrey from the paper called for an update as to whether they should continue asking the public about the van. Marc told the man about the Gould family and that the van was no longer any concern, they'd located it and it belonged to an everyday citizen who deserved as much privacy as anybody else. The reporter pressed and Marc went as far to say that the man was not from here but was staying in Copper Falls. Marc reiterated that if anyone sees the van, they should go about life, it was only a probe to find more information. He hung up before Ernie Humphrey got his next question out.

"My method is simple when it comes to getting your dollars' worth from a Chinese buffet. You load every other plateful with fruit. No meat. No veg. Only fruit. The healthiness offsets the bad and staves off the sick feeling you inevitably get," Jody said over her shoulder as Marc followed her along the buffet line.

"Seems reasonable enough."

They returned to the table to find their water glasses filled and a pitcher sitting next to them. Jody set down her plate and lifted her index finger to state she'd be only a moment. She returned after a quick visit to the buffet with a small white bowl of chili pepper paste.

"Also, hot sauce. It's the cleanser of all things bad."

Marc shook his head at this. "No thanks, but it's good you reminded me." He pulled out a fresh tube of Rolaids and popped six into his mouth, chewed, took a mouthful of water, and then swallowed. "A little pre-emptive defense."

"I'm kind of glad I never became a real cop. Everywhere I go, you guys are munching antacid like it's candy."

"The badge causes the funkiness in… Maybe it's my wife. I've had it bad since she…well, no. It's been pretty loveless and that's damned stressful on its own, but the split brings out a lot of ugliness, and then the boy's acting up. Skipping and mouthing off. You don't have any kids?"

Jody had the chopsticks between fingers and had a clump of rice and kung-pow chicken ready to enter her mouth. "Nah. Not interested. Not all that interested in putting down roots either. I mean, I like having a home base, but the world has a lot to see." She shrugged with her left side and moved the food to her mouth with her right hand.

"As it is now, my boy feels like more trouble than it was worth, but this split is hard on him. Me too. Hard on Alice too. She's my young—" Marc stopped talking about his kids, recognizing a glaze falling over Jody's eyes. "Tell me about FBI training."

"Oh geez. Let's wait until dessert for that one. I'll need some chocolate for comfort."

"Okay, how about you really tell me why you're so invested in this case."

"All the good questions, huh?"

"Well, you follow it all over. You could take other cases, why this case."

Jody opened her mouth, but the waiter came by and asked if they needed anything and changed the subject.

***

They got to the show late and waited until between songs to get to their seats. They were in the fifth row from the back of a two-thirds-packed house—granted the Roxy only seated a little shy of 150 bodies. The woman on the stage was pretty, but had a good pink scar on her face, suggesting a relatively fresh heal. She dressed like a cowgirl without the hat and strummed on an acoustic guitar as she sang. Her range with the guitar was obviously limited, but her voice was strong and hit everywhere it should hit and then some extra on top.

For her last song, she sang an original about moonlight and love. As they were walking out, Jody leaned into Marc's shoulder and reached for his ear with, "Seems like everyone's thinking about full moons, huh?"

"Ten days," he said.

He drove her to the motel, and they sat for a few minutes in his personal car—a Ford Taurus. The red light shined down on them from the vacancy sign.

"Think we'll catch them?"

Marc rolled his head on his neck as if kinked, and said, "I think you will."

"We had a breakthrough today. It's going to come together. Everybody makes mistakes, it just can't be us making them."

"That Talia Grey was a fine singer, huh?" Marc said, looking forward.

"Yeah. Won't get anywhere doing so many covers, but I like what she does, slowing them down, making them quiet. Cool to hear the heavy metal ones really sang and not screamed."

Marc shivered. "My son has been listening to this group Body Count. The lead singer is that rapper who made the song *Cop Killer*."

"I know *of* that one. Never heard it."

"It's mostly a Rodney King retaliation song. I don't know what to say to the boy to get him to smarten up. He's some small-town hick kid, and acts like, I don't know…"

Jody shook her head. "If you're looking for advice, you're talking to the wrong chick."

"Yeah."

"Yeah." The pause went on for about a minute before Jody grabbed the door handle. The door opened a crack and the interior light lit. "Tonight was fun. You're a good guy, probably things'll work out with the kids. Sounds for the best that you and your wife are split."

"Could be. See ya tomorrow."

"Yeah-huh," Jody said and opened the door. Ten steps from her room, she stopped and turned around, came back to the car. Marc rolled down the window. "The Goulds didn't have a camper or anything and their van was still home, what are these people driving now that they left behind the Winnebago at the Jalinski farm? If it's multiple people and it's part of their cover, don't they need another camper? Where does someone get a big camper like that?" Steam puffed from her lips as she spoke.

Marc tapped the steering wheel. "Have to make some calls tomorrow, but there can't be too many places around here."

Jody slapped the roof of the car and turned abruptly. "Little crack eventually lets out the flood," she said as she walked away.

"With the good and the bad alike," Marc said and rolled up the window with a button's push. He backed out of the parking lot and headed for home, sad, lonely, and needing an easy win, somewhere. "Ten days," he said again.

Chapter Twenty-Six

March 21, 1994 – Copper Falls, Ontario, Canada

The Hydro bill came in and put Jake in a mood. The trip was already a set thing, and though the others were paying for him, he had to cut some of Ben's losses to bring him along.

The snowfall through the night was heavy enough that he sheared the lynchpin from the spout on the blower attachment as he cleared the lane. He had to run and push the blower double time once he swapped out the pin. He watched from the end of the lane as Kit charged toward him. Down the road, the bus was about a minute away. It was his fault she was running and it pissed him off all the more for it. He started back in the lane once she climbed aboard the bus. On the final corner, he sheared another pin.

"Godfuckingbitch!"

He slammed his palms against the steering wheel. He was snow-covered and damp and cold. He pulled into the driving shed, parked, climbed down onto the slick cement floor, and slipped, though managed to remain upright.

"Now what?"

Ben was breaking from the old hay barn down along the path by the main barn. He carried a big steel gate and the fencing pail. Jake hurried that way, feet crunching the fresh snow that climbed past his shins—through an area he still had to clear, once he put in another new pin. His breaths puffed in great steamy clouds and his lungs burned once he saw over the slight rise and down the hill to where Ben was.

Ben had the big gate pressed against the fence next to where they'd put in the feeder lean-to. The bull was on the other side, nudging. No bigger asshole in the whole animal kingdom exists than a bull.

Jake got down to the spot just in time to shove up against

the gate while two cedar rail cracks echoed over the pasture and into the swampy bush behind them. The bull backed off a moment and Ben got the fencing wire wrapped around the post and the gate, at the top anyway.

The bull was back and had rammed the spot. Jake dropped to his knees and tried to push the gate back to the post when the bull let off the pressure, only to butt his incredible head back against it. The fresher cedar posts groaned and Jake took the bottom of the gate to his chin, sending him sprawling sideways and onto the ice, before falling through into the shallow creek below.

"Fucking cuntsucker!"

He crawled to the gate and put his back against it and while the bull had relented again, Ben got a second piece of fencing wire around the gate and the post. The bull nudged and the fence moved, but as a whole and no more than a quarter inch. Ben dropped the wire snips into the bucket and sighed in relief.

"That was close, would've been a bi—"

Jake popped up and drove his fist—mitted as it was—into Ben's mouth. Ben snapped his arms out and pushed Jake away. Jake leapt and latched onto Ben, rolling over him and driving blows into the thick material of his coat. Ben began slamming his fist against Jake's back. The top of Jake's head came up and got Ben in the chin, forcing him to bite his bottom lip. Ben brought his knee up as they rolled and pushed into Jake's thigh, this gave him space to free his shoulder and drive a mostly decent punch into Jake's face. Jake growled and forced Ben flat and got on top of him, screaming that the bull wanted out by the lean-to and that the lean-to was Ben's idea and that if he didn't show up, Ben would've let the goddamned bull out of the pen and then what? Ben said, "Fuck you," and tried to roll out from beneath Jake, but Jake clasped on, so that when they rolled, they continued over the laneway and onto the ice-covered swamp on the far side. Jake started to shout something more when the ice broke and they dropped a foot in the startlingly frigid water. Startling for Ben, Jake was hardly fazed, already soaked as he was. "Get off me!" and "Get away!" and "You prick!" came from Ben in a high shout, but he latched onto Jake with renewed vigor and drove his fist into Jake's eyes three times before Jake could send them both back into the freezing swamp water. They rolled; water and hard mud splashed their faces and necks. Jake drove his fist into Ben's ear and Ben shouted a string of pained vowels while he brought his knee up into Jake's testicles. The pants protected him, mostly, but the sensation travelled through his body and lingered in his guts. He moaned and Ben punched him in the center of the chest. Jake fell sideways and Ben scrambled to get out of the swamp, but Jake dove and grabbed his legs, brought him back down. That was all though, no more remained in the tanks and they both huffed, gripping each other tightly until Jake rolled over and Ben got to his feet, said nothing, and stormed to the house. Jake gave him a minute and then followed. By the time Jake stepped inside, he heard the shower running. He stripped out of his wet clothes, put on his good jacket and boots, grabbed his cigarettes and lighter from the shelf by the coat rack, and then grabbed two cans of beer from the fridge.

He sat in the cold garage, sipping and puffing, before going into the shower.

***

Kit fixed two boxes of Kraft Dinner and made the tuna melts from the *Meals on a Budget* cookbook she found amongst the other cookbooks. The publication date had to be somewhere around 1960, but what's changed about tuna melts? The atmosphere at the table was thick and she'd looked close enough before sitting down: Jake had a light bruise by his ear and Ben had a weak black eye and a cut and puffy lip.

"Did you get in a fight or something?" she said, looking from one face to the other, both of the men kept their eyes on their plates.

"Don't worry about it," Jake said.

"You heard him," Ben said. "Jake just owes me an apology."

Jake finally looked at Ben and Ben lifted his face from the bright yellow mound of noodles. Kit's eyes were huge. Jake wasn't exactly the apologizing type.

Jake sighed and said, "Sorry."

Like lightning, Ben reached across the table and slapped Jake in the side of the head. "Even," Ben said.

Kit said, "Uhh," and Jake started laughing. "You guys are so weird."

Jake waved this off and then around a mouth full of mashed tuna and hamburger bun, he said, "It's still good you're going to Alana's for the whole weekend, right?" Kit nodded as she chewed. "Guess what else."

Kit swallowed and said, "What?"

"Darren Wiseman called this afternoon. I guess old Harold passed the word along. Darren needs all the cedar rails; said he won't go higher than three bucks apiece." Jake grinned while he chewed.

"That's like three hundred dollars," Kit whispered.

"Not really, some of those posts are dollar posts, but I bet it's two hundred. Now what I'm thinking, we fill up the truck, there's thirty," Jake snapped his fingers, "we tally a nice lunch for you, me, Ben, and maybe Alana, and then you still have a little better than a hundred to blow on clothes. Perfect birthdays get away for you. Late by a few days, but it'll work, huh?"

Too quickly, jumbling her words together, Kit said, "Alana's mom'll give her money for her own lunch does that mean we're going to the mall in Guelph?"

"Sure thing, say first weekend in April...unless Darren Wiseman decides he don't want our rails." Jake added this point as if it had only right then dawned on him.

"Good rails. He'll take them," Ben said.

Chapter Twenty-Seven

March 22, 1994 – Sprucemont, Ontario, Canada

There was no more leaving Jody out, if it could be a lead, she was in on it. At the station first thing, Marc told her to keep her coat on, they were going for a ride. Port Hampton was about an hour and a half away and gave them time to go back over what they already knew, after Marc explained that he'd gone out of town the night earlier and purchased the Andover Post and the Owen Sound Sun Times. The Sun Times was daily, but the Post was six days old and a weekly. It included an update on the Pierson RV dealership fire.

"Did it read like it suggested arson?"

"It read like the lamest duck from their reporter pool went, snapped a shot, asked one question, and then filled in two paragraphs beneath the shot. As much as Humphrey and a couple of the others get to me sometimes, the Confederate is the upstanding paper around here."

"So, it only just fits the timeline?"

"Not entirely. After I read the thing, I asked one of the old guys at the Andover Tim Hortons about it and he said they were rebuilding with insurance money, but leaning in a different direction, he said, and I quote, 'hardly any of them big units like they used to have, getting into them Jet-Ski things.'"

Jody bit the inside of her cheek and kept her eyes forward. "So, they're acting like it's a windfall."

"Yeah, my guess either they burned it or someone burned it and they're changing things up. It would all depend on what was in the main building when it went down."

"I'm guessing it's like typical RV places with a big lot and most of the product out on display?"

"Correct."

They stopped once to grab fresh coffees and a couple

donuts before continuing up to the dealership. The construction was busy in the back—fenced off from the public—and a rental business trailer had been installed out front. Plastic, multi-colored triangular flags on strings danced in the chilly wind. There were two cars in the lot overcrowded with campers, pop-tent units, and truck bed campers. The manager came out as they pulled in, probably desperate for some winter business.

"Hey, hello. Welcome," he said. He then tilted his head and seemed to understand the heavy wheels on the big car. The double antennae on the back. "Ah, hey."

Marc said, "We're here to ask some questions."

The manager didn't invite them into the trailer, instead stood in a knit sweater, cradling his arms at the elbows. "Well, I already talked to you guys."

"Not us. We're from Sprucemont. Can you tell me what burned, exactly?"

The manager jerked his head back slightly and puckered his lips. "Two brand new thirty-four footers and two small campers in for repairs. Plus, all the tools and equipment. It'd be a damned tragedy if I didn't have insurance."

"Insurance doesn't work the same for theft though, right? I mean, the insurance company doesn't dish right away, they look for your product and then if they can't find it, they'll give you what you're insured against, correct?" Marc folded his arms to mimic the manager.

"Yes, that's kind of how it works, but that's nothing to me. Not in this situation. You telling me you think something's different than what I told the local police?"

"Only wondering if it was possible there was a fire and something also went missing," Jody said.

"Sprucemont, huh? What are you even doing here?" the manager asked.

The portable office door opened and a young man in a parka waved and nodded, said, "I'm off. See ya tomorrow, Todd," and continued on to one of the two cars. A late eighties, gold Ford Tempo. He was out of the lot before anybody spoke another word.

"Cops make him jumpy?" Marc asked.

The manager shivered and said, "No. He had to finalize a sale, it's one of his days off, but commission is commission."

"Ah," Marc said.

"Look. I don't know what you guys think you're getting at, but I suggest you talk to the Port Hampton OPP, okay? I have stuff to do. Losing your main building isn't exactly good for business."

"In your case it wasn't exactly bad for business though, was it?" Jody asked. "I mean, getting into Jet-Skis is quite a shift. You'll have to buy the specialty trailers for them and maybe put in one of those test tanks. Places out west have those, they let the public come in and test machines in tanks, chained, so the Jet-Skis just float and churn water—great for business, my guess."

"Hmm, hadn't thought of that tank thing. That's a good idea. Like I said, talk to the local cops." The manager said nothing further and mounted the steps to his portable trailer.

Marc and Jody sat in the car a minute, letting the windows un-fog. Marc suggested it was a bit of a bust and Jody suggested she thought the man was lying, but probably only to avoid the costly waiting game of stolen property.

"Guess me might never know."

Marc started the car, pulled back onto the two lanes of Highway 21, and turned left to head south. They didn't make it into the town proper before Jody pointed out her window to a gold Tempo merging from a gravel road.

Marc said, "He's flashing us down," and pulled over.

They waited in the car and the young man ran up to the passenger's side after parking on the shoulder behind them. Jody lowered her window.

The man said, "Hey."

"Hey," Jody said.

"Uh, I saw the shop before the cleanup. Doug lied."

"Oh?" Jody said.

Marc reached for the lighter above the ashtray and pushed it home. He didn't take his eyes off the young salesman.

"Can we go somewhere to talk? I been so danged mad."

"You take the lead, and we'll follow," Marc said.

The lighter popped.

***

The young man led them to a former railway car turned coffee diner. In the summer, they served huge crowds outside, but in the winter, the line of eighteen stools and two small tables were mostly vacant.

The waitress who came to their table said, "Hi, Mike. What can I get yas?"

They ordered a round of coffees and the salesman, Mike, got into his story: "I was working the afternoon before the place went up and this chick came in. She was being super open, like her shirt was open and her tits…and touching arms and stuff. I figured just trying to get a good deal but didn't hardly argue on price and had to go over the in-house financing with Todd. She was joking and talkative and always leaning over so her tits poured out…sorry." He looked to Jody, as if he might've offended her. "Anyway, there was a bing noise from the door opening when we were talking to her and I looked around, but nobody came in and Todd didn't acknowledge and neither did the woman, so I thought I imagined it. But then, after she was gone and we were leaving, the alarm wouldn't set. Todd said it would take the alarm company 'til Monday, so we left it be. He told the cops about the alarm thing but suggested maybe that had to do with the wires shorting."

During Mike's story, the waitress had come and gone, left behind coffees.

"Is that how the fire started?" Marc asked.

"Yeah. Started at a wire right by the oil bins. They go out for recycling or something. Some new idea. I don't know."

Jody said, "Go on with the important bits."

"Right, so we did have two thirty-four footers in the bay, but I think only one of them burned. I think the other one was gone by the time the roof came down. I didn't think of it 'til this week when I saw this movie on in the middle of the night called *Elvira Mistress of the Dark*. See the woman called herself Elvira something. The next morning after that, it hit me, I was out picking up garbage—people toss stuff out their windows on the highway—and I found most of the padlock that was on the gate. It was broken and I asked my cousin who's on the fire department and he said the gate was open when they got there."

Marc drained his cup and then said, "That's all?"

"No. See Todd couldn't sell those thirty-four footers. They were just too much money for the locals and he told me if they didn't both sell, it meant he'd come up short for the new smaller stuff. People buy new stuff, even with campers, though year-to-year they're just about the same, just have better microwaves and recliners and stuff. We had a couple trailer campers stolen last year and the insurance company didn't pay until last month. I heard you talking about this with him through the window; I know you know how it is. It would be so easy for Todd to fake having that second one in there without proof."

"I still don't get what you're saying. It's pretty loose that you're suggesting only one burned," Marc said.

Mike shook his head in small, quick increments. "No, but, the keys, remember?"

"What?" Marc and Jody said at once.

Mike squinted at them. "I forgot, okay, I thought...so, okay, there's a steel, fire-proof box mounted in the shop manager's office—all the shop people are laid off until the rebuild—and someone jimmied open that box with a screwdriver or something. The roof didn't come down over the showroom, the firemen got there in time, so that box was still hanging, but it was missing two sets of keys. Todd made me walk through with him the next Tuesday so he could get all sad eyed and tell me I was the one guy he was keeping on 'cause I sell so well. Wouldn't be a business if I didn't sell so well. I get papers from all over the province and call up anybody advertising about wanting to sell their camper or wanting to buy a camper. I go the extra mile, nobody else does that. One time I drove six hours to buy a cherry Airstream and sold it to a guy who lived only forty miles from the first guy. Made four grand, wham bam, thank you, ma'am."

"Nice job. Any chance both sets of keys would just be missing?" Jody rolled the base of her mug on the tabletop beneath her palm as she spoke.

"No way. Todd's nuts about the keys. The padlock keys for the trailer campers go in there too. He's been a nut case about the key box since those two were stolen...don't know why. The thieves broke the locks, didn't use the keys at all, but I guess it's like control what you can."

"So you're thinking you have this Elvira woman showing you her tits to keep you busy while her partner comes in, dismantles the security, and once everybody is gone, lights the building on fire and steals a huge RV?" Jody said.

"Uh or has like an electric bomb to short the wires or whatever," Mike said.

Marc flipped open a small notepad then and said, "Give me the makes and models of the RVs."

"Both the same, one was navy and green on beige and the other was red on beige. Ninety-four, Fleetwood Pace Arrows. Top drawer. Thirty-four footers. We had them on the lot since the day they came off the line. Don't know why they do this, but the ninety-fours came out in about June of ninety-three. Those two spent the whole camper season being walked through and never had so much as a real nibble."

Marc wrote and turned the pad so Mike could see. Mike read and nodded, and Marc turned the pad back and said, "Tell me about Elvira."

"Thin. Pretty face. A pink scar up her cheek, but real pretty. Wore a coat with a fur hood. Uh, dirty blonde hair, I think it's called. She was a little shorter than me, so maybe five-nine. Didn't notice if she had heeled boots. I don't know...very pretty face."

***

At the station, Marc got on the phone to local campgrounds and got a hit almost immediately. In Aystadt, a group of five adults had a brand-new Pace Arrow, a real sweet one according to the woman on the line. They'd signed in under the name Paula Cruz, an older woman. Ontario plate: 490 1LL. Unfortunately, they'd left the park sometime in the last thirty-six hours. In the off-season, the park ran on an honor system.

"Feeling close." Marc unwrapped a new Rolaids tube and popped four pills into his mouth.

"Twenty-seventh. We're running out of time. Hell, they might be in a whole new province already."

"Come on, this is good. We have a real lead here."

March 24, 1994 – Sprucemont, Ontario, Canada
The long days were made longer by a game of phone tag. Chip Hancock had called the hotel and left a message for Jody but hadn't bothered to call the additional number she'd left. When she called back at the end of the day, Chip was performing. She asked the assistant to implore Chip to call immediately. He called the station and asked for Jody Penrose as if the woman actually worked there.

"I've seen you live," Jody said after greetings passed.

"Always nice to chat with a fan," Chip said.

"I'm sure. What I need from you is to know if any of these people have filled out questionnaires from your shows." She was three names into the list when Chip stopped her.

"We don't keep that stuff. It's a liability, either we use it or we don't." The showman had fleeted some from his voice. "It's possible...hey! You know what, one-time, years ago, someone stole all of our files. Broke a lock and left off with the boxes. I figured it was this singer I had to fire...what the hell was her name...? Anyhow, the files were gone and maybe that's what's happening."

Thinking aloud, Jody had the biggest aha moment since starting the case, "That would explain why your people told the Goulds to fill out new sheets after they'd already filled out multiples!"

"Hey, yeah, sure. It's not our fault though, the door was locked and someone had to know what they were getting...what the hell was that chick's name? Twyla? No."

"Okay, so when was this? When did the files go missing, Mr. Hancock?"

"Uh, let me get somebody. They'd know. Night before I had one of my assistant's throat chewed out by a rabid dog that somehow got into the arena. Give me a second."

Jody's breathing increased and goose bumps paraded her skin. This was it. This was the break. Everything was coming together.

Chip came back on the line. "That was August sixth, nineteen-eighty-eight."

Jody scribbled. "Okay. That's...where were you when this occurred?"

"Montana." Chip turned his face from the phone receiver, and said, "What was the venue again?" A voice replied, but not loud enough to come through the telephone. "Great Falls. I never went back there...what the hell was that woman's name?" The voice spoke as Jody added the city name to the notes. "Talia Grey."

Jody gasped. A brand-new, biggest of big break. She had to swallow her breath and said, "Say that name again."

"Talia Grey. She was pretty good, but she skipped a show,

and you don't skip a Chip Hancock show. It was a big piece—"

"Talia Grey."

"Yeah."

"Late twenties, early thirties? Dirty blonde hair? Pretty face?"

"That's her. She have something to do with this? I always thought those freaks she rolled around with in that old Winnebago were weird."

Jody shook in her seat. "Names! Names!"

"I don't know. Hey," Chip spoke across whatever room he was in, to his assistant. "There was a tough guy named Ryder, he ran the tapes. I met him when I discovered Talia in some Vegas shithole. He pretended to play the piano, but it was all tapes. Then there was an old girl called Paula—No, Polly Harp. The other two never did much, but were always there in the Winnebago, middle aged or so, no names for them."

Jody's teeth chattered as she wrote, the words on the page as sloppy as it got while still remaining legible. "Anything else you can tell me about them?"

Chip exhaled into the microphone and then said, "I only remember little bits. My assistant is looking at the notes. She takes good notes, I could fax you all the hiring stuff and her notes on the firing and whatever. She's good."

"You do that, Mr. Hancock."

Marc had just come into the boardroom and Jody spun on her chair to face him. His expression suggested her expression and he stopped dead, holding a coffee tray with a box of donuts and a pack of cigarettes cradled on top.

"Thank you, goodbye."

"What?" Marc said.

Jody cradled the phone, barely. Her entire body thrummed. She took a deep breath. "In August eighty-eight, boxes of questionnaires were stolen the night after a rabid dog killed one of Chip Hancock's assistants, tore out his throat. Just before the questionnaires were stolen, Chip fired a singer named Talia

Grey."

Marc's hands momentarily ceased function, and everything he'd been holding dropped to the carpet.

Chapter Twenty-Eight

They walked from the school to Alana's and Alana spoke the entire time, her breaths coming out like a mist on the cold afternoon air. The sidewalks were slim gullies and they had to go single file.

"It's gonna be bitchin," Alana said. "Aaron Lansdowne has his license already and his dad bought him a Lumina."

Kit scrunched up her face beneath the collar of her coat. Aaron Lansdowne was seventeen and had pimples all over his cheeks and drove around with fourteen-year-olds in his car. Jake said there were always guys like that, usually they were harmless, but just don't let them convince you, you owe them something for a ride.

"He's bringing his little brother and two of his friends and April Fergusson, remember her?"

Kit didn't answer. April Fergusson was two years older than they were and got suspended in the eighth grade for smoking pot at lunch hour on the walking bridge by the Olympia restaurant.

"Aaron says he's gonna bring beer and stuff too."

They got to Alana's house and Alana immediately shut up about the plans. Her mother was home. Alana came up with the idea of having a party at Kit's about five seconds after Kit explained that her brother and the hired help were going on a snowmobile trip all weekend and Kit needed to sleepover. Alana then lied to her mother and her mother was going to drop them off at the farm and they wouldn't even need to lie once they got there because it was often enough a farm truck wasn't parked in front of a farmhouse.

Alana whispered through much of the movies they'd popped in and all the popcorn they snacked on. She wanted to give someone a hand job, probably not Aaron, but maybe Aaron. Kit was too grossed out to say anything more than that everybody had to be gone by Sunday afternoon and if they made a mess, they had to clean it up.

Chapter Twenty-Nine

March 26, 1994 – Sprucemont, Ontario, Canada

Janelle Humphrey looked out the living room bay window at all the snow. She and Ernie sold the house in town once the girls went to college and bought a house a little smaller, but with three times the property, located two miles out of town. A bungalow plopped in the middle of several small farming operations. In the summer, when the farmers spread manure, the shit stink made her eyes water, but other than that, soft-country living was the way to be. She sipped coffee and listened to Ernie getting ready for his day. His being a reporter meant he didn't follow regular hours, it also meant he overworked. He'd been out late covering the Patriots Junior C game and was up with the rise of the sun—late as that still was.

A gentle rumble turned her attention to the laneway next to her front yard. A huge camper rolled in and a young woman in green coveralls led the exodus, followed by a young man also in green coveralls. Intrigued, Janelle tightened the string on her robe and shuffled in her fluffy pink slippers toward the door. The knock was much slower in landing than she expected and when it came, it was only the woman.

"Hello?" Janelle said after opening. The chill nipped at her bare legs and at her neck.

"Hi. I'm here to see Ernie."

Janelle looked past the woman and out to the driveway. Behind the wheel of the big machine was an old woman. The situation was strange, and in that oddity, it suddenly smacked of danger.

"Sorry, he's not home," she said and tried to close the door, but a bare foot blocked the way.

***

Ernie exited the steamy washroom in his boxer shorts and a white tee undershirt. He heard noises but thought nothing of them as he dressed. It was a Saturday, and he worked most Saturdays, though often took good chunks of Sunday through Wednesday off, but rarely an entire day. He dressed in jeans and a yellow button-up with short sleeves, tails tucked into his waistband. He pulled on white socks and then filled the right front pocket of his pants with his wallet and change. He stepped out of taster bedroom and walked down the hall. He passed the living room and then stopped before entering the kitchen. A strange man and two women sat on his couch. In the kitchen, a man and a woman sat at his dining table.

"Who the hell are you?" he asked, and then in afterthought said, "Where's Janelle?"

"She had to run out for sugar," Ryder said. He was in the kitchen, wearing rumbled and splotch-stained green coveralls.

Ernie looked around some more. The ones in the living room had their boots on in the house, trudging soggy prints everywhere. The man in the kitchen was barefoot. Seeing it made him shake.

"Where did you put her? Did you kill her?" He looked at the people in the living room. "You're the ones who killed the Gould family, aren't you?" He took a deep breath. "You can't kill me. You can't kill me. Nobody will write your story and get it out. That's what you want, right? You can't kill me."

"Nobody's been killed and nobody's gonna kill anybody," Talia said. She stepped out from the pantry, also barefoot in green coveralls. The stains on her getup were much more abundant and soaked both arms as well as her abdomen and collar.

Ernie pointed a finger. "I know you. You did the Roxy. You're," he paused and closed his eyes, opened them, "Talia Grey."

The woman clapped her hands.

"You're Talia Grey and—" Ernie stopped dead.

Recognizing home invaders was bad business. It meant an end to all things, where he was concerned. His legs gave out beneath him, and he sank. A wet patch from a boot print seeped into the seat of his jeans. "You're going to kill me. You killed Janelle and you're going to kill me. I was going to write a book. I was going to retire next year and write a book. I already wrote the plan. Twenty-five chapters. About a reporter who finds out a town councilman's working for mobsters, burying illegal landfill junk, a money laundering scheme, but a body shows up and then Hell's Angels. I was going to write a book, but you're going to kill me."

"Not if you cooperate," Ryder said as he stood from his chair. "All you gotta do is tell us where the blue van is."

"What blue van?"

"From your story. In the paper. From the A&W," Polly said from the living room couch.

"Oh, the witness. It's an American, he's living somewhere in Copper Falls, but I don't know where exactly. I'd tell you. You don't have to kill me. I'm going to write a book."

"Think real' hard now," Talia said. "Think real' hard and we'll let you go."

"I'll call Marc Foster. He knows. He's the detective. I won't tell you guys are here. I'll call him and make him tell me and then I'll tell you. I'm going to retire next year. I'm going to retire sooner in fact. You don't need to kill me. I'll call—"

"Shut it. You're giving me a headache. You don't know. You. Don't. Know. Not your fault, but it really sucks for you. Ya know? That book, you're not gonna write it," Ryder said. He stood over Ernie and bent into a crouch and put his hands on Ernie's throat, massaging the carotid artery. "Last chance."

Ernie stiffened, looked around at the faces, the ones in the living room didn't look happy or excited, but the pair in coveralls did and they obviously called the shots. He took a deep breath, closed his eyes, and said, "Eat shit, you goddamned cunts."

"Tisk, tisk." The hands left Ernie's throat and Ryder grinned before he winced and let the dog out.

Ernie tried to backpedal but found the trio from the living room had come to circle him during Ryder's transformation.

***

Thelma Robinson knocked on the door. She was supposed to have a late lunch date with Janelle, but Janelle didn't show up. The lights were off, but the door was open a crack and she stepped inside, calling out, "Janelle? Janelle, it's me, Thelma!" She ran her hand over two walls before finding the row of switches behind the door. She hit all four at once. "Oh God! She ran over to Janelle who lay face down next to the kitchen island. Her throat had been torn and a puddle of blood haloed her shoulders and head. Thelma felt her wrist, found no pulse. She popped up then and looked around more.

Ernie was dead on the rug, his eyes bulged and were pink all over. Beneath him was a huge black stain. She screamed, ran for the phone, found it had no dial tone, and then broke from the house.

Chapter Thirty

They arrived at the rental place the afternoon earlier. Jake and Ben were the only two without sleds of their own and both got Ski-Doo Safaris. Each had an emergency pack fastened over the rear of the seat. They guys had joked that the big trekking sleds would never keep up, but Jake and Ben did fine, to start.

They stayed in the first of three lodges in the looped trip and headed out the following morning, once the sun was up. The world was much colder that far north—a seven-hour drive from the farm—and humanity was sparse. They'd gone by one farm the night prior, but after leaving the lodge, they saw nobody else.

Jake was second to last in the line and followed the tracks of the sleds in front of him. They passed elk and deer. A massive jackrabbit ran alongside Jake for a few hundred feet, as if racing. Jake checked his mirror off and on. Ben had a stomach thing that morning and had spent much of that time on the can, tending to false alarms while his insides were burning. He bought a pack of Imodium at the lodge and popped three before they left. Just in case.

At midday, the route started winding around trees and rock faces. Jake did his best to follow the tracks before him, but it was obvious several other parties had used the route recently. The snow was clumpy with tread-spill and divots. Jake's right ski had struck the stone rock face a handful of times attempting to avoid bumps and eventually tipped himself over, going about twenty miles an hour. He laughed into his helmet from his knees and looked back the trail for Ben to catch up. After a minute, he rose to his feet and righted the sled.

He watched the trail. Ben was not coming. He took off his helmet and listened. He didn't hear another snowmobile.

"Damn," he said and popped his helmet on and set to yank the machine around by the left ski to have it face back the way he'd come.

Within five minutes, he came upon Ben. Smoke rose from beneath the hood of the sled and the word Ski-Doo on the right side of the hood had burned through. Jake took off his helmet and mitts and rubbed his steamy head with a steamy hand.

"Grab the keys and your stuff, guess we're riding doubles."

Ben nodded, the visor on his mask up, but his helmet covered any expression he might've had. Muffled, but clear enough, he said, "Better take this too, don't want to get fined if someone steals it." He strapped the safety pack to his back and Jake had just enough room to turn his sled around.

Trying to play catch-up, he thumbed the gas. The speedometer went more than twice as high as it had been, potential obstacles be damned. Too quickly, the sun was starting to go down and he felt Ben clenching at his sides.

He shouted over his shoulder, "You all right?"

"My guts!"

They stopped and Ben ate several handfuls of snow. Jake offered to take them back to the lodge, but Ben straightened himself and said, "Probably we're closer to the next one by now."

They continued and kept right, passing a fork in the path that Jake did not see. He flipped the lights on, and worry began sinking deeper. Ben clenched and moaned. Jake hit an open space and thumbed the paddle hard, unnoticing that he'd begun to plow a new trail. The Safari had an extended track and with double the weight, cut the untainted powder with an ease that kept Jake unnoticing.

"Stop!" Ben wailed.

Before Jake had the sled stilled, Ben fell sideways from the seat. The night was dim, but a nearly full moon gave them plenty of light to see one another. Jake's hands and feet were no longer hot, and they ached at the cold. Ben had to be worse.

He'd essentially only clung to Jake's back for the last four hours. Jake looked around while Ben held his stomach. They were alone on the edge of a forest and the stalled sled had sunk into two feet of snow. Later problems.

He knelt next to Ben and Ben spoke through chattering teeth, "I'm so cold."

"Fuck."

Jake stood straight and then broke for the forest. Under the trees was near-black and he dragged his mitts through the snow—much less beneath the canopied limbs—looking for sticks and branches. He found several hunks of birch and a brown branch of cedar and dragged it all back to where he'd left Ben.

He dropped the load and dug through the safety pack attached to the back of his sled. He flung out a silver emergency blanket, folded to the size of a sandwich, and kept looking. He tossed two flares to the ground and took out the liter of gasoline in a plastic container. He set that aside and found the collapsible shovel he'd sought was still strapped to the seat at the rear of the sled. He dug a fat, open-ended oval next to the path he'd trekked, piled the wood in as best he could, sprayed it with gasoline, and then searched his pockets beneath the borrowed thermal snow pants. He gave up, looking at the flare.

The fire whooshed an orange flash before settling. The wood was wet, but the flare was relentless, and the gasoline had the liquids trapped within the wood crackling. Jake sloshed more fuel onto the fire and then dragged ben closer to the flames. The emergency blanket went over him and Jake took off for more flammables.

***

The second flare burned until it died over in the forest. Jake had scratched the tip and stood it in the snow like a nightlight while he gathered enough wood for an extended stay. They obviously weren't going anywhere. He was exhausted and scared and starving by the time he wrapped the blanket from Ben's pack around him. Ben shivered violently and then stopped suddenly. His lips were blue even by the fire's glow and Jake popped to his feet and ran his hands over his face, thinking, thinking, thinking, there was something you did for extreme cold, thinking, for hypothermia, thinking, thinking, think—

He set out his blanket like a mat next to the fire and pulled the blanket from Ben. He then rolled Ben onto his back and began stripping away the layers. He left only his underwear. Quickly, Jake stripped himself and spooned tight against Ben's back. He then pulled the second emergency blanket over them and then wrangled the coats and snow pants on top of that.

It wasn't long before Ben began shivering again and Jake rubbed the man's arms and legs to get the blood moving. Intermittently, he slid partway out of the nest to feed the fire and explore their packs. He ate two granola bars and drank from the little bottle of whiskey he'd brought.

He'd fall asleep and wake up cold and feed the fire. The third time he did it, Ben was awake and said, "You saved me again."

"Shh, it's okay."

The night was long, sundown to sun-up was fourteen hours. With a few hours left of dark, Jake was rubbing Ben's shoulder and hip as much to keep Ben warm as himself. Ben was awake and whispered, "You saved me again. You saved me again." Jake was rubbing and telling him, "Shh. Shh," when Ben spat into his palm and reached back for Jake's erect penis. No more words were spoken for about three minutes after Jake penetrated Ben and then Jake moaned, "I'm gonna cum."

March 27, 1994 – Sprucemont, Ontario, Canada

Marc wasn't answering his phone and he wasn't at the station. It was Sunday, but it was also the full moon. Jody was frustrated and called all the leads back, the only connections she made were at the RV dealership, the manager held fast to his story, but had been willing to talk about the not-so-mysterious Elvira, but no, there was nothing more to elaborate, and with the manager of the Roxy. He'd been the most helpful when it came to the man named Ryder, but even that was simply a description and an impression. An honest to god bad man.

Jody pulled into the Tim Hortons drive-thru and ordered a coffee and a half-dozen donuts. She rolled out to Aystadt to the trailer park and asked the two sets of campers. One had only just gotten there while the other pair remembered the RV in question well. They were an old couple who travelled every other winter in their 35-ft Coachmen. They'd sold their home and lived in the camper full-time, survived on a benefits package from when the couple both worked at Ford.

"Was a real beaut'," the woman said. Her name was Ruth, and she had an under bite and a curly black 'do, coarse as pubic hair. She had that same black hair coming in at the corners of her upper lip. "We look at those new ones now and then, but we're on a budget."

The husband piped in, "Not that we got to scrimp, we just have to be awares." His name was Bruce, and he wore a thin combover atop a shiny bald head. He was forever fidgeting with his gut and when he caught Jody noticing, he said, "You ever had a hernia?"

She told him no and he got into the surgeries and the eruptions and then more surgeries. It was well after one when Jody got out of there and made for Sprucemont. When Marc wasn't in the office, she knocked on Charles McCarthy's door.

"I wish you worked here. You'd be a damned fine officer."

"Thank you."

"I've never seen someone so dedicated to a case. What is it about this?"

Without pause, Jody said, "Money. You haven't heard from Marc today, have you?"

"I take it you tried him at home…maybe him and the wife—you know about all that, right?"

She tilted her head back and said, "Ah. Right. That's got to be it. Family trumps work."

"Not for you."

Jody offered a lopsided smile. "Says the guy in on a Sunday."

"I like Sundays. It's quiet." The chief slapped the desk then and pointed at Jody with his right index finger. "It's the full moon, isn't it? These guys do it on the full moon."

"See, that's why I'm here and that's why I'm surprised Marc isn't."

Charles picked up his cigarette pack. He lit a cigarette with a green Cricket brand lighter, took a good drag, and then exhaled. "I don't know what to tell you. You could always drive by his house, or I guess over to—"

"Jesus, imagine they're on the mend and some woman shows up. Hey, wife, I'm the woman your husband's been spending his days with."

Charles laughed humorlessly. "You're right. I got nothing else. Sorry."

Jody went back to the boardroom and began flipping through the latest information, she'd questioned all of them twice, at least…though not Ben Lynch. She'd never spoken to him. Marc had done that on his own and it might be worth a shot. "To hell with it," she said and grabbed her coat and purse. She was out the door a few seconds when the call came in about a dead reporter and his wife.

Chapter Thirty-One

March 27, 1994 – Copper Falls, Ontario, Canada

Marc's hand ached enough that he forgot about the pain in his head. He'd been leaving his house when he pitched forward, and the ground came at him while a great black ink smear blotted out his vision. He'd been dragged, that much was obvious by the sensations under his armpits and in his toes. He came to, tied to a kitchen chair. There was a clock above a small TV, it stood out against the vinyl wall. Two hours had passed since he heard the telephone ringing on his way out the door.

Ryder—this man before him had to be Ryder. He recognized Talia Grey, too. Ryder leaned over him and said, "Tell us where to find the blue van and you'll live."

Marc had looked around some more then. The room was slim, but long. A microwave. A small stove and a small refrigerator. The brown couch. A recliner. A breakfast nook with two disinterested looking people, a husband and wife by appearances. Two captain's chairs about twenty feet away. The gentle rock and sway of motion. His gun and his wallet on a table next to a set of pliers.

"What van?" Marc said.

"You get one pass 'cause you're groggy from where I conked you, and that was it. The blue van from the A&W, where is it?"

"I'm sorry, I think you have the wrong guy," Marc said.

Ryder sighed and looked out the window. He picked up the pliers with the red rubber handles and fell onto the couch next to Talia. He glanced over his shoulder often, out the window.

It was Copper Falls. Marc imagined a series of events, thinking there was an APB on a big, new Fleetwood Pace Arrow RV, but would that silly ass Robert Mink acknowledge it if he saw the thing? Not likely.

So, they'd hit him, dragged him into a different vehicle, made it out to where they'd parked the RV, and then headed to Copper Falls. No doubt they'd read the paper and the point he'd let slip about location. They had his wallet, so they had the right guy, and they knew they had the right guy. Did his lie really matter? Was this Ryder as hard as he'd impressed upon Chip Hancock?

The RV took a right at the stoplight in Copper Falls and then a right at the first corner past the town limits. Into farm country. The RV came to a halt on a road that separated hundreds of empty field acres. Ryder snapped the pliers and stared into Marc. Marc didn't flinch until the pliers clamped on the index finger of his right hand, just above the first knuckle. Ryder said nothing as he did this, simply squeezed and then wrenched and twisted until the bone snapped and Marc groan shouted.

"Where's the blue van?"

The pain in his head was secondary to the throb in his hand. This Ryder was indeed as hard as he seemed. In a flash, Marc saw the photos of the body count they'd left in their wake, these freaks. He needed time.

"How do you pick who dies?" he said, gasping.

"Where's the blue van? Tell us and I'll let you run free."

A lie. This Ryder was a liar and a killer and Marc just needed time—the pliers clamped on the index of his left hand, and he screamed, "No! No! No! Nonono—" The snap and crunch were louder inside than out, and Marc wailed at the pain.

"I'm not foolin', you keep this up, I do your fingers, then your dick, then your balls, then your eyes, then your lips, then...fuck, I guess then your tongue and throat. I mean, you won't be able to tell by then. So, make it easy, you say where the blue van is, and I'll let you run free."

Marc licked his lips and swallowed. His throat was hoarse, and his vocal folds strained tight at the top of his chest. The clock on the wall suddenly suggested it was after two.

"There he is," Talia said.

Ryder picked up the pliers from the table, they had strings of sticky blood trailing. Marc looked at his hands. Six fingers were crooked. He'd missed four breaks. He blew out a wheeze.

"Gary says I should do your dick and balls last because he'll get sympathy pains and thinks you'll crack before then. I get it, you probably get it too. See a guy get his nuts squeezed 'til they burst, and you feel your nuts burst a little bit right along with them." Ryder was grinning. "Now, where's the blue van."

"Outside Copper Falls. On a farm, but I don't know exactly where. I'd tell you if I did." Marc's words spilled in a jumble.

Ryder slammed the pliers down on the table and charged at Marc. The hot breath hit his ear a tenth of a second before the mouth closed over it. Marc screamed and Ryder bit and shook like a dog on a rope until the ear came away. Ryder smiled around the flesh and cartilage, blood trailing like a Van Dyke goatee.

Marc vomited into his lap, onto his hands. The hole seared and yet was freezing inside his head. The air getting into that cavity stung and the ink seeped slower, and he blinked.

"He's going out again," Talia said.

"Fucking guy," Ryder said and delivered a punch.

Marc rocked his eyes open, and now the clock read minutes to five. They'd let him run free if he told. They would. He didn't need to protect anyone. They'd let him go free and he could see his kids again and tell his wife to fuck herself and tell Jody to leave it alone, trailing these people would only get her killed.

"It's straight north of the town and then turn left at the first road, but that's not for about five minutes after the water tower. Then you go for a while, like three or four miles maybe."

"What did he say?" Polly asked from the driver's seat.

"He's trying to give directions." Talia stood up and shook him. "Say it again but separate the words."

"North of town. First left. Go a few miles."

The washroom door accordioned open and Ryder popped out. "Is he talking?"

"Yeah," Talia said and then called over her shoulder, "North of town. First left. Drive a few miles."

"He mean off the main highway?" Polly asked, the RV rumbling to life.

"You mean off the highway?" Ryder swatted at Marc's good ear.

He groaned and nodded.

"Yeah. He nodded, yeah," Talia said and then clapped. "I've got butterflies. It's crazy."

"It's something." Ryder flopped down on the couch and watched out the window.

It was another twenty minutes before one of them spoke to Marc again. Ryder had him by the chin and was looking out the window onto a long laneway with a house, a barn, a big shed, and two more outbuildings. "Yes." Marc hissed, his heart coming to life. He'd be free to run. They said so and they'd let him go. Sometimes you did things, trade-offs, but you still got the win.

"What's the name on the mailbox supposed to say?" Cynthia asked.

Marc blinked. A final question before his freedom. The answer was there, right there, if he could just... "Gerber! Guy's Ben Lynch, but the farm is Gerber."

"He can't see the mailbox, right? No way he read it and can see it?" Polly asked. "Better to go in peaceable and take what we need quiet."

"Nah, he can't see it." Ryder stood over Marc, looming. "Guess you want to run free now, huh?"

"You said." Tears slipped into the blood on the side of Marc's face, sending pink tendrils into the collar of his shirt.

"I did." Ryder began untying Marc's legs. He then untied his arms. The motion made Marc shiver. "You should've told us sooner, see how easy it could've gone?"

Marc began stumbling. He blinked; a tepid euphoria lapped at his shores. A free man. Sure, he'd lost an ear and most of his fingers were broken, but he had his balls and he had tomorrow. They'd let him go. This was his win, finally.

Down the steps, his feet crunched and the cold air bit something awful inside his head. He began stumbling toward the highway. He'd get there and someone would see him and give him a ride, better yet, he'd come across someone along the way and they'd rush him to the hospital.

He wasn't ten feet from the door of the RV when he heard, "Your turn, Gary." Ryder's voice said this, but it meant nothing because Marc was free, and he could live everyday with the knowledge of his second chance.

Something clicked against the RV steps and Marc stopped again. He watched the door over his shoulder—bending his neck into the wound on the side of his head to shield some of the cold burrowing in. What he saw made no sense and all the sense. The victims with their necks torn to look like a vicious dog attack, all that work to mimic, and why? Why would anybody mimic when they had the real thing? The wolf was grey and brown and stood on its fours almost five feet high. The mouth was open and slobbering and the eyes were on him.

"No, but I'm free," he said and pushed to double the stagger-pace he'd held up before.

Falling again, the snowy road coming at him, four paws pressed to his back and teeth sank into his neck. Marc had no screams left.

***

Kit stomped around the house. She'd awoken in the afternoon, alone. Everyone had left and nobody had picked up after themselves. The first thing was to collect the empty bottles and cans, plus the food wrappers and dirty dishes, then she could get to the vomit and spilled liquor. Some of that vomit was hers. She gagged as she scrubbed. At two, she stopped and put a freezer pizza in the oven before hearing the mewling of cats. They'd come up to the house...because she hadn't fed them, or the chickens, or the cattle.

She had to feed herself first. The pizza came out of the oven, and she watched TV while she ate. The hangover wasn't in her head, but in her arms and legs and she stretched on the couch. She awoke to a plate with three slices of cool pizza remaining on it. The sluggishness had abated some and she took the plate out to the kitchen. She drank fruit punch from the plastic jug she'd mixed it in on Thursday evening and then wiped her mouth. The cats were still mewling around. She got dressed and put on her boots, was surprised at how dim it was already.

The cold nipped and she kept her head down, put her hands in her armpits, and followed her old boot prints to the barn. The cats that'd gone to the house, followed close behind her. The cattle were livid, mooing to the evening shade.

"Shut up," she whispered.

The guilt was there. Jake left them with enough feed to do them from Friday to Sunday morning, though they'd do what they usually did, and pig out right away and then stupidly moo about where the food had gone. The chickens were better, but the cats were just as bad.

To keep from stumbling over the cats, she fed them first. The Co-op sold fifty-kilogram bags of Barn Cat brand cat food for next to nothing and they had it in a green garbage pail in an unused corner of the granary. She took the Chapman's ice cream container, full to just below the middle line and dumped it into one of the two aluminum pans set out on the floor. The cats' water was a block of ice, but that would have to wait. She grabbed the closest pitchfork and began forking down hay from a round bale. Jake would've told her to do the mixed chop first, but she wasn't in the mood to do what was right, because what was right was a little more effort. Cattle were stupid and stank and weren't worth half the trouble they were.

The water dish in hand, she went to the house rather than to the tap. Too cold for all that effort. Flipped over, she ran hot water over the bottom of the dish until the big ice chunk let go. She filled the dish three quarters of the way up with hot water and started the careful trek across the lawn. She still spilled onto her hands, making her fingers ache with the cold. Probably even hot water would freeze in an hour or so out there.

"Drink it while you can," she said.

The feeding cats ignored her.

She hurried over to the chicken coop and closed the door behind her once inside. She rubbed her hands and basked in the shit-smelling warmth. It was always damp and balmy in with the chickens. She lined the chicken feed in the trough and put the scoop back in the steel pail behind the door before closing the lid on it.

A rumble approached outside, and she paused to listen. She opened the door at the sound of voices—there were no windows in the coop—and was surprised when the sound wasn't Jake and Ben home early...because who else would be at the farm on a Sunday night?

A big RV parked by the shed and four people got out. One of them immediately went to Ben's van and climbed inside. The others started for the house. A huge dog prattled in the lane behind them.

Kit crept back, pushing the door open with her butt and then pushing it back closed with her hands. Something was funny. The .22 was on the wall to her right.

Chapter Thirty-Two

March 27, 1994 – Abitibi Canyon, Ontario, Canada

The sun wasn't all the way up when Jake and Ben started trailing back the way they'd come. Knowing the route pushed Jake to move faster. He wanted a meal and a proper bed, to finally get warm.

It was about two-thirty when they arrived at the lodge. Ben said he still wasn't feeling great and that his insides were twisting themselves apart. The sleeping lodges were individual rooms fashioned like a motel set-up with a washroom built on, two twin beds, a TV, and a nightstand. In one corner was a closet with a tall fan next to it for drying out gear. They were in room nine.

They had burgers and fries ordered to go and sat on beds, quietly eating, not looking at each other. Ben finished his food first and said he was going to have a shower. Jake turned on the TV and flipped without stopping anywhere longer than a few seconds—the lodge had satellite with more than twenty-five channels. He finished eating and left his trash on the bed. The shower stopped and he waited outside. The door opened and they stood a foot apart and Jake joked that there better be hot water left. Ben dropped his towel and kissed Jake. Jake couldn't undress quickly enough, hands hungry as mouths, they explored and pushed and pulled and stroked.

Ben joined Jake in the shower until there was no hot water left.

After that, they shared one of the twin beds and explored all the pent-up emotion and attraction they hadn't fully explored in the cold night, though stopping now and then to drink from the little whiskey bottle Ben had packed to match the bottle Jake had packed. By six, Jake was out, face down and naked in a room that reeked of sweat and semen. Ben was up and licking the tinfoil wrappers from the food they'd eaten. That deep fryer scent under the mask of all that they'd done had him wild.

His guts stilled their twists as he paced the room. He looked at Jake in a different way and drew to within a foot, sniffed at hands and found they didn't smell like what he wanted. He then stared down at Jake's neck, watching the pulse. He licked his lips and that fever dream memory exposed itself as truth. Coarse fur began sliding from his pores and his hands began to change, fingers shortening. He moaned and crawled to the door. If he changed like he had before and was in a room with Jake... He pawed at the knob, but it wouldn't turn. He rolled sideways and his bones snapped and rippled.

Jake kicked from bed. "Ben?"

"Open the door," Ben managed to say.

"What?"

"Open...the...door."

Ben's knees jutted up with great snaps and his face began to transform.

"What's happening?" Jake took two steps closer. "What's happening to your—"

"Open the fucking door," Ben said, the words rode a growl beyond the human norm. "Open the door and get into the bathroom and lock it!"

Jake watched. The transformation was incredible, and quick. The jaw stretched and the body curled. His hands were gone and then his feet. His ears elongated to points. He began to roll and suddenly he was all fur and teeth and glowing eyes.

Jake leapt for the door handle, yanking it wide before he stumbled back. Ben was looking at him, but it could hardly be described as Ben, it was a wolf. It stepped toward Jake and Jake crab-walked in reverse into the washroom, never breaking eye contact. Cold stone underhand, then ass, then feet. He kicked the door shut a few inches from the wet nose and dripping maw.

Ben howled.

Jake covered his ears, feet pressed against the door.

March 27, 1994 – Copper Falls, Ontario, Canada

"They haven't been gone long. That pizza hasn't gone hard and look'it that big ice cube in the sink," Cynthia said.

Talia leaned over her shoulder. "Not so conclusive, Holmes. You don't know how big that ice was before and who can tell yesterday's day-old cardboard pizza from today's cardboard pizza?"

Polly reached past Cynthia's shoulder and picked up a slice. She bit and talked around the food. "Not old at all."

"Do we care to ambush?" Talia said. She held a blanket from the basement under her face.

"Doubt it." Polly took another bite.

"This is his." Talia inhaled deeply from the blanket.

"Don't let Ryder see you do that. He'll get jealous." Cynthia picked up a slice of pizza as she unbuckled her belt. The sun was going down and, in a few minutes, none of their discussion would matter.

"Maybe I want him to get jealous," Talia said.

Polly lifted her left eyebrow and said, "Doubt that."

They began to strip then—though not Polly. Ryder was out in the van and was surely ready for the call of the moon. Gary hadn't changed back and was in the yard, somewhere.

"This is going to be a waste of a moon," Talia said.

Cynthia pouted a lip. "I saw a wee chicken barn." She was naked and rotating her shoulders.

Polly passed by behind her and started the coffeemaker brewing. "Maybe there are deer. Probably are somewhere," she said.

Talia had made a pile of her clothes and left them on the dining table. She crossed the kitchen and opened the garage door. A chilly, manure-flavored scent wafted through.

"Guess there's a bull if you all get too bored." Polly opened and closed cupboards until she located the mugs. "I never understand how people don't put the mugs right over the coffeemaker."

"You ever try a bull?" Cynthia asked.

Polly smirked at her. "I heard of another wolf who did."

Cynthia said, "Did it get the bull"

Polly shook her head gently. "Kicked him and before he could get hisself righted, it pinned him to a wall. He was partway back to man by the time he died, guess he was hoping the bull didn't shine on killing men. Mattered none to the bull."

Cynthia was on the floor, looking up, huffing and puffing, panting as fur began to sprout and coat her flesh. Polly set the mug she'd found on the counter and went to the garage door, stepped through and opened the second door to the outside. Talia watched her, full wolf.

***

Jody reached across the seat to her purse for the Spearmint gum she kept in the zippered center compartment. When she put her eyes back on the road, she had to swerve hard to avoid a sprinting deer. The nose of her rental tipped and slammed into the ditch.

"Well, shit," she said and pulled the shifter to the R, then gassed it. It didn't rock or sway. "Shit."

She grabbed her purse, the keys from the ignition, and stood from the car. She looked around. Sundown was minutes away. To her left were miles of road. To her right, about a quarter mile away, was the Gerber mailbox. She locked the doors of the car and started off. Ditching her car wasn't exactly a professional leg to stand on to question a witness. Then again, it gave her a second reason for showing up at the door.

***

The sound of crunching snow approached the chicken coop. The door rattled inward, banging against the wall and the feed pail. The chickens became flustered, jumping and squawking. The huge wolf stepped closer, almost licking its lips. It turned around and nudged the door closed with its nose, the movements practiced and sophisticated. The hen called Alpha charged near the wolf, as if trying to scare it off. The wolf moved in a flash, spinning and clamping long yellow fangs into the bird. Feathers danced on air and blood squirted, freckling the walls. One, two, three jerks of the great jaw; four, five, six— the shot echoed from where Kit hid herself in the rafters of the squat building. The wolf stopped shaking and teetered sideways. Kit pulled the bolt and the hot casing fell to the floor eight feet below, only a few inches from where she dropped the Crown Royal bag after she loaded her pocket with ammunition. She fired again, missing. She repeated, frantic as the wolf climbed to its feet, growling. Kit fired, puffing fur, but hitting nothing of consequence. She chambered another round, turning on the loose board where she lay as the wolf scrambled past the hysterical chickens and jump-kicked off the wall into the rafters.

Kit fell sideways and landed hard on her ass. The pain stung upward and outward and into her hands and feet, but she kept hold of the .22. The wolf leapt again, and Kit fired.

The wolf yelped and rolled back. It immediately began pawing at its face and charging in reverse, as if to get away from the pain. Then it stopped and fell sideways against the shelving that held the chickens from the ground. It panted and whined, barely audible over the din of the terrified birds.

Kit chambered another round and remained on her ass, watching. She began panting herself, letting out a low moan as the wolf started to change. The bones began flexing and popping and the fur thinned. The muzzle crunched and fell into the very human face of a woman. Blood spurted and oozed from the hole through her left eye. The woman blinked at Kit with her good eye and forced through a high and heavy breath,

"Best…re…load…girl."

Kit popped to her feet and pressed herself against the door. She fumbled for the rounds from her pocket and filled the tube magazine beneath the barrel. She remained leaned against the door.

It was minutes before the first scratches and the first thump came from the other side.

***

By the time Jody was most of the way in the lane, the sun was down, and that goddamned full moon was high. She kept her eyes low, looking anywhere but to the sky. That moon. People would be dying somewhere, and she was too late to do anything…

There was the RV.

She stopped for three heartbeats before she sprinted from the laneway into the packed snow piles next to the shed. Climbing, the cold in her hands burning the flesh and aching beneath. Crawling, the pain the same, but gravity on her side. She made it to the wall of the shed and pressed her spine tight to the rippled steel. She jerked to her right and looked around the corner, at the RV, and beyond that to Ben Lynch's van, and then back to straight. She took six deep breaths and ran for the RV.

She was so close. She'd tracked them and had them, but certainty was in quick exploration…hell, maybe she'd drive right out of there. She swung open the door on the passenger side and quietly mounted the stairs, pulling the door closed behind her. She first went to the driver's seat and found the ignition empty.

New plan. Be sure and then get out, haul ass on foot up the lane and jog until hitting the closest neighbor. She slipped in something wet and sticky as she crossed the linoleum floor to the bathroom. She flicked the light on inside the cramped space—a better bet for going unnoticed than flipping the main switch and illuminating the entire hull.

The light revealed that she'd slipped in blood. The light revealed a bolted chair with ropes puddled around it, on top of the blood. The light revealed a wallet and a pistol on the foldout dining table.

Jody picked up the wallet and carted it back to the light. Her hands shook. Given the juxtaposition between the gun and the wallet and that she hadn't reached Marc, it suggested exactly what she found when she opened it up. She groaned and set aside her purse. She picked up the pistol from the table, and returned to the light of the bathroom. Quick check, loaded, sixteen in the clip. Safety off. Fifteen in the clip, one in the hole.

She had a decision to make. She owed nothing more than to report to her employer that she'd located the murderers—she already had IDs on two. If she could just…but people lived at the farm, and what in the hell were they doing? Killing a witness?

Shots rang out. Something with a small caliber, more like popping. She looked out through the window and saw the improbable. A giant wolf loped over the snow toward a squat outbuilding. It scratched at the door and another pop sounded.

Marc had told her the make-up of the folks living on the farm. The memory of just what kind remained beyond reach. She had to do something. What if there were kids?

The air was crisp in her lungs as she ran a huge U around the building. The wolf was scratching and finally it began barking. There was another dull pop. The drills and the obstacle course and the training scenarios—Jody had done so well on paper, but when it came time to act, she'd failed. The strength wasn't there. The speed wasn't there. The lightning thought wasn't there.

She crossed around the building and stopped dead as the wolf stood in her path. It growled, lowered to its forepaws, ready to leap. The gun remained heavy against Jody's side. The wolf shook, still growling, somehow drawing nearer without taking a step. There was nothing to do. Jody's eyes could widen no more and her lungs could hold no more air.

Then the pop and the yip. The wolf fell sideways and turned. Jody looked at the tail and the haunches and acted. She fired three shots into the wolf's back. The clucking chicken sounds were loud and wild. Kit then rushed from sight and the chicken sounds immediately abated. Jody rounded the building.

"Who're you?" Kit hissed, aiming the .22 at Jody's chest.

"Jody Penrose. I came to talk about Ben…I'm an investigator. Do you know, are there more dogs? How many people?"

"Why is this happening?" A long pause. "At least four, but they're not people or dogs, they're both."

"What?"

"Look." Kit pointed behind Jody and the wolf was gone. Instead, there was a middle-aged man.

Jody spun, trying to catch up with her head and every shadow that might potentially be something more. "The van we can take—"

"I saw one of them go in the van."

"Then we need to get inside."

Kit said, "They were already inside."

"We can't stay out here."

***

The wolf had not left her completely. The heightened senses, the smells she picked up, the things she heard, what she saw. Through the cracked door to the garage, Polly Harp caught two unfamiliar voices talking about how they'd get into the house and where the phone was once, they got there. She set down her coffee mug, grabbed a knife from the butcher's block, and walked swiftly to the door that opened onto the basement. The fuse panel was almost always in the basement, usually right next to the main telephone panel.

She'd kill them if the opportunity presented itself, but really all she needed was time and a scene that leaned into the skills of the wolves and away from the skills of the humans.

***

Ryder terrorized the cattle until he grew bored and killed one. He drank his fill and then took the path out of the barn toward the forest, sniffing. He found the old tracks of a deer and the recent tracks of a muskrat down by the swamp but ignored both. His hunger was for the flesh of man.

He ran in great circles, seeking out the scent of Talia, but hit a snowshoe track and changed his destination. Happy and excited, his tongue dangling from the side of his semi-parted jaws, Ryder came to a stop and looked around. He heard the shots but did not incorporate them as something to consider. They were so far away.

Suddenly, he was on a back-forty dirt path where ATV tracks stole the snowshoe tracks. He looked over his shoulder. It was possible the man with the blue van had returned, or someone else. He looked down the ATV path. The possibility also existed that this path was short and that he'd come upon other people. Edible people. He sniffed the air, seeking farm scent and found the farm scent came from only behind him. He turned back.

***

"The phone's just in there," Kit whispered, pointing into the darkness.

They'd hurried to the garage and locked the door behind them, and then tested the light switch. When that didn't work, Jody put her left hand on Kit's shoulder and followed her lead.

"Maybe you should go in front," Kit said.

They were by the washer and dryer at the side door, a few feet short of the opening to the kitchen.

"I don't know where I'm going."

"I know. I'm scared."

"Me too."

"I need my hands to see…I'm…it's okay," Kit said and started poking the rifle barrel, swinging it gently through the air. She stopped at the switch next to the fridge and tapped the wall until she found the familiar shape. She flicked it three times. "Does that mean the power's out?"

Jody whispered back, "Maybe cut."

"Cut."

"No. Thinking worst case. Probably not cut. Go."

Kit shuffled her feet and swung the rifle before her. The moonlight shined through the small windows to her right and cast a great swatch over the living room to her left. She pinched the rifle against her side and lifted the phone receiver. Not even static.

"It doesn't work?" she said.

"Is there another one?" Jody whispered.

"Yes. In my room." Kit then repeated an unanswered question. "Why is this happening?"

Jody said, "We'll get to your room and shut the door."

"Okay."

The path was a straight line to the hall and a right turn through the last door. Kit had wandered the hall in the dark for as long as her memory stretched. She reached her bedroom door and stopped when Jody said, "Did you hear that?"

Kit scrambled then and pushed through the door, escaping the nearly full dark hallway. Jody trailed her after a second and Kit pushed the door closed. Jody was next to her, pressed against the wall.

"What did you hear?" Kit asked.

"I don't know. Something."

Kit was on her knees, the .22 laid aside, feeling for the

telephone. She found the long grey cord and began pulling the multi-colored keypad telephone her parents bought her for Christmas when she was ten. She lifted the receiver to her head. She fingered the paddle, and listen, but nothing. The phones were dead.

"No dial tone. Why is this happening?" she asked. That hole in the woman's face played on a loop in her mind. "How is it possible?"

"They want to kill Ben Lynch, I think."

"He's snowmobiling with my brother." Kit faced upward from the shadowy floor to look at Jody. Jody's chest heaved much faster than the pace of her words suggested.

"Will they come home soon?"

"Not until tomorrow."

"Damn, okay, I guess we—"

Paws thumped against the window—about six-feet from the ground at its lowest point—and a large head and pointed ears silhouetted like a horrid shadow puppet. Kit rolled in reverse, bumping up against Jody's shins. A great steam puff clouded the glass from the hidden nostrils of the beast.

Jody raised the pistol but did not fire. To break the glass was to invite a wolf inside. She tugged at Kit's armpit, forcing the girl to stand. Kit whined but complied.

"We need light and strong walls. Where?"

Kit blinked at this, her breath hitching as she spoke. "Basement...no, uh...uh, the fireplace! There's the bricks and the barbeque lighter!" She gasped then. "They won't get through walls, will they?"

"Not stone ones. Where's the fireplace?"

"The living room, where the other phone is."

Jody led and stopped in the kitchen, bumping a table. "Did you hear that?"

"Did you hit a chair?"

"No, another noise."

"Oh."

Jody grabbed Kit by the coat sleeve and pulled her to the cusp of the living room. The huge moon cast a light that thickened the shadows where it didn't touch, and it didn't touch much of the room.

"Where now?"

Kit pushed Jody into the shadows of the right side of the room, before sidling by and dropping to her knees to feel around the cold hearth for the barbeque lighter. She found the stack of penny saver flyers, the bucket and shovel, and then the lighter and the wood. She handled the grip and flipped it blindly. Her finger played over the trigger, clicking it as she stood and turned. Each click brought a flash and Kit clicked twice more before understanding what she saw in the flashes.

"Look out!" Kit shouted as the flame finally lit.

The knife nailed into Jody's lower spine, and she fired a round into the floor. Kit backed away; the flame still lit on the end of the skinny tube. She watched as the old woman bent over Jody and reared back for another strike with the knife as Jody brought her hand around to cover. The knife jabbed through the skin between the bones of her ring and pinky fingers of her left hand. She brought up her right and the old woman punched her in the eye. The gun left Jody's grip and clattered into the corner by the rarely used front door.

Jody shouted and groaned. The old woman growled. The flame went out as kit reached for the cast iron poker. Her hand found a tin jug of accelerant—the one she and her bother used whenever they didn't feel like looking for dryer wood. She turned it at the humped shadow amidst the empty shadows and began spraying. She touched flame a jet of fluid that sluiced through the dark. It lit and the container lit and the old woman's head and back lit, and Jody's arm lit. The old woman began howling. The room was suddenly bright with her burning hair. Kit threw the accelerant container at the fireplace, it banked just inside the lip, popping with flames.

"Help!" Jody shouted. She was bloody and writhing, her

hands and coat on fire.

Kit ignored Jody and went for the gun while she knew where it was. On her knees, she slid and turned. She pointed the gun at the smoldering shape trying to put out flames with the burnt sweater she'd pulled off. Kit began squeezing. She got off four shots before her finger was too tired and numb from the effort and recoil. At least one shot hit the old woman. She was on the floor, panting, a high wheeze sound trailing each breath until gurgling began and the breaths became gasps and then became none.

Kit's heart pounded wildly, and her ears rang. She watched the insane tableau until she recognized that Jody needed help. She crawled over, dropped the gun on the floor and took off her coat, began smothering the wet fire while Jody writhed and wailed. The high ping noise in her ears began to abate two seconds before the living room bay window shattered. Paws skittered and clopped on the hard floor. Kit felt the wolf pounce on her before she had a chance to turn. Slobber and teeth and bovine blood rained over her shoulders and cheek. She screamed as the jaws came down and—

The shots rang out, one after another—bangbangbangbangbangbang—until there was nothing but clicks remaining. The wolf was flung into a corner and began blinking wetly in the moonshine, a growl crossed from dog to man that sounded much like the word *mommy*, and there the figure stayed, moving, but without life. The bones cracked and snapped. Flesh sagged before tightening. Fur began to disappear like swallowed smoke.

It was almost a minute before Jody said something about finding keys and Kit went to work, in shock. Afterward, she'd have no memory of dragging the woman or of driving Ben's van to the hospital or of talking to the police.

March 27, 1994 – Abitibi Canyon, Ontario, Canada

Sylvia Brown and Lanny Hopkins were on their way to the lodge after a long day on the Abitibi Canyon trails when they stopped for a piss break. The sun was already down and pushing themselves was likely only going to make them uncomfortable, better to take the trip in stride and piss when they had to piss.

"Wanna fool around?" Sylvia leaned against Lanny and spoke over the rumble of the still running engines. The machine's vibration kept her in the mood most of the day and Lanny had confided that it did much of the same for him.

"I think we're pretty close to the lodge, like another twenty minutes. Let's say we ride and take ourselves a nice warm bath."

"That's a date."

Lanny straddled the seat of his Yamaha Vmax-4, gave a look back before closing his visor and thumbing the paddle to boogie onward. Sylvia rode a Yamaha Ovation, a bit smaller, but kept up fine for trail riding, and she stayed about twenty feet from the red running light at the back of her husband's sled.

It was three minutes before the first glimmers of the lodge lights appeared through the treeline. Lanny was in the midst of turning for a glance to be sure Sylvia was looking and then something slammed him sideways. He barreled off the seat, into the trunk of a spruce tree. He gasped and choked for oxygen. Sylvia didn't have time to react, and she cranked to the left, but her ski still clipped the bigger machine and sent her headlong over the handlebars, onto the seat and into the windscreen of her husband's Vmax-4. It cracked and tears sprung instantly from her eyes. She fell sideways hard on the packed snow floor. She fumbled with her visor and began crawling.

"Lanny? Lanny?" she said, muffled by the helmet.

She dropped a mitt and fingered the nylon loop belt holding the helmet tight to her chin. She tipped her head and the helmet fell to the snow and spun six revolutions. The engine of her sled was quiet and the engine of her husband's had just begun sputtering. In seconds, it died as well.

"Lanny? Lanny?"

She heard the wet snapping then and shut up. She took three steps and the eye shine of the wolf devouring her husband sent her in reverse. She turned and went for the pack strapped to the back of the seat—they had a hatchet…but that was on her sled and her sled was upside down. She cast a look over a shoulder to Lanny's wasted body, the wolf had stopped eating and was looking at her, she put her head down and reached for the handle of the recoil rope that would start the engine, she pulled it once, it growled, she pulled it twice, it growled again, a little closer to starting, she was about to pull it a third time when the growl was in her ear and had nothing to do with the snowmobile.

***

Jake got dressed and forced what he saw from his mind. It was a hallucination, the whole thing was one wild revelation after the last, internally, and his head had malfunctioned.

A snowmobile buzzed close, and light flashed his window. He put on his coat and boots, grabbed his cigarette pack, and spat into the snow while he stood in the doorway of the rented room.

Lot lights shined diamonds in the frosted powder and the cold of the atmosphere bit at Jake's lungs, froze the hair in his nostrils together. The cold made the cigarette smoke stick to him, tasting fresh, cleansing. He ran a hand against his jaw and up over his head. He tossed the butt with his other hand and then reached into his pocket for the pack. He needed clarity and the cold northern air was like a balm. What he'd done with Ben. What he'd felt. What he became, what he was.

What Ben became.

"A wolf. He…" His words trailed in a smoky, steamy exhale. Through the blackness, he saw the eyes. They were brown, as they'd always been, but the amber flecks seemed alive and on fire. "Ben?" he whispered.

The wolf across the lot let its snout come into the light, blood dripped and oozed. Jake swallowed hard and took a step back. The world was lifeless in that moment, as if all but Jake and the wolf—Ben!—had gone greyscale and the only colors remaining did so because blood pumped veins and dripped from parted jaws.

Thirty feet away, the doors of the main building slammed against a wall and men were shouting. A snowmobile started and then another. Jake kept his eyes on the wolf and the Wolf kept its eyes on Jake. Fully into the light, the wolf's head peaked at close to five feet. Its paws were mammoth, and the pink slobber ran so thick and steady that it dragged the snow before sticking and separating. Jake found himself against the wall, saying Ben's name, over and over.

The wolf stopped ten feet away and tipped its head, growling. Jake kept the mantra going, "Ben. Ben. Ben," and snapped his eyes closed. The way the wolf looked at him suggested zero percent recognition and one hundred percent hunger.

The gravel beneath the snow crunched and Jake tensed, just as someone shouted, "Hey!" and shotgun blast sprayed wide enough after striking a beam that pebbles sliced Jake's coat sleeve and burrowed into his flesh and that the wolf turned, yipping, as it departed.

Jake moaned and grabbed his arm, sliding down the wall with a grimace on his face and a cigarette still dangling between his fingers, all but burned to the filter.

"Holy, Elgy, you hit that guy!"

Men ran past Jake, and he rolled to his knees. Suddenly a man had his arm and Jake was standing.

"Let's get you some help."

Jake pulled back toward his room and said, "It's not bad, just give me a sec'. Just a sec', okay?"

"Sure, guy, no worries." The man lifted his hands, palms out.

Jake opened his door, looked around the messy, stinking room, and grabbed a piece of cardboard from the floor. Discretely as he stepped back out, he pulled the door closed on the cardboard so it wouldn't lock. In case Ben returned.

Hands or no hands, he didn't have a key.

Chapter Thirty-Three

March 31, 1994 – Copper Falls, Ontario, Canada

Ben had much of his memory back and buckshot wounds a little worse than what Jake had. They'd snowmobiled to the truck first thing in the morning. Ben remembered everything he'd forgotten. He explained about half of his life before coming to the farm on the trip home. Little conversation volleyed in return, but he kept talking. He was feeling himself again and told Jake it was because of him, though that wasn't true. Jake sat in the passenger's seat, head against the glass, listening.

When they arrived, the mess was incredible, and Kit was in the hospital for observation. The doctors suggested she receive counselling for shock. She confided in Jake that werewolves were real. He told her he knew that.

Returned from the hospital, Ben had boarded windows and swept glass. He mopped the blood in the house and moved around straw in the chicken coop. He dragged the dead heifer out of the barn with the tractor and left her in the forest for the coyotes. Jake thanked him. Awkwardness stood between them like a brick wall.

Alley Oates was there to do what she loved and took care of everybody, even if they all didn't need it. Jake asked her for space at night, but please come back tomorrow. When Ben knocked on his door, Jake told him he was confused and please go away, but don't leave.

The rental movies were in a stack on top of the pizza boxes that Alley carried. Ben sat at the table with Kit and Jake was up getting glasses for the two-liter bottle of Mountain Dew that came with the pizza. A triple rap at the door stopped everyone doing what they were doing for a second and then Jake emptied his hands at the table.

"Start, I'll tell whoever it is to go away."

He opened the door to a beautiful woman with a pale pink scar on her face, wearing clothing that appeared scavenged from boxes stacked in the rafters of the driving shed. His grandfather's stuff that his mother had kept, for whatever reason—flannel jacket and loose, blue woolen slacks, black dress shoes that appeared clownish on her too small feet.

"Can I help you?" he said.

"I'm here for the man with the blue van," Talia Grey said and then leaned in and sniffed Jake.

Jake blinked at her and rubbed his head, turning. "Ben, you know this woman?" Ben rose from the table and began crossing the kitchen. "Ben?" Jake said again.

"Hello," Ben said, and then sniffed the air, his eyes wide and excited.

"Hi," Talia said.

"Don't hurt them."

"What?" Jake said, putting his hand on Ben's shoulder. Ben did not look at him.

The woman pouted her lips and said, "Okay. Get your things."

Ben nodded and spun out of Jake's touch.

"What's going on?" Kit said from the table and Alley tried to get her to eat, put her mind on something meant for children. Pizza.

Ben had a garbage bag packed and his keys in hand when he returned to the main floor.

Jake said, "Ben. What in the hell is happening? You can't leave."

"I'm not Ben. This isn't me. This isn't where I belong," Ben whispered and looped a pinky with Jake's pinky, leaned in, and kissed his mouth. "Sorry. I'm not Ben. I'm Troy, and I'm hers."

Talia Grey grinned at them from where she stood. Ben passed her through the doorway and she followed. Jake rubbed furiously at his head and turned. Nobody saw him. They hadn't seen the kiss.

"Guess Ben knew her, and he's moved out," Jake said, fighting tears as he stumbled back to the table.

July 19, 1994 – Moreland, British Columbia, Canada

The movers were finally gone. Jody Penrose looked at the living room of her new home. They hadn't hung anything or filled any of her shelves, and maybe that was okay. The doctors suggested she'd be lucky to stand and reach any top shelves ever again.

Her employer gave her a mighty bonus after she'd explained the rational bits of the gunfight and the dead police and the serial killings. That bonus let her move to the new place and gave her time to sell her old place. It almost felt like the end of something, or a new beginning, but not quite. She'd called Detective Bourque and Buddy Maroon to explain things. The conversations were somber, and Buddy didn't ask for her hand, probably worried she might accept.

She wheeled to a box marked office and dug until she found the two items she sought. Then she wheeled to the spare bedroom, down the hall next to the bathroom. A plain room with a small window and soft white walls. She opened the container of pushpins, pinched one, and leaned up as far as her limp legs could muster. The pin travelled through the photograph and into the wall at about eye level. She sat and stared at Talia Grey's beautiful face.

It wasn't over. She'd failed becoming an agent of the FBI, but she wouldn't fail this. The sum of her life wasn't going to be failure…and this wasn't over. The news was big and bloody. Chip Hancock's right leg and most of his head had been in the basement of his Phoenix, Arizona home. He'd been eaten alive by very big dogs, according to the forensic pathologist working the incident.

April 22, 1995 – Copper Falls, Ontario, Canada

Jake's eyes glazed…I object! I object! Ben's voice carrying over the crowd and Jake turning and running into his arms. Fuck what anybody thought about—

"Jake?" Alley said, holding his hands, beautiful in her white dress.

"Oh, sorry. I do."

The minister nodded and continued. Her side was full. Friends, family, former classmates, and coworkers. His side was mostly friends, plus a handful of distant relatives from Quebec. Nowhere among these faces was Ben. Jake eyed the crowd. He would eye every crowd, looking for Ben, and would do so for a very long time.

About the Author

Eddie Generous is the author of close to 40 standalone books, has edited 6 anthologies, and put together 19 issues of Unnerving Magazine. More than 100 of his short stories have seen print in anthologies or magazines. He created and operates Unnerving, a small press responsible for publishing 85 titles and counting.

For more about Eddie Generous, visit:

www.jiffypopandhorror.com